THE IRON SPEAR

The Sequel to "IronHeart"

By Victoria Kasten

To: Kelsey

Love
Victoria

Books by Victoria Kasten

Mighty Stallion Series:
Mighty Stallion
Mighty Stallion 2 Fury's Journey
Mighty Stallion 3 Glory's Legend
Mighty Stallion 4 Dancer's Dream
Mighty Stallion 5 A Stallion's Heart
Mighty Stallion 6 The Civil War (2009)

The Leyowan Scrolls:
IronHeart
The Iron Spear

In the Shadow of Your Heart Trilogy:
In the Shadow of Your Heart *
The Shadows Darken *
Out of the Shadows *
* Coming soon

For the latest information on Victoria's books, appearances, and more, log on to **www.EpicScrolls.com** or write to:

Epic Scrolls
5465 Glencoe Ave
Webster, MN 55088

THE IRON SPEAR

By Victoria Kasten

Original cover art by Sara Enderle
Photography by Scott N Briggs Photography
Cover Layout & Design by Victoria Kasten

The Iron Spear

First Printing • 750 copies • Mar 2009

Library of Congress Control Number: 2009901556

ISBN: 978-0-9788850-6-9

Published By: Victoria Kasten

Printed in the USA by
Morris Publishing
3212 East Highway 30
Kearney, NE 68847
1-800-650-7888

Dedicated with love

To all the fans of IronHeart who encouraged me to write this book... I hope

it lives up to your expectations.

Acknowledgements:

A huge thank you to my fans for getting me motivated to write this book. If it weren't for you, I probably wouldn't have written a sequel to IronHeart. So thanks, because I'm very glad that I did.

Another big thank you goes to my parents for listening all those nights that I crawled up on the foot of your bed and read to you when The Iron Spear was still in its "baby stages".

And to Mom for all of your help in editing. Even when both of us were really sick, you still sat diligently at the computer with me and helped me get through all twenty-one chapters. ☺

A big thank you to my friend Bob (aka Ben Tecken) for some great ideas and awesome writer-to-writer brainstorms. I had some great inspirations come from our phone conversations.

A thank you my best friend Sara, who always motivates, encourages, and inspires me in all the writing I do.

Thanks also to all of my family and friends for their support, and most importantly my loving Savior for giving me the talent and passion for writing that I have.

Pronunciation Guide

Aewin (AY-win)

Aliano (Ah-lee-AH-no)

Aren (AHR-in)

Brooz (bruise)

Cika (SEE-kah)

Falkiro (fall-KEER-oh)

Geria (gehr-EYE-ah)

Getane (Guh-TAYNE)

Kazih (kuh-ZEE)

Kona (KOE-nah)

Leyowan (LAY-oh-wahn)

Lumere (loo-MARE-ay)

Nobio (KNOW-bee-oh)

Noora (NORE-ah)

Pernog (PEAR-nahg)

Quetoro (kay-TORE-oh)

Roniki (Roe-KNEE-kee)

Sarra (SAH-rah)

Sesthuine (SESS-thoo-eene)

Sumeria (sue-MARE-ee-ah)

Terikanha (tare-eh-KAHN-ah)

Vanddai (VAN-die)

1.

The Queen's head fell back, and her mouth opened in a silent scream of agony. The spear cracked and split, falling to the ground in two halves. The man behind her backed away, an evil smile on his face. Hoofbeats sounded, and then faded into silence. All that could be heard was the labored breathing of the queen. All that could be seen was the slow dripping of blood to the ground, staining the hard packed earth a deep crimson. A scarlet river of royal blood...

"NO!"

The sixteen year old girl bolted upright in her bed, throwing the blankets aside in her haste to rise from the dream. She heaved in a deep lungful of air, shaking her head to clear the nightmare from her mind. The door to her bedchamber opened, creaking softly.

"Princess Kona? Are you alright?" said a familiar voice. The girl turned her head slightly, looking at the big red stallion that had just entered the room. She sighed in relief at his presence.

"Quetoro! I am so sorry that I woke you."

The old stallion regarded her kindly. "No matter, Princess. That is why I am here. What ails you?" he asked quietly, eying her with a look of concern. His graying muzzle betrayed the gleam of youthful vigor that shone in his dark eyes. Kona looked down at her hands.

"It was the nightmare again, Quetoro. I saw her...I saw her die. I saw the spear, the blood...it was so real," she whispered, her long eyelashes brushing her cheeks as she closed her eyes tightly.

Quetoro shook his head. "Ah, poor child. Many nights I have wished that it was your mother, not I, who came to comfort you. But it was not meant to be. The dream is terrifying, but you must know that it is only a dream, nothing more. Your mother would not have wanted you to be so afraid."

Kona blushed and felt the heat rise in her face. She lowered her head so that the soft tendrils of her golden hair fell between Quetoro's eyes and her face, keeping her embarrassment hidden. She felt so sorrowful whenever she thought of her mother. The mother that she had never known but had so much wanted to meet. The great Kikpona of Leyowan, whose name was spoken in reverence by everyone in Utomia.

A soft breath blew aside her hair, and she saw Quetoro standing next to her. His eyes surveyed her comfortingly.

"Try to sleep, my Princess. Dawn comes swiftly, and tomorrow does not wait for anyone. You must rest." The old stallion's logic was inarguable, so Kona lay back against her velvet cushions and closed her eyes. This time, however, her sleep was peaceful and undisturbed.

. . . . .

Kona rose from her bed, her linen nightdress trailing behind her. She sat down in her vanity chair, picked up her hairbrush, and ran it through her golden tresses. Reaching for a navy blue ribbon, she wound it through her hair, tying it back away from her face. She grimaced as a slight ache throbbed in her left leg. She stretched it out next to her and rubbed the tender muscles.

Many years ago as a young child, Kona had fallen beneath the wheel of a heavy wagon. The bones in her leg had been crushed. She could walk now, but with a pronounced limp. Running was very difficult, and because of her limited agility, she had so far been unable to learn the ways of weaponry.

The princess's brush was placed carefully back in its jeweled case. She looked up into the mirror, and felt a lump form in her throat. Her fingertips brushed the gold necklace that she wore at her neck.

It had been a gift from her father, on her fifteenth birthday, nearly a year ago. She still remembered the words her father had spoken as he handed it to her, tears in his eyes.

"Guard this carefully, my daughter. It belonged to your mother. I gave it to her when we were married, and now I think she would want you to have it."

A wistful smile came to Kona's lips as she looked into the small hand mirror that she held. So many people had told her that she looked like her mother. Except for the honey blonde hair, of course.

Kona tried to imagine her mother's face in the mirror, with the dark red hair framing her ice blue eyes. But the image was fuzzy. Kona had very little memory of her mother. So how could she see the face she could not remember?

Her thoughts were stopped when she heard the blaring trumpets from Utomia's outer wall. Setting the mirror down, Kona hurriedly wrapped herself in a thick robe and hurried out of the palace as fast as she could.

She was joined by her aunt Vanddai in the hallway. The older woman wrapped an arm around Kona's shoulders and gave her niece a quick hug.

"Good morning, Sunshine," Vanddai said with a smile. Kona smiled back. Sunshine was her special nickname from her aunt. Vanddai had called her that ever since she was a baby.

The two of them walked outside and headed for the main gate. A group of horsemen were just dismounting inside the city. Among them was Kona's uncle, Jathren, the brother of Kikpona.

When Jathren saw his niece, a huge grin spread itself over his face. He moved forward and caught her up in his arms, spinning her around.

"Greetings, niece! Have you kept things under control while I was gone?" he asked her, pretending to be stern. Kona laughed as he tickled her sides.

"Uncle, I cannot answer your question with you doing that!" she giggled. He laughed and set her down, raising his hands as if to surrender. Kona blew a wisp of hair from her eyes and then glared at him half-heartedly.

"In answer to your question, Uncle Jathren, yes I have kept everything under control. However, with my father as king, there is hardly reason to worry," she replied. "Come inside the palace, I am sure you are hungry and tired."

Jathren smiled and nodded his agreement, following her inside the palace. Morgo came up to them from the hallway and embraced his brother-in-law.

Kona watched her father carefully. She felt a pang of sadness in her heart. No matter what, her father's eyes were always sad. He rarely smiled, and Kona wasn't sure if she had ever heard him laugh.

"Come to the dining hall, Jathren. We have much to discuss, and I am sure that you are famished after that long journey to Sesthuine. Tell me, how are our Sumerian allies…"

The two men moved off toward the dining hall, leaving Kona by herself in the hallway. She clenched her fists. She would make her father smile again.

"Kona, are you alright?"

The deep, familiar voice of Quetoro caught Kona off guard. She clamped down her sorrowful musings and turned to face him with a smile.

"Of course I am alright, *hhateh!*" she spoke quickly to reassure him, using the ancient word for "master".

To her surprise, a shocked light filled the old red stallion's eyes. "Your mother used to call me that very same thing," he said, a soft look of memory passing through his eyes.

Silently Kona berated herself. Why did she always have to remind her loved ones about her mother?

"Do not be angry with yourself, Princess."

The old stallion's words reminded Kona that she could rarely hide her emotions from him. He saw through all the false facades she vainly tried to set up around her. He was the one living being that truly understood her. He had known Kikpona since her birth, and had known Kona for all of her sixteen years as well.

"Forgive me, *hhateh*. I just…"

Understanding came to Quetoro's eyes. "Do not speak it, Princess. I understand. Your mother was the same way, always concerned about the feelings of those around her. She would get very angry with herself if she caused them pain."

Kona looked up at her teacher. "Quetoro… you have never really told me my mother's entire story. I have heard bits and pieces of it from you and Aunt Vanddai, but I want to know everything. What she was like, her childhood…if she was like me as much as everyone says she was."

The old stallion sighed. "You know how your father feels about speaking of your mother. I would not wish to anger him."

"It is my desire as a daughter to know my mother's story," Kona replied softly.

Quetoro let out a soft grunt, and Kona realized that he was laughing. "You are so much like your mother. She would have said the same thing."

Anxiously, Kona waited as Quetoro regarded her, deep in thought. Finally, the old stallion nodded his head. "Very well. I will tell you everything I know about your mother. But you must understand that it will not all be told in one day, and some things will be hard for me to remember. My memory is not what it used to be."

A bright smile came to Kona's face. "Thank you, *hhateh!*" she said. Turning around, the young princess limped down the hallway, a bit of extra spring in her step. Quetoro smiled to himself as he watched her go.

Indeed, she was like her mother in so many ways. Her determined spirit and her stubbornness were the foremost of those similarities. Quetoro closed his eyes. Kona had spoken truthfully. It was time she knew about Kikpona's life. But if Morgo learned of Quetoro's telling the story, there was no telling what might happen.

. . . . .

Morgo sat across from Jathren at the dining table, watching his brother-in-law eat. Jathren devoured the fruits and soup that were in front of him as though he had not eaten for days.

"How was your journey, my brother? Are the Sumerians still our allies?" Morgo asked. Jathren swallowed his food, and wiped his mouth with the cloth on his lap.

"They have fallen on hard times. In Sesthuine, everything is dry and the crops are failing. Their food is getting scarce, and they have had to nearly empty their treasury to trade for food with other countries."

Morgo felt a slight unease building in his mind. "A famine, do you think?" he asked worriedly. Jathren shrugged.

"What else could it be? My only hope is that we stay out of its path. A famine in Leyowan is the last thing we need right now." The two men sat in silence for several minutes, each thinking the same thoughts of famine and what would happen to their country if such a disaster should come.

"Perhaps…we would be wise to prepare. It could save us fortunes and lives later," commented Jathren. Morgo glanced at the younger man and nodded.

"So it would. I will have our farmers raise an extra crop this year, and use more of the lands outside the city walls."

Jathren nodded again. "I will begin making arrangements today, if you wish it."

"Of course. Have Kona help you. The experience will be good for her, and she needs to make herself useful," replied Morgo, his voice low and neutral. Jathren watched his brother-in-law carefully. He opened his mouth to speak, but decided against it when he saw Morgo's jaw harden.

Jathren pushed back his chair and stood. He gave a short bow to Morgo, and then strode out of the room.

Watching him go, Morgo sighed deeply, and then returned his gaze to the chair that Jathren had just left. An image of Kikpona sitting there flashed through the king's mind. Her bright laughter echoed through his head. Dropping his face to his hands, Morgo closed his eyes, trying desperately to close off the memories that were flooding back.

. . . . .

On his way around the palace to find Kona, Jathren found himself walking toward the Council Hall. Opening one of the oaken doors, he went inside. The large circular room was lined on one side by columns. On the other side of the columns, at the end of a walkway, was a single door.

Beyond that door, was a memorial chamber. Feeling strangely drawn to it, Jathren walked down the walkway. Flanking each side of his path were statues of the heroes that had died in that long ago battle.

All the heroes were there...except two. Jathren opened the chamber door and then closed it behind him.

The chamber was lit by several candelabras that were placed around the room. The tiny flames flickered, casting eerie shadows on the faces of the two solid gold statues that faced each other with sightless gemstone eyes.

The forms of Atoru and Kikpona looked almost real, as though you could reach out and touch them and they would somehow come to life. Jathren stood before the statue of his sister. Feeling a lump in his throat, Jathren impatiently forced it down.

"Sister..." he whispered, touching the sandal of the statue. "Why did you die? After all this time...I still feel my heart tear in two every time I think of you."

The only answer was profound silence. Jathren raised his misted eyes to those of the statue, wishing desperately that he could somehow bring the likeness of his sister to life.

"Why did you leave Morgo alone to rule the city you built? And your daughter, she is being raised without her mother, and nearly without her father. Morgo will hardly even look at her."

Clenching his fists, Jathren sank down to his knees. A low cry of pain came from his lips.

"Jathren..."

That voice. The young man lifted his eyes, full of hope. There, standing in the doorway, was Vanddai. Disappointment and pain fell over Jathren's face once more.

"Oh...Lady Vanddai...it is you."

Sensing the distress of the young man, Vanddai kept her silence. Instead of speaking, she glanced up at the golden statue behind Jathren. At the gigantic golden bull, with onyx eyes and thick golden horns.

"I know, Jathren...I miss them too. Leyowan doesn't seem like home without them. I remember the day I met your sister as though it happened yesterday," said Vanddai quietly. A smile touched her lips. "We hated each other. I thought she was a pompous fool, and she thought I was an uncivilized barbarian."

Jathren couldn't help the small smile that came to his face at the thought of his sister's reaction to Vanddai.

"But when I finally realized how majestic and powerful she really was, I began to think of her as a sister. I loved her as though she were my own flesh and blood. As I love Morgo."

Wiping his eyes, Jathren stood up. Looking at Vanddai, his eyes glinted with determination.

"My sister gave her life to build this city. Who am I to despair, when she left us with the task of keeping this city alive? How better to keep Kikpona alive than to make her city prosper?"

Vanddai placed a hand on Jathren's shoulder. "Wise words indeed, my friend. You speak truth."

Straightening his shoulders, Jathren moved toward the door. "And Vanddai...thank you."

The tall woman smiled. "You're welcome."

2.

"Come, Kona!"

The princess turned at the sound of her uncle's voice, and smiled when she saw him waving to her from the other side of the training field. Grasping her walking stick tightly, she began walking in his direction.

When she reached him, Jathren gave her an impulsive hug. As she returned his embrace, Kona asked, "Uncle, is something wrong?"

"No, my heart. I am simply glad that I have such a wonderful niece," Jathren replied, cupping her face with one hand. Kona's bright smile rewarded his words. Looking at the two swords that Jathren held in his hand, Kona grew puzzled.

"What are those for?" she asked curiously. Jathren brought them forward and gave one to his niece. Kona accepted it hesitantly, the leather bound hilt a strange feeling to her hand. Jathren put a hand on her shoulder.

"I have decided that it is nigh time you learned to handle a sword. I should have started your training earlier."

Fingers trembling, Kona followed her uncle out to the center of the training field. Noticing her hesitation, Jathren decided to start by getting his niece more comfortable. Sitting down in the grass, he motioned for her to do the same.

Kona sat down awkwardly, her leg making the simple movement difficult. Jathren smiled.

"When does Cika return?" he asked her quietly. Surprised but pleased by the topic of conversation, Kona's thoughts traveled to her best friend and animal companion. Cika was a young elephant. She was a grand-daughter of Pernog, who had been a faithful friend to Kikpona.

"She will be home in two days time. I hope she enjoyed her visit to Avorak with her parents. I have heard that it is a beautiful city, with every kind of merchant's ware… someday, I would like to travel around Leyowan and see all the cities," mused Kona dreamily.

"Would you like that?" asked Jathren with a smile. Kona nodded, still deep in thought over the prospect of travel.

Jathren leaned forward slightly. "Kona, as the ambassador, you know that I travel to our cities quite frequently. Perhaps your father will allow me to take you to several of the cities with me for your next birthday."

A look of pure joy flashed over Kona's face, but was quickly quelled. "He will never allow me to go," she said softly. "He does not let me go outside the city gates."

But Jathren was still smiling. "I think I could convince him. As long as a properly armed escort went with us, I think he would let you go. Perhaps he will even allow us to take Quetoro along, because then you could learn the history of each city we visit. It would be a good experience for you."

Looking down at the sword in her hands, Kona couldn't help the shudder that raced down her spine. Everyone expected her to be a great warrior like her mother, but Kona felt only uncertainty and dread when she held a weapon in her hands.

"I...Uncle Jathren..." Kona's voice trailed off. Her uncle looked at her expectantly.

"Yes Kona? What is it?"

The princess' blue eyes lifted to Jathren's as she spoke. "Never mind, it was not important."

Although Jathren was not convinced, he said no more and let the subject drop. Standing up, he helped Kona rise to her feet. Adjusting the sword in his hand, he held it point down.

"The first thing to remember when you are fighting is that the sword is simply an extension of your arm. It must become a part of you."

Kona imitated her uncle's pose, but the sword's weight nearly caused her to lose her balance. Jathren felt a strange foreboding as he watched his niece fumble with the sword. Kikpona had always been a natural with weapons. She could pick up a weapon she had never used before and instantly be comfortable with it. It seemed as though Kona did not share her mother's natural talent.

"Relax, Kona. You fight the sword too much, instead of letting the sword do the fighting for you," Jathren reproved gently.

Biting her lip, Kona held the sword still, lightly letting its point touch the ground. Jathren nodded.

"Much better. Now, pick it up and move it around a little to get more acquainted with the feel of it. Let the sword flow naturally. Do not force the blade or you will end up falling over again," Jathren said with a hint of amusement. Kona managed a small smile, but dread filled her as she once again attempted to raise the sword.

A dark image of her mother raising a bloodied spear and calling out a battle cry flashed through Kona's mind. With a small cry, she released the blade, and it fell to the ground with a resounding thud. Losing her balance, the golden haired princess landed hard in the grass.

Jathren knelt down and gathered her up in his arms. "What is wrong, Kona?" he asked her gently.

Drawing a shuddery breath, Kona looked up at him. "Uncle Jathren, I… do not want to learn the ways of the sword. I have another dream… one that does not require bloodshed. I will never lift a sword again."

Her softly spoken words amazed Jathren. "Kona…"

Tears welled in the sixteen year old's eyes. "I cannot lift such a burden, the one that my mother carried. No, if she shed her blood to build this city, I will not shed mine and destroy it."

Jathren had no answer to those words. The tone of his niece's voice was completely foreign. He had never heard her speak so firmly, yet so sorrowfully.

For a long moment, neither Jathren nor Kona spoke. The only sound was that of the far off city bustle, and the breeze rustling through the grasses.

"There is a Council meeting, Kona. We…your father wishes for you to attend. It is your duty as the heir of Utomia to be there. Your father has a very important matter to discuss with the council today."

Kona flinched, but nodded. Jathren helped her to her feet, and the two of them walked toward the Council Hall.

. . . . .

Kona found herself seated at her father's side in the Council Hall, the eyes of all the Council members upon her. There was Pernog, the elephant chieftain, still as wise as ever. And Aewin, the ambassador from the Black Panther city, her midnight tail twitching back and forth over the floor. Falkiro, the representative of the cattle tribes, was a large white ox, with sweeping horns that were tipped with gold.

Also present were Quetoro, and Makkiu the cheetah chieftain. The retired messenger cat was blind, his lifelong scar from the battle against Orluc and his dark Morbian minions. Bringing the group to completion were Morgo, Kona and Jathren, along with Vanddai.

Morgo's strong voice carried out over the room. "Welcome, my friends and advisors. There is much to be discussed this day. My brother Jathren informs me that in our neighbor country, Sumeria, there is a great famine that is sweeping over the land. I propose to send food to the people there, in an effort to help them."

17

Murmurs broke out among the Council. Aewin spoke up, "But my lord, mustn't we also prepare ourselves, if it should so happen that the famine spread to our land as well?"

"Aewin speaks wisdom," commented Quetoro. "We must strive to help our allies in what ways we can, but we must also look to our own welfare."

Morgo nodded. "I have given my brother Jathren permission to begin preparations to do exactly as you have said. Store houses are being built, and the farmers are using the land outside the city walls to plant more crops. I have already readied several caravans with supplies to send to Sumeria. I believe that this is the wisest course of action."

There was no objection, so Morgo continued, "There is…also another matter that bears discussion. And that is the welfare of the throne of Utomia."

Kona glanced at her father, an uneasy feeling growing in her stomach. Morgo did not look at his daughter.

"As you all are aware, my daughter Kona is the heir to this throne, and will sit upon it when I am gone, or perhaps before. Her mother would have wished it, and I will uphold that wish. However, she will need a suitable husband to rule as king beside her, and to provide an heir. Therefore, I propose that a young man be found for her to wed, and a betrothal issued."

Silence fell over the hall. Speechless with horror, Kona could hardly breathe. Her knuckles whitened as she gripped the arms of her chair. After several minutes, Quetoro was the first to speak. His tone was even, but surprise emanated from it.

"My lord...from her reaction to this announcement, it would seem right to guess that your daughter has not been informed of this decision."

Falkiro, after a deep grunt, added his opinion. "However, I agree with the king's sentiments precisely. It is very important that the throne be secured for future rulers. Kona should have a husband, and to seek a betrothal would be most wise."

A pleased look came to Morgo's face. But Vanddai spoke up, "My brother, I think it would be most wise to reconsider. Utomia is a city of peace and freedom. Do not make such a choice for your daughter. Let Kona have a say in her future. I think her mother would agree. Besides, Kona is still very young."

Morgo stood up with a jerk, his angry eyes staring at his sister. "Do not speak of her again, sister! I will decide the future of my daughter, and I will do what is best for her."

Tears rolled down Kona's face. Her clenched hands whitened even more as she struggled to compose herself. She received a reassuring look from Quetoro.

"Father...I..." Kona could not bring herself to speak. She stood up, bowed quickly to the council, and retreated out the side door toward the palace.

Limping through the courtyard as fast as she could, Kona felt hot tears sting the backs of her eyes. Impatiently wiping her face with her hands, she lost her balance and fell, landing on the stone path. Sharp pains jolted through her crippled leg. Curling up in a ball, Kona felt utter despair wash over her, and she cried openly, her thin body racked with sobs.

"Ahhh…what sorrow is in your heart, Little One."

Kona sat up quickly, and looked around. Behind her on the path into the courtyard, was Makkiu. The blind cheetah was sitting on the stone, his sightless eyes gazing at her intently.

"Lord Makkiu, I…" the young princess's voice faded. The cheetah sat quietly, his tail sweeping back and forth over the stones.

"My heart is divided. I am loyal to my father, as I have always been. But this….why does he ask this of me? I am barely old enough to be wed, and I have no desire for it. I only want to help my father, and become a better ruler for this country."

When Kona finished, Makkiu stood up and walked over to her stiffly, his old legs trembling slightly as he stopped in front of her.

"I too, believe that your father's heart has been hardened. Your mother's death cast this country into a dark void. You are the only one who can mend it again, for you and your mother's hearts are one and the same."

The old cheetah's voice gave comfort to Kona. "Then, you believe that I am not ready to be wed?" she asked.

A grave nod was her only reply. Kona smiled and bowed her head respectfully to her mother's old friend. Reaching out, she stroked a hand down Makkiu's silky fur. A deep rumbling purr began in his throat, a sure sign of appreciation.

"Makkiu…may I ask you a question?"

There was a long pause before Makkiu finished his purring and answered. "Of course, Princess."

"I've been told a great deal about my mother's rule and her kind way of treating our people. But Quetoro, I think, leaves out many things about who she was as a person. What her favorite places were, what she liked to eat… I was wondering…do you remember when she…how she reacted when she discovered she was with child?"

A smile came to the old cat's face. He sat down, and his tail resumed its steady sweeping motions.

"Aye, I remember that day well. She announced it to the city, and it was a day of celebration. Lord Morgo was as proud as could be. And so was our Queen. She was so anxious for you to be born, and she used to sing to you as she walked around the palace."

A faint voice echoed through Kikpona's memory, tiny bits of songs. "I … I remember her voice."

Makkiu's purr began again as he continued. "She had a beautiful voice. She could charm the very birds from their nests," he said. His sightless eyes opened and turned to Kona. "I have never heard you sing, Highness."

Surprise emanated from Kona's eyes. "I rarely sing, Lord Makkiu."

The cat's purring stopped. "Ah...this is most unfortunate. For if you have inherited your mother's voice... what a gift it would be to hear it again."

Swallowing hard, Kona realized that Makkiu had so much missed hearing her mother sing, and that it had meant a great deal to him. The least she could do was try to bring him the small joy of hearing her sing, if she did indeed sound like her mother had.

Opening her mouth and trying to calm her racing heart, Kona began to sing an old Ichodian song that she had learned from Quetoro.

Dawn comes to bring a new day
Chasing the shadows of night away
I don my sword and shield
Called to fight on the battlefield

For love and land I fight this day
To free my people from darker ways
I fight until the setting sun
The battle and the victory's won

Here I stand to face all fear
With fellow warriors far and near
I follow King and follow Queen
To bring peace unto this land again...

As the last notes of the song faded away, and Kona stopped singing, she glanced at Makkiu, and saw moisture lining his blind eyes.

"Highness, you have the gift of your mother's voice," the old cheetah finally said with a smile of gratitude. His words warmed Kona's heart as she repeated the words to herself over and over.

"Many thanks, Lord Makkiu."

The cat stood up, and turned to face her. "Now, perhaps you should return to the palace. The Council Meeting is no doubt finished, and your father may wish to speak with you."

Dread crept into Kona's heart, but she knew that Makkiu spoke truthfully. She bowed her head again, and stood up, limping slowly toward the palace. Back on the path, Makkiu's sightless eyes watched her go.

. . . . .

Kona heard a knock on her bedchamber door. She put her scroll away in its box, and turned around in her chair.

"Come in."

The door opened to reveal her father. As expected, his scowling expression and rigid shoulders revealed his anger with her. Kona gripped the back of her chair. Morgo stopped a good ten feet from his daughter, and looked at her sharply.

"I am gravely disappointed in you, Kona."

His tone was painfully strained, as though he was trying his utmost to control his anger. Slowly, he continued.

"You will not leave in the middle of a Council Meeting again. You have not yet earned that right. And you will never question my decisions. Do you understand?" he asked her sternly.

Kona felt a burning at the back of her eyes. "Father, I..."

But Morgo did not allow her to continue. "I did not ask you for your opinion, daughter. I asked if you understood me."

Realizing that she had no choice at the moment, Kona nodded miserably. Morgo turned brusquely and left the room, closing the door sharply behind him. Kona turned back to her study table. The scrolls that were arrayed upon it held no interest now. Kona had always loved reading the old tales of the ancient warriors. But now, she only wanted to get away from the palace, the city, and her father's anger.

She stood up, balancing herself against the table's edge while she reached for her walking staff.

"I come back to find that you got yourself into trouble, Kona. I thought you could handle being alone for a few weeks," said a teasing voice from the doorway. Kona turned, and gasped in delight and surprise.

Cika, her best friend and animal companion, stood before her. The young elephant's eyes were sparkling with good humor, but there was an edge of concern in them.

"Cika!"

Kona was overwhelmed with happiness. She reached her friend and wrapped her arms around Cika's neck. The young elephant's long trunk wrapped gently around Kona's shoulders, returning the embrace.

"You weren't supposed to return until tomorrow!" exclaimed Kona. Her friend smiled, and her eyes sparkled again.

"My father decided to return home early. All of us were anxious for home. I like traveling and seeing new things, but nothing compares to Utomia. I am content to stay here forever now."

Kona laughed. "I am so glad to see you! I never thought you would return, and I missed you so much."

Suddenly, Cika became more serious. "What is this rumor of betrothal that I'm hearing, Kona?" she asked. The young princess looked down, unable to meet her best friend's searching eyes.

"My father wishes me to wed, Cika. I...I feel torn in two. I cannot disobey him, but I do not want to marry someone that I do not love."

Cika sighed. "Kona, just because you have not met him yet does not mean that you will never love him. There are many kind-hearted, worthy young human males in this city, and all around Leyowan. Your father has your best interest at heart, and you know that he will choose someone who is well qualified."

"I am just afraid that he will choose a young man who is better suited for the country than for me," Kona voiced her fears for the first time.

Cika regarded the princess quizzically. "Would that not make you happy? To marry someone who loves this country and is anxious to care for it?" she asked softly. Kona did not know what to say. She just did not want to talk about it anymore.

"Will you sleep here in my room tonight, Cika? I have been very lonely of late."

Concern filled Cika's eyes once again. "Kona, have you been dreaming nightmares again?"

The young elephant's sensitivity to Kona's true emotions never ceased to surprise the young girl. But she nodded hesitantly in answer to Cika's question.

Cika's long trunk once again wrapped around Kona's shoulders, and understanding replaced the worry in her expression. "I will stay," she said quietly. Silent gratitude emanated from Kona's relieved appearance.

That night, Cika slept on the bedchamber floor, a velvet blanket draped over her broad shoulders. Kona slept against her friend, her fur robes tucked securely in around her. Wide awake, the young princess' eyes scanned the room, but she was no longer afraid of the dark. Cika's warm presence comforted her. When she finally dropped off to sleep, it was to the soft sound of Cika's steady breathing.

3.

"Kona! Get up, Highness! Your father requests your presence in the Council Hall!"

Quetoro's voice came through Kona's bedchamber door. The young princess awoke groggily, and rubbed her eyes. Beside her, Cika grunted and made a whuffling sound as she drifted awake.

Shakily getting to her feet, Kona reached for her robes, realization dawning on her that it was most likely a meeting regarding her betrothal. She put on her dress and the robe over it.

Cika waited for her by the door, and then followed her out into the hallway when she was ready. But even her best friend's presence did not calm Kona's raging nerves.

When the two companions reached the Council Hall, Kona saw Quetoro waiting for her, as well as a well-dressed man and a boy that she didn't know. Her father sat upon the throne, a satisfied smile on his face.

"Welcome, daughter."

Kona bowed stiffly, and felt Cika's trunk touch her hand ever so gently in reassurance. The golden haired princess glanced to her left at the boy who stood silently, fiddling with the tassel on his cloak.

"You called for me, Father?" Kona inquired, keeping her tone respectful and quiet, as she had been taught. Morgo looked pleased with her reaction, and stood up from his throne.

"So I did. Princess Kona, this fine man is Lord Albios of Kepwick. He has been a loyal ally to Utomia and to this royal house for many years."

Lord Albios turned and bowed slightly to Kona. He was a handsome looking man, with a neatly trimmed gray beard and kind blue eyes. He reached out and took Kona's proffered hand in his own, and smiled at her.

"It is an honor to meet the daughter of our most respected king," said Albios. His voice was warm and his way of speaking mirrored his noble heritage. Drawing back, the nobleman gestured toward the boy who stood beside him. "And this is my son, Nobio, future lord of Kepwick Hall."

The boy knelt down on one knee, and bowed his head. His reddish brown, curly hair swirled in every direction, as though it had a mind of its own.

"Your Highness," he said softly, as though he were afraid to speak too loudly. He hesitantly raised his hazel green eyes to hers. The uncertain look in his eyes was that of a boy who had been brought by his father to an unfamiliar place, to meet a girl he'd never known.

"It is a pleasure to meet you, Nobio," Kona replied with a small smile. The boy stood up, and Kona was surprised to see that up close, he looked to be about her age. He was tall, nearly a head more than Kona herself.

Freckles were spattered across his cheeks. He was thin, and his cloak hung precariously from his slight shoulders. His tooled leather belt hung loosely about his hips, and he stood leaning slightly to one side.

Morgo came down from the dais. "Albios, my friend, we have much to discuss. Kona, perhaps you would like to show Nobio the palace gardens."

There was an unspoken order in the king's voice. Without glancing at her father, the young princess motioned for Nobio to follow her.

The two of them left the Council Hall in silence. As they walked, Kona glanced at her companion out of the corner of her eye. His eyes followed the path in front of them, and his shoulders were slumped. Obviously he had no more interest in this whole affair than Kona did. But the young princess felt as though perhaps, at least, they could be friends.

"What sort of hobbies do you have, Nobio son of Albios?" asked Kona lightly, hoping to start a conversation.

"None that would interest a princess, my lady," he replied quietly. Kona was keenly aware of her limp as they walked outside, and that Nobio was watching her closely.

"You give me no credit, young sir," Kona countered smoothly. She felt strange; talking so courtly to one that was the same age as her and only a boy, at that. It was as if she was speaking through the lips of someone else. She stopped at a bench and sank down onto it, smoothing out the folds of her gown in front of her. After a moment's hesitation, Nobio sat beside her, but as far to the side of the bench as he could be without falling off.

A pang of sadness struck Kona's heart. "Oh, let us be friends, Nobio!" she said finally, unable to bear the formality of it all. The boy looked at her in complete surprise, and it was clear that she had caught him off guard. He stammered as he tried to respond to the unexpected words.

"I...of course...Highness."

Kona smiled warmly at him. "Now tell me, what hobbies do you enjoy most?" she asked again.

Nobio studied her for a long moment with his dark brown eyes, looking every bit a thoughtful philosopher. But then, he smiled through his shyness, and began his response slowly.

"Well...I enjoy reading very much. Studying, really. And I love history..."

. . . . .

Cika watched the pair of them through the branches of a young tree across the garden. She let out a relieved sigh when Nobio turned to sit facing Kona, and the two of them began talking more animatedly.

"Spying on the princess, are we?"

Cika whirled around, speechless with horror at being caught eavesdropping. She looked up at an extremely amused Quetoro. The old red stallion laughed aloud.

"At ease, young one. I only meant to teach you a lesson. Eavesdropping is not a task for one as noble as you."

Cika lowered her head, and her ears flapped back and forth. "Forgive me, Lord Quetoro. I should not have listened

30

to the conversation. I just wanted to make certain that the princess was happy."

Glancing through the leaves of the tree, Quetoro replied, "I believe they are both happy, Cika. It is good that the princess has someone her own age to talk to, who is also a human."

"Do you...do you think I am not a fitting companion, Lord Quetoro?" asked Cika quietly, her eyes downcast. The very thought of it horrified her.

But the stallion only chuckled. "Quite the opposite, my dear. Now go and tell the palace baker to make some of Kona's favorite treats. I am sure she would like to share them with her guest."

Quetoro watched the young elephant as she trotted back toward the palace kitchens. Looking back at the princess one last time, a wistful thought crept into his mind as he remembered another young princess, long ago. Kona was indeed her mother's daughter.

. . . . .

Kona and Nobio's conversation was cut short as Morgo approached them from the path. He smiled, but Kona felt the satisfaction in his gaze.

"I see that the two of you are getting along well. Quite excellent," he said. Kona lowered her eyes, trying desperately not to let her father see the anger in them. Nobio instantly scooted farther away from the princess, and his gaze also became downcast.

"No need to be shy," Morgo said. "I am not staying. Kona, it is time for your studies. Perhaps you would like to take Nobio with you."

"Of course, Father."

Kona stood up, and limped down the path toward the palace. Nobio followed her dolefully, glancing at Morgo as he walked past the king. Inside the palace, Kona led the way to the large study room, her limp pronounced as her angry strides carried her to the desk.

She sat down on the chair, and pulled a quill out of the inlaid box on the desk. She looked at Nobio, who had settled himself at one of the smaller desks.

"Forgive my father, he…is not himself," Kona said apologetically, keeping her gaze fixed the blank scroll in front of her.

Nobio shrugged and dipped a quill in the small inkwell. "I suppose that it is a hard task, to be king. I would never wish for it. Perhaps your father is afraid for you…because of…" he didn't finish his sentence, but Kona knew what he spoke of. And she knew the truth in his words. Her father was deathly afraid of losing her just as he had lost her mother long ago.

The door to the study opened, and Quetoro entered quietly, looking at his two charges. "A pleasure it is to have you join us, young Nobio," he said, inclining his head slightly. Nobio stood up swiftly, nearly knocking over his inkwell.

"I beg your pardon, sir…but are you really Lord Quetoro? I did not have the chance to meet you when I first arrived." Nobio had the look of one who had met his hero for the first time.

Quetoro looked pleased. "I am indeed."

Nobio's face nearly glowed, but he blushed and bit his lip as he sat back down. It was clear that he longed to ask a million questions but did not have the courage. The old red stallion watched the boy for a moment and then turned to Kona.

"Your Highness, would you be good enough to find the Tales of Taldari scroll? I believe we left off in one of its passages."

A smile came to Kona's face. She loved learning the old tales of Leyowan's ancient warriors. She stood up and made her way to one of the scroll shelves. After scanning the contents for several seconds, she selected one and brought it back to her desk.

"I have it, *hhatch*," she said. Quetoro nodded his majestic head in acknowledgement.

"Please read from where we left off yesterday," he told her. Kona opened the scroll and smoothed her hand carefully over the parchment. Eagerly, she scanned the writing for the passage that they had last read.

"Ahh, there it is."

She glanced up at Quetoro, who nodded for her to continue. Kona began reading in a clear, enchanting voice.

"When Lopan became king of Terikanha, he set a new rule over his people, banning the acceptance of all dark arts and witchcraft. He also ruled that anyone harboring a fugitive practitioner of these arts would be charged with treason. He had been tutored by a great man by the name of Reneldo, a monk and well known healer from Leyowan.

Reneldo brought a new religion to the barbaric ways of the Terikanhians. It was a religion that honored one God, and put an end to all the cruel practices that the pagan gods demanded. At first, the people of Terikanha rebelled against these new rules, but eventually, they learned to accept, and then love the new religion."

Quetoro grunted softly, a signal that Kona was to stop reading. She did, and looked up at the red stallion for further instruction.

"Kona, what risks would Reneldo have faced by teaching Lopan the way of our religion? At the time he introduced the idea, Lopan would have been only a prince."

The princess smiled and brushed aside one of her golden tresses. "I suppose that he would have risked his life, and perhaps war with our country. If Lopan's father, the king, had discovered his son's secret tutelage under a new religion so against his own, he would have put Reneldo to death, and perhaps attacked Leyowan for attempting to undermine his rule."

Quetoro nodded in approval. But Nobio looked thoughtful. "Well, I think Reneldo was not the only one to risk his life in this story. Lopan himself, although he was the son of the king, could have lost much as well. For the old religion of the Terikanhians was very strict about secession from its ways. It stated that all those who abandoned it must be either forced to recant, or be sacrificed to one of their innumerous gods. In which case, Lopan could have lost his life and his throne. His bravery is perhaps the greater of the two."

The old red stallion's eyes sparkled. "Truly, this is so. Well met, Nobio son of Albios. It is apparent to me that you have studied these legends in some depth."

A slight flush spread over Nobio's cheeks. "I...yes, I have. My tutor has introduced me to many of the cultures of our world, as well as their religions and patterns of monarchy."

Quetoro nodded. "So I see. It will be an honor to include you in our studies then. Please read on, Princess Kona."

. . . . .

That evening, the atmosphere in the dining hall was much more than tense. It was nearly unbearable. Morgo, Albios, Nobio, Kona, Jathren, and Vanddai were seated at the long table. The feast was eaten in silence except for a few quietly spoken sentences. Finally, Morgo put down his knife and clapped his hands.

"One would think a funeral procession had passed through! Let us be merry, and have music!" he said. A group of musicians came from one corner of the room, and began to play a melodious tune.

The king smiled. "Much better. Vanddai, you told me that there was an urgent matter that needed to be discussed."

The dark haired woman looked up at her brother with a blank expression, her eyes carefully neutral. But she nodded, and took a scroll from her belt.

"There have been many reports that the famine is spreading to our borders. The crops are failing, and we have not had rain for months. Our people are growing fearful and they look to you for guidance."

A frown replaced Morgo's smile. "So it has reached this far. I was afraid that it would. But there is little we can do to change it now. Jathren, have provisions been made for extra housing and crop harvest?"

"Yes, Sire. The building goes as planned, and more crops are being harvested every day. I believe that we may be able to hold out until the rain comes," Jathren replied.

But Morgo did not look relieved. "We can, but that says nothing for our neighbors in Sumeria. I had hoped to lend them aid in these dark times."

Jathren was shaking his head. "We have already sent them all that we can spare. Lord Albios was very generous in giving of his own harvest to add to the wagons that we sent. But it was not enough to stem the famine's spread. Sumeria is still in dire need of help. And we cannot give it."

"Surely the famine has not spread to all of our neighboring countries," offered Kona quietly. "Perhaps we can go to Nenamene for help; they have been our allies for years."

Morgo shot her a sharp glance. "Ridiculous notion. The Nenamene people are too afraid of their own country's well being to help us, and it has only spread to half of their lands.

They will not send us aid. Let the adults handle the matters for adults."

The words her father spoke felt like thorns driven into Kona's heart. She set her knife and fork on her plate and stood, bowed to her father, and limped painfully from the room. She could hear the dull drone of voices begin behind her as her father carried on the conversation without her.

She entered the hallway and stopped, leaning against the cool stone wall. She felt a strange void in her heart, and she knew why.

Without losing another moment, she continued down the hallway, and toward the Council Hall. Her hands clenched the sides of her gown as she struggled to keep her balance. A sharp pain lanced through her bad leg, causing her to misstep and nearly fall, but she kept going. Her footsteps echoed through the chamber hallway as she passed by the golden statues and came to the heavy door at the end of the passageway.

Kona gasped as another, sharper pain went through her leg. She pulled open the door and entered the dimly lit chamber. She took three steps forward, and an explosion of agony wracked her body as her leg buckled, and she fell at the foot of the golden statue that was the only piece she had of her mother.

Her tears rolled down her cheeks and splattered on the tiles of the floor. Sinking down, Kona came to rest against the ground.

"Mother, why does Father harden his heart..." Kona whispered. She tried to lift her eyes to those of the statue, but her vision blurred, and she felt dizzy. The pain in her leg was nearly unbearable now. Slowly, the golden haired princess slipped into black unconsciousness.

4.

Nobio walked slowly through the Council Hall, his footsteps echoing through the stone passageway. He stared up with wide eyes at the huge golden statues. He felt as though he were trespassing in some hallowed place.

"Princess Kona?"

His call was barely louder than a whisper. Swallowing, Nobio called out again, this time a little louder. He saw a large oaken door at the end of the hallway, partly open. Inside, he caught a glimpse of a gown's hem spread on the floor. Doubling his strides, Nobio entered the small chamber, and saw Kona lying on the floor before the golden statue of her mother. Her eyes were closed, and her hand was stretched out, white and pale.

"Your Highness!" exclaimed Nobio. The fifteen year old boy knelt down and shook Kona's shoulder gently. There was no response.

Biting his lip worriedly, Nobio put his arms under Kona's shoulders and knees, and lifted her up. Even though she weighed little, Nobio still strained to lift her as he stood up.

Slowly but surely, the boy made his way out of the Council Hall. He saw Quetoro and Cika in the garden, and called out to them.

"Lord Quetoro!"

The old red stallion turned and saw Nobio walking toward them with an unconscious Kona in his arms. The boy was obviously struggling to hold the princess. Cika rushed to them and touched the Kona's cheek with her trunk, and Quetoro went immediately to the palace.

"What happened, Nobio?" she asked. "Where was she? Is she hurt? We must summon a healer, quickly!"

Unable to supply any answers to the young elephant's long string of questions, Nobio knelt down and gently placed Kona on the grass. He looked up at Cika with an expression of confusion.

"I found her in the Council Hall, in that chamber with the two golden statues. I do not think she is injured."

There was a shout as Morgo came running toward his daughter from the palace, followed closely by Vanddai, Jathren and Baka the Healer. The old healing woman dropped to her knees beside the princess and felt the girl's wrist.

Nobio related what he knew to the small group. Morgo was pale, and his hands clenched and unclenched as they waited for Baka to finish her examination. Finally, the old woman glanced up.

"Her leg muscles have tightened; I believe she fainted from the pain. Carry her to her room, and I will give her some herbs to sooth the ache away. Don't worry, she will awaken shortly. It is not serious," she finished reassuringly. Morgo let out a long breath of relief.

Jathren moved forward, and lifted the princess effortlessly, carrying her toward the palace. Morgo turned to Nobio.

"Are you sure that you did not see anything?" he asked. There was a barely audible edge to his voice that made Nobio tremble. The hard gaze of the king was like red hot metal searing into his face.

"…yes, my lord."

The boy's quiet reply seemed to sooth the king's anger. Nobio stepped aside as Morgo followed Jathren back to the palace.

. . . . .

Kona could feel someone holding her hand. She opened her eyes slowly, taking in the sights. She was in her room, and her father was sitting beside her bed, holding her hand. He was asleep, leaned back in his chair.

A warm feeling raced through Kona as she looked down at the strong hand that held hers so gently. She could not remember the last time her father had held her hand. She wiggled her fingers slightly, and Morgo stirred from his sleep. Opening his eyes, he looked at her, and smiled.

"Ah, you are awake."

Kona nodded, and looked down at their entwined hands again. "Yes, I am awake. I am sorry that I have worried you. How long have I been asleep?"

The king sighed. "Since yesterday afternoon." Morgo paused. "Kona, I... forgive my words in the dining hall. They were spoken without thought, and I am sorry for them now."

Joy filled Kona's heart at this small sight of her father's true self - the caring, compassionate father that she loved so dearly. She squeezed his hand reassuringly.

"It is forgiven, Father. Let us talk no more of it."

Morgo looked up at his daughter. "Have you thought any more about what I have said concerning your betrothal?"

Kona frowned and Morgo instantly patted her hand. "No, we will not talk of this now. Perhaps later, when you are better rested. Sleep daughter, and regain your health."

The king stood and left the room, closing the door softly behind him. Kona sank back against her pillows, feeling as though all the air had been drained from her lungs. Every time she thought her father had softened toward her, he brought up her betrothal again.

There was a soft knock at Kona's bedchamber door. As much as she didn't want to see anyone, the princess called softly, "Enter."

The door opened slowly to reveal Nobio. The young lad came in and sat down in the chair that Morgo had recently vacated. His expression was a mixture of relief and concern, as well as the slight blush of shyness.

"Are you well, Highness?" he asked quietly. Kona smiled and shook her head in amusement.

"I would be much better if you called me Kona," she said. "We are friends, are we not? There is no need for formalities."

Nobio looked uncertain, but he nodded in agreement. "Very well, Hi-...Kona." He fell silent then, and watched her for a long moment. She gazed back at him, waiting for him to speak. There was a question hovering about him, she could tell. She only wished he would just say it.

Finally, he did. "Kona, there is something I have always been curious about. I have read many tales about your mother. My tutor included the stories of her into our studies. She is... well she is much like a hero to me, I suppose. I have always greatly admired her."

Kona waited until Nobio spoke again. "Do you suppose that she... was she always a warrior? Or did she enjoy quieter life as well? I have always wondered that."

Unexpectedly, tears formed at the corners of Kona's eyes. She lowered her head, hiding her crying from Nobio behind the long tresses of golden hair. The boy did not say anything, but he knew that his question had awoken a tumult of emotions in the young princess.

Finally, Kona lifted her eyes. They were red-rimmed, but her voice was steady as she answered him.

"Truthfully, I do not know. My father has always been very quiet about my mother's life. He has not really told me anything about her, and he has forbidden my tutors to speak of her with me." She paused. "But I believe that she would have enjoyed peace, as I do."

A smile came to Nobio's face. But then a shadow passed over his expression once more. "Kona, there is something else that I feel you must know." His voice had a barely audible plea for understanding behind it. Kona sat up straighter and looked at him carefully.

"Of course, Nobio."

The young lad clenched his hands together. "I know that I can trust you, which is why I must tell you this. My heart...belongs to a peasant girl on my father's estate. Her name is Lilleth. My father does not know of this, I could not find the courage to tell him."

Shock and then relief flowed through Kona. She reached out and touched Nobio's hand.

"Nobio, thank you for being brave enough to tell me. I never wished for this betrothal. I hope we can be friends. And now perhaps, we shall both get what we wish for."

"But how?" asked Nobio, confused. A spark of hope lit his eyes.

"I am not sure yet, but I will find a way to free you from this betrothal, so that you can return to Lilleth," Kona said determinedly, then paused before continuing. "Tell me about her...what is she like?"

There was a new light in Nobio's eyes as he spoke. "She is not fair like the sunshine, as you are, Highness. She has hair that is dark brown as the earth. Her eyes are a beautiful green. They out sparkle the greenest gemstone. She is quiet and kind. She loves to nurture things that grow, plants and animals alike."

"You love her very much."

Kona's soft comment surprised Nobio, and he looked at her for a moment in silence. But then he smiled and nodded slowly.

"Yes, Highness. I do."

.....

Later that afternoon, Kona felt well enough to leave her chamber and walk around the palace gardens with Cika. Their progress was slow because of the princess' pronounced limp, but both of them were used to it, and kept up a lively chatter. The conversation soon turned to the problem of the approaching famine. Kona was the first to bring it up.

"I do not know what Father intends to do about the famine, Cika. It is approaching faster than we originally thought, and he does not seem to be interested in sending for help. He seems convinced that we can survive without any aid."

Cika looked thoughtful. "Perhaps we can. Besides, what country would give us aid? Our neighbors are suffering already from the famine, they have nothing to spare for us."

"None of the countries surrounding Leyowan can help us. No, we would have to go farther north," Kona observed. "To Terikanha."

There was a barely audible gasp from Cika. "Please tell me that you did not just suggest that *we* should ask *that* country for help. Surely you know the tales, Kona. That land is full of greedy, good-for-nothing thrill-seekers. They would never help us."

Kona looked at her best friend sharply. "Cika, how do you know that? Have you ever been to Terikanha? Since you have not, perhaps you should not judge them."

"They say that the queen of that country is evil," replied Cika warily. Kona sighed and her shoulders dropped slightly. She stopped walking, and turned to face her friend.

"There are some who would say that my mother was an evil, vicious, dark ruler. But those who knew her know the truth. That she was...beautiful, strong, and courageous."

Kona's eyes grew distant, and Cika didn't speak. She felt her heart ache for her best friend, a young human who had never known the mother that she loved so much. The young elephant tucked her trunk in towards her mouth, not knowing what to say.

"Your Highness!"

Kona turned slightly to see a young cheetah messenger standing behind her, looking proud of himself, with an urgent expression on his face.

Cika chuckled. "Young Rath. I see you have been given your first message to carry. Well then, let us hear it."

"Her Royal Highness, Kona, is wanted at once by her father the king in the Council Hall," finished Rath breathlessly. A short pang of dread raced through Kona's mind, but she did not show it. Instead she smiled brightly at Rath and limped toward him. Reaching down, she lightly stroked the soft fur on top of his head, as a sign of favor.

"Thank you, Rath. Your message is heard."

The young cheetah positively glowed with pride as he bowed, and then turned to leave. Cika came up behind Kona and lightly touched the princess' shoulder with her trunk.

"Come then, we had better go at once," the elephant said quietly. Kona nodded and followed her best friend toward the Council Hall.

. . . . .

Morgo sat on the throne, his head cradled in his hands. The council was quiet, and there was a tense atmosphere in the room. Lord Albios sat on a carved bench with Nobio, as guests of the council meeting.

Sitting beside her father, Kona could see the grim expression on his face. Jathren walked forward to stand before the dais.

"My lord, the famine has reached our borders. There are refugees coming in from the outermost cities, asking us for food and shelter until the famine passes. We have had to make new homes and expand the city to make room for them. We are still taking crops into our warehouses. But they are coming less and less by the week. We have perhaps a few days before there will be nothing left to add to the store. There are reports from Sumeria that their death tolls are rising every day. People are starving, my lord."

Jathren's report left a dark silence hovering over the rest of the council. Vanddai slumped in her chair, looking haggard

47

and drawn. She had been working in the city and running the stocking of the warehouses for the past few days. Quetoro's eyes were less bright than usual. Aewyn and Falkiro looked no better.

Jathren turned to face the Council. "If we do not seek aid from the northern or eastern countries beyond our neighbors, we will be destroyed by this disaster."

"No."

Morgo's voice was strong and sharp. Jathren turned to face him in surprise, and the heads of the council members lifted to look at their king.

"We will survive this...on our own."

The king's statement shocked those who heard it. He had lifted his head and was looking at each of them intently, his gaze shadowed.

Jathren wore an expression of incredulousness. "My...my lord? Surely you cannot mean..."

"That is exactly what I mean!" exclaimed Morgo, rising from the throne. He strode down the dais steps and came to stand right in front of Jathren. He glowered at the younger man.

"Those countries never came to our aid when we fought the Morbians all those years ago! They never came to our aid then, what makes you think they will help us now?"

Vanddai rose from her seat. "Brother! Think rationally! Even if the Northern or Eastern countries had helped us in battle, Kikpona may not have survived. You cannot think of her at a time like this!"

She barely finished her sentence before Morgo lunged toward her. His hand flew up to her neck and he pushed her into the wall. Leaning in to her ear, he spoke quietly.

"If you ever speak her name again..." he said. He didn't need to finish his sentence. Vanddai's expression of anger disappeared, and a blank mask veiled her true feelings.

Kona could not believe the aggression that her father was showing. He had never treated Vanddai so roughly. After all she had been through with him, after all she had done for him and for Leyowan, what right did he have to do that?

"Father! You forget our guests!"

Kona's desperate exclamation worked. Morgo released his sister and turned around, walking stiffly back toward the throne. Taking a deep breath, he sat down on it and looked at the council.

"I have spoken. We will not call for aid."

5.

The dark halls of the palace were familiar to Kona after she had lived in them for so many years. She easily made her way through the passages and to the door that led to her aunt's room. The candle she held in her left hand trembled slightly as she knocked on the door with her right. She waited for several seconds, the moonlight casting a dim light through the windows.

"Come in," came Vanddai's voice through the door. Kona opened the latch and entered the room. There were no lit candles, only the dim moonlight shining through the single window. Vanddai stood before the window, her arms crossed, and her back to her niece.

"Aunt Vanddai..." Kona spoke softly, afraid that speaking too loudly could result in breaking the fragile atmosphere in the room. She moved forward toward the older woman, and could not hold back the soft gasp that escaped her lips.

A single tear's trail shone on Vanddai's cheek.

Kona had never seen her aunt show emotion like this. She never cried; never let anyone see her true feelings. She was the strength that had kept the royal family together for so long.

"There is something I want you to know, Kona. Your father is a good man, he always has been. There is a darkness that has hardened him now, a darkness that began its work the day your mother was murdered. He has never been the same. But I have never given up hope that he will be the man he was once again. And you must not lose hope either. We must be strong and help him find his true heart once more," Vanddai finished, determination lining her face once more, all traces of sorrow gone. She turned and held out her hands.

Kona choked back a sob and walked into her aunt's open arms, which closed around her protectively.

"I am so afraid of what will happen," whispered Kona, tears running down her face. "I do not want our country to be in a famine. I do not want Father to be so angry, and I do not want to marry Nobio."

Vanddai put her hands on either side of Kona's face, looking at the princess with an intent gaze.

"Nobio is a fine boy, Kona. I understand your apprehension concerning marriage, but surely you cannot find fault with your father's choice."

Kona shook her head. "No, he is a wonderful friend and he has a gentle heart. But he loves someone…a girl from his father's estate. And I do not wish to be his wife…only his friend."

A faint smile touched Vanddai's lips. "Well then, I will do my best to change your father's mind. Perhaps we can find you another husband. Thank you for being honest with me," the older woman finished. She patted Kona's cheek.

"Alright, it is time you were in bed and asleep. Thank you for coming to visit me," Vanddai said.

Kona murmured a response, and left the room. Suddenly exhausted, she limped back to her own bedchamber and crawled into the warm blankets. She was asleep as soon as her head hit the pillow.

. . . . .

The next morning, breakfast was quiet. Vanddai was not present at the table, but no one commented on her absence. Morgo ate with a ferocious appetite, but Kona just picked at her food. Nobio, who sat beside her, kept glancing at her worriedly.

"A princess needs nourishment, daughter," said Morgo. His tone was neither kind nor harsh.

Kona looked up at her father and put down her knife and fork. "I cannot eat, Father. I cannot help but think of those poor people who have nothing to eat, who have been struck by the famine. And here I have more to eat than I wish."

Setting his jaw, Morgo replied, "Then you are dismissed from this table. Quetoro will be waiting for you in the study."

Kona rose from her chair and curtseyed. For the first time in her life being around her family, she was intensely embarrassed about her limp. She tried to conceal it as much as possible, but she felt the stares of those at the table burning into her back, especially her father's. She was the imperfect replica of the daughter he should have had.

The thought stung Kona. She had never seen herself in such a dark light before. But now that she had, it filled her with the desire to do something that would make her father proud.

Limping down the hallway toward the study, Kona thought very hard about what she could do. But every idea just seemed too unworthy of her father's approval. Except one. Kona stopped walking, and looked around. She could not believe she had actually thought of such a daring plan. But if it worked, she might save her country and her father's honor.

Determination filled her, and she entered the study briskly. Sitting down at her desk, she smiled at Quetoro. The old stallion gave her a quizzical look, but didn't mention her expression of excitement.

"Are you ready for your studies, Highness?" he asked. Kona nodded and opened the scroll in front of her.

. . . . .

"WHAT?"

Cika's voice rose to a near wail as she responded to what Kona had just told her. The young princess jumped and put a hand on her best friend's forehead.

"Hush! Do you want to tell everyone in Utomia what I am going to do? You know that my father will never let me out of the palace if he hears of this! Now, are you with me or not?"

Cika's ears flapped back and forth nervously. "Of course not! What a foolish, impulsive, dangerous, imprudent, irrational, reckless - "

"Brilliant idea?" offered Kona with a smile. Cika paused for a moment, and then shook her head vigorously.

"No, it is not. How could you even think of going against your father this way? If he would not send a commoner to ask Terikanha for help, what on earth makes you think he will be happy about you going? You are the princess of Utomia, and all of Leyowan will one day be under your rule! It is far too dangerous. And besides, you know you cannot travel on foot!"

Kona bowed her head. "My father is not right in his heart. Perhaps this will do more good than just saving our country from starving, Cika. If I am going to rule Leyowan, I must know the people who will be my subjects. Besides, if I can save them from this famine..."

The young princess did not need to say more. Cika sighed. "When are you leaving, then?"

Kona perked up happily. "I will leave tonight. Are you coming with me?" she asked. But Cika shook her head.

"I cannot Kona. I do not want to support you in this. It is far too brash." she said quietly. Kona's shoulders drooped, but she set her jaw in determination.

"Very well. I will carry on alone then."

Cika's ears flapped again. "Alone? You mean no one else is going with you? What about Nobio?"

"Nobio is not obligated to follow me, and I do not want to jeopardize our friendship by asking him to come with me on a journey. I am trying to end our betrothal, and this will be one way to do that. My father cannot possibly give me in marriage if I am not here, and Nobio will be released from the betrothal," finished Kona triumphantly.

Cika eyed her skeptically. "You have really thought this entire plan out. What if something goes wrong? What if someone finds out about you leaving?"

Leaning into Cika's ear, Kona whispered, "If you do not tell anyone, no one will."

The young elephant's head lowered slightly, and Kona could tell that she was struggling.

"I shall not give away your secret," promised Cika. With a smile, Kona murmured grateful thanks, and limped back toward the palace. Cika remained in the garden, watching the princess leave.

Kona re-entered the palace and felt a rush of excitement flowing through her. One friend told, one left. She knocked on the door of Nobio's room.

"Enter," came the expected voice. Kona went into the room, and saw Nobio bent over a scroll, furiously writing with a long black quill. The scritch-scratch sound of the writing instrument filled the room.

He looked up and the sound ceased as he rose from his chair. "Kona! I was just going to visit you after I finished writing this poem."

The young princess chuckled and sat down on a stool across from Nobio's desk. She held out her hand.

"May I read what you have written?" she asked.

Nobio did not hesitate, but handed her the parchment. He sat back down, leaning toward her, waiting eagerly for her comments on his work. Kona let her mind wander over the words, letting them sink into her heart.

See the sunrise over the mountains
A royal, golden hue
Casting light over sapphire waters
Deep, majestic blue
The forests sing their morning song
Wind sings harmony
I have found here a perfect home
Beauty lies before me
See the city's timeless walls of stone
Protecting her children
They have found a home in Leyowan
New lives here begin

Kona was silent as she read the poem once again. Finishing, she set the parchment down on the desk gently, and lifted her eyes to the boy sitting in front of her.

"That was beautiful, Nobio. You painted a perfect picture of this country," Kona said quietly. Nobio smiled, and looked immensely pleased. He replaced the parchment in its place on his desk, and put the quill in a wooden box. Kona clenched her hands.

"Nobio, there is something I must tell you. But you have to promise not to breathe a word of it to anyone. Cika is the only other one who knows of this," Kona said.

With a slightly worried expression, Nobio replied, "I promise, but what is this thing, that you are so secretive about it?"

"I am leaving Utomia, Nobio," Kona began. "I am going to Terikanha to find food for our people. I will convince their queen to help us. My father need not know of it until I return."

Shock was plainly written on Nobio's face. It was a long moment before he gathered his thoughts enough to speak. "Please, your Highness...reconsider! This is a very dangerous plan! Surely you could send someone in your stead."

Kona shook her head. "No, I will go. This is something I must do for my country and my father. I think...perhaps his heart will be softened when I am not here. Perhaps...many good things will come of it."

There was an awkward silence for several minutes before Nobio spoke again. "Your Highness, allow me to accompany you."

"No...you must stay here. If you come with me, then you will never be free of our betrothal. If I leave, my father will have to release you from all the bonds he has set upon us. I want you to be free of me."

Nobio stood and moved around the desk until he was next to Kona. He knelt in front of her, and took her hands in his own.

"I would have loved you, Kona. I would have cared for you and been a good husband to you. Do not do this because of me."

Tears formed in Kona's eyes as she squeezed Nobio's hands lightly. "I know you would have, Nobio. And I am not leaving because of you, but because of the famine. You must return home, and find a way to marry Lilleth, if she loves you as you love her."

Bowing his head in respect to the princess, Nobio replied, "If anything happens to you, I will hold myself completely responsible. Leyowan needs you. Please do not ask me to carry such a burden on your behalf."

"My mind is set Nobio. You cannot dissuade me."

"Then please do not travel alone," Nobio replied. "With the famine, it is a much more dangerous path than it would have been before. And you are too precious to this land and to your family and friends."

"I will find someone to travel with me, Nobio. I promise."

Nobio nodded, and as he stood up, he leaned forward and placed his hands gently on either side of Kona's face. She looked up at him as he bent over her and placed a kiss on her golden head.

"Whatever may happen, Kona of Leyowan, as a sister I have loved you."

Kona smiled up at him. "Then forever are we bound, for you are dearer to me than any brother could ever be."

Rising from the stool, Kona limped to the door. "May the stars shine over you," she said, using the ancient blessing. Nobio bowed slightly as he spoke the response.

"May God guide your footsteps."

"And may you find peace," finished Kona. She opened the door and left the room, leaving Nobio alone in his room. He sank down into his chair, resting his hand against his forehead. After a long moment he picked up a fresh piece of parchment. He was going to write to Lilleth.

. . . . .

Darkness settled over the city of Utomia. The crescent moon cast very little light over the shadowed buildings. The wind blew through the streets, fluttering the canvas walls of the marketplace huts.

The stars watched a lone figure limping away from the palace, a heavy sack secured from her shoulders, a sturdy walking staff in her hand.

Kona's night had begun with secretive preparations. She had gotten food from the kitchens with Nobio's help. Thankfully the cook was a heavy sleeper. Nobio had once again asked if someone was going to travel with Kona, and she had reassured him that she would yet find someone. Kona smiled slightly as she remembered Nobio's final goodbyes to her. Her hand strayed to the leather thong necklace she wore, and the silver medallion that hung from it.

Nobio had taken it from his own neck and hung it around hers. His words still echoed through Kona's ears.

"Take this. It is very precious to me. My mother gave it to me before she died, and told me to give it to the girl I married."

Kona looked confused. "But, Nobio, that is for Lilleth. Why have you given it to me?"

"So that you will have to return to give it back," replied Nobio firmly. "In giving you this, you have to promise me that you will come back."

Kona embraced Nobio tightly. "Of course I will. I'll guard it carefully, and when I return, you will have it back. Then you can give it to Lilleth."

Closing her hand around the pendant, Kona whispered her promise to return once more. Looking up ahead, Kona stopped when she saw a dark shape hidden in the trees alongside the road. The shape moved toward her ominously.

Kona lifted her staff, terrified. "Who...who is there?" she asked, trying to keep her voice steady. The figure moved into a patch of moonlight, and Kona gasped when she saw who it was.

"You do not really think I would let you go off on this ridiculous quest all alone, do you?" asked Cika. "You would get yourself killed or worse...lost."

Kona stifled a giggle, relieved that it was Cika and not someone else. "Do you not mean lost or worse...killed, Cika? Because personally I would much rather be lost than killed."

The young elephant huffed in irritation. "Of course. You know what I meant. Now you must get on my back."

Cika lowered herself down to the ground so that Kona could climb up onto her back. The princess pulled herself up onto her friend's broad back, and clung to the silver chain that Cika wore around her neck.

"Are you ready?"

Kona's excitement traveled through her voice, and Cika shook her head in despair.

"I do not know why you are so excited. We could get attacked by robbers, bandits, snake tribes, wolf tribes, spies, and who knows what else. And we could get horribly lost and die of starvation…"

Kona laughed softly as Cika continued to tell her every possible thing that could be dangerous to them on this journey.

The stars sparkled as they watched the two companions move briskly down the worn road away from the city that was their home.

6.

Kona awoke to the sound of Cika's snoring. The golden-haired princess looked around, and felt a strange ache in her back. Very early in the morning, the two companions had left the road and found shelter under a rock ledge. Lying on the hard ground was not as bad as Kona had thought, but the rock under her lower back certainly was not appreciated.

The princess was suddenly aware of the slight scuffling sound coming from within her sack of supplies, which was laying a few feet away from her. She saw a bump under the sack's cloth side that was moving.

Curious, Kona reached out and pulled the sack closer. The bump went very still, and did not move, but Kona thought she heard a panicked squeak.

Lifting the sack's opening, Kona peered inside, and saw a small rodent cowering inside, clutching a piece of bread that had a bit of the top nibbled off.

"Hello?" said Kona. She wasn't sure if the little animal could speak the common language or if it could speak at all. But she wanted to try. "I suppose you are hungry. Go ahead and eat the rest of that."

The rodent cautiously crawled out of the sack and into the morning light. Kona smiled. The rodent was a small rat, about half grown. A small red dot painted on its shoulder identified it as a female. Kona silently thanked Quetoro for her studies of all the different animal tribes.

"My name is Kona."

The rat looked at her quizzically for a moment before chuckling merrily. "Is a Roniki!"

The sound woke Cika, who snorted as she opened her eyes groggily. When she saw Kona and the rat, she was wide awake. Her trunk coiled backwards in distaste, and she stared at the newcomer.

"What on earth!"

"Cika, may I introduce you to my new friend, Roniki," said Kona with a broad smile. The elephant's expression clearly stated that she thought Kona had lost her mind.

"She is a…mouse!" exclaimed Cika in exasperation. At this, Roniki chattered wildly and scurried over to Cika. Reaching the astonished elephant, she stood up on her back feet and crossed her front legs.

"Not mouse! Is rat!"

"What is the difference?" retorted Cika, scooting her front feet away from the irritated little rodent.

Roniki spread her front arms wide. "This mucha difference, elephant," she said sagely. Kona tried to hide her mirth by covering her mouth with one hand, but she could not hold back the giggle that passed her lips.

Shuddering, Cika replied, "Go back to wherever it is that you came from and leave us alone."

To both Kona and Cika's surprise, the little rat's head drooped. "Roniki sent away by family. Finder of food. No food left for Roniki family to eat. Starving weather comes here."

Saddened, Kona asked, "You mean the famine?"

Roniki nodded. But Cika was not touched. "Well then you had best be on your way. You do not need us to search for food."

Kona was about to protest. Cika gave her a glare. But Roniki was not so easily defeated. She began to walk away very slowly.

"Roniki go away, find food for family all alone...probably Roniki die. Never go home to family. Family probably die."

Baffled, Cika groaned. But Roniki was not finished. She spread her front arms wide once again.

"Probably whole rat tribe dies. Maybe whole world die. Then there be no more elephants."

Nearly choking with laughter, Kona rolled onto her side and buried her face in her blanket. Cika was bursting with frustration and puzzlement over what to do with this rodent.

Roniki paused and turned to look back at Cika with drooping ears and a look that was so sorrowful and anguished, that Cika couldn't stand it.

"Alright, alright! Stay with us then. But the minute I catch you stealing any food, you are on your own...understand?" the elephant said in exasperation. Roniki's ears perked up and she bounded back toward Kona and Cika, glee written in her eyes.

"Roniki not steal food! Bigga elephant worry much."

The little rat clambered up onto Kona's shoulder and chuckled. "Where we go now, pathmates?" she asked enthusiastically.

Cika's eyes narrowed. "Pathmates?"

Kona explained. "She is calling us her friends, like companions. You know, since we are traveling together."

Rolling her eyes, Cika touched Kona's supply sack with her trunk. "I do not suppose that you have a map in there?" she asked. Kona grinned triumphantly, and after fishing around in the sack, brought out a carefully folded parchment map.

Opening the map, Kona spread it out on her blanket and studied it for a moment. Jumping down from her perch, Roniki bent over it as well, paws on hips, pretending to look at it carefully.

"Well, we should cross the Melduine River today," said Kona. "Then the next village we will come to is Terar, but to get there we have to go through most of the Sidasor Jungle. When we get to the country of Sumeria, we will have to take a longer way if we want to miss Goraphel's Desert."

Roniki nodded gravely and pointed straight ahead. "We go thatta way, then. To north city of Terar!"

Chuckling, Kona shook her head. "No, Roniki. That is south. We want to go north."

Undaunted, Roniki spun around and pointed the opposite direction, and repeated her enthusiastic comment. Kona laughed and refolded the map, returning it to her supply sack.

"Come Roniki. You can ride on my shoulder. Just do not jump down onto Cika's head," teased Kona. The young elephant huffed and looked away. Roniki scrambled back up to Kona's shoulder.

"I cannot believe I am doing this, Kona. This is madness," said Cika. "We should return to Utomia now before we get into something that is too dangerous for us."

"Have you so little faith, Cika?" replied Kona with a smile.

Cika grunted. "Kona, to get to Terikanha, we will have to cross some of the most dangerous land in the world! The Sidasor Jungle is a labyrinth run by robbers and thieves, and misfits of the worst kind, not to mention rogue animal tribes that bear no loyalty to the rulers of Leyowan."

"Cika…" Kona began.

But the elephant was not finished. "And then, we come to Sumeria! No matter which way we go, we run into the same problem! Goraphel's Desert is hundreds of miles across, and there are innumerous dangers within it. But if we go the other way, we will have to pass over the Rihanor River, go past the Lake of Secrets, and cross the Welkali Mountain Range, which has defeated many stronger than we are. So yes, I have very little hope that we will even make it to Terikanha. And even if we do, the Queen may turn us away without even a proper greeting."

There was a brief silence before Kona replied, "Cika, I cannot say that we will not face any dangers. But I will continue until I have no breath left in my body to try to save this country and the people in it."

Roniki puffed out her chest. "Roniki too. No breath."

With a sigh, Cika lowered her head. "I just...I would feel better if someone actually knew where we were."

"Someone does know where we are. And that Someone knows everything, and what lies in every heart. God will protect us, Cika. Besides, Nobio knows where we are going. I told him too," said Kona, securing her sack to her shoulders.

Climbing up on Cika's back, Kona rested her hand on the top of her best friend's head, noting the slowly flapping ears indicating Cika's nervousness.

"Please trust me, Cika. If we do not do this, many will die."

The elephant did not respond, but Kona could sense her best friend's agreement, for Cika moved northward with a determined edge to her stride.

For a long time, they traveled in silence, Roniki sleeping on top of Kona's supply sack. Kona was intrigued and fascinated by the scenery. Having never been outside of Utomia since she had been a tiny child, seeing more of her country was a dream come true for her.

The forest soon gave way to heavier jungle territory. But Kona noticed that the leaves were not as green as they should be.

Dry underbrush crackled and broke beneath Cika's large feet. Birds flew overhead, some gliding silently through the air, some chasing after bugs and other edible items. Some were perched up high in the trees, and sang out unique and beautiful melodies. Kona breathed in a deep lungful of fresh air, reveling in the foreign feeling of freedom that was rushing through her.

Soon, the faint sound of rushing water came to Kona's ears. Roniki awoke and sat up, peering curiously over Kona's shoulder. Cika's ears began flapping, but Kona was too enthralled to notice. The three companions moved out of the jungle and onto a rocky slope that ran down to a wide river. Cika stopped on a ledge overlooking the swiftly racing water.

Kona caught her breath as she marveled at the beautiful sight beneath her. The sun's rays caught the glistening waves that the water made, making the river sparkle like a diamond road.

"Oh!" Kona exclaimed in delight. Roniki was also excited and jumped up and down.

"Time for bath, Roniki thinks!" the little rat said enthusiastically. Cika began making the descent toward the river, and Kona tightened the straps on her sack, preparing for the swim.

"I will have to swim, so hang on tight, and keep the supplies above the water, Kona," said Cika. For the first time, Kona realized that Cika was trembling, and her voice was unsteady.

"Are you alright Cika?" asked Kona worriedly. But Cika did not answer. She just stepped into the water one foot at a time, going slow and feeling out the currents. Kona clamped her legs around Cika's sides, and Roniki gripped Kona's supply sack with her paws.

Soon, Cika was up to her shoulders in the water, and the currents were getting stronger. Kicking off from the river bottom, Cika began swimming, her powerful shoulders and hindquarters moving her through the rushing water.

Kona felt the cool water splashing against her legs and thighs. Roniki chuckled and climbed down to Kona's lap. The next splash had them both drenched and laughing. Cika kept moving, focusing on her progress through the water. The opposite shore came closer and closer.

Finally, Cika's feet touched solid earth once more, and she moved more quickly now. Kona threw her sack up onto the shore, and slipped off of the elephant's back. She gasped as she was completely engulfed in the cool refreshing river.

Cika's trunk wrapped around her waist. Kona laughed as she shook her head, her soaked golden hair showering the elephant with watery drops.

Releasing Kona and walking closer to shore, Cika shook herself. Water sprayed everywhere. Roniki jumped from her back and swam over to stand in the shallow water where she could touch the ground.

Playfully, Kona whisked her hand back and sent a large splash up against Cika. In surprise, the young elephant stared at her best friend. In all the years she had known the princess, Kona had never actually played like this.

"Kona, are you sure we should be - "

Cika's comment was cut short by a glob of mud that struck her forehead. Roniki, the culprit, chuckled merrily, armed with another pawful of the gooey substance.

The warning look that Cika gave the rodent was ignored, and the other pawful of mud struck Cika's shoulder. Kona, thoroughly excited by the prospect of actually getting dirty for once in her life, reached down into the water and picked up half a handful of mud.

She threw it at Roniki, who was struck square by the glob. Kona nearly fell over with laughing at the sight of the young rat completely covered in mud. Using her paws to wipe her eyes clean, Roniki chuckled again and looked up at Kona with a gleam in her eyes.

Then a true battle began. Mud and water flew everywhere, completely drenching and covering the three companions. Even Cika participated after her protests were ignored and she had been pelted with a few handfuls and pawfuls of mud. When the furious fighting began to cease, all three were wet through and very dirty.

"How are we going to clean this off?" observed Kona, looking down at her muddy dress. At least she had worn a very simple old dress, and not a fancy one.

"We in water, silly human!" giggled Roniki. The little rat jumped up into the air and dived down under the water. Kona smiled and sank down beneath the surface, and discovered that by kicking her feet and simultaneously moving her arms and hands, she could clumsily but effectively glide through the water.

Opening her eyes hesitantly, Kona could see all the beautiful rocks that lined the river's bottom. There were plants growing up into the water, and they waved slowly back and forth. Kona reached out and touched one of the plants, and it's slimy yet soft feel surprised her.

Coming up for air, Kona saw Cika splashing the mud off herself by sweeping up sheets of water with her trunk.

"Cika, have you seen under the water? It is so beautiful! Who would ever guess that there was such a world under the river?"

In surprise, Cika looked at the awestruck princess. "Of course there is, Princess. Remember all the studies that Master Quetoro had you and I go through to learn the different types of land and water kingdoms."

Kona nodded. "Yes, but I did not know they were so wonderful!" she said, and then dived back under. This time, Kona saw a school of tiny fish floating around near the bottom. She reached out to touch one, but they darted away. Kona barely held back her giggle as one of the long water plants brushed against her leg, tickling her.

How could she have missed all of this her whole life? She had been so sheltered in Utomia, and had never known anything about what her country was really like outside of the city walls.

Gliding through the water, Kona reached down and picked up a handful of rocks and mud. She watched as the mud sifted through her fingers and floated back toward the bottom like muddy rain. She inspected the rocks carefully, and found one that was a clear blue color, and smooth like silk. Gripping it in her hand, Kona began kicking her way back up toward the surface. She reveled in the knowledge that her leg didn't ache when she was in the river.

A swift movement next to her alerted her to danger. A white and black striped snake darted past her, moving through the water at great speed.

Kona tried to call for help, but her voice was lost under the river's surface. She realized her mistake as water rushed into her nose and mouth. Frantically kicking, she raced toward the surface and air. The snake turned and came back toward her again.

The long reptile was nearly upon her when it stopped suddenly a few feet from her face, and looked at her quizzically. It was about to turn and swim away when a huge gray foot smashed down into the water, pinning the snake against the river bottom in some rocks.

Kona lunged to the surface, breaking clear of the water with a loud gasp. Coughing, she felt herself being pulled toward the shore. She dragged in a huge lungful of air, but that caused her to erupt into another coughing fit.

Cika stood next to her, her ears flat back, her sides heaving. "What did I tell you about the dangers?"

The elephant's 'I told you so' tone was lost as Kona smiled up at her. "I am alright. I realize now the snake was not going to hurt me. That was so *exciting*, Cika! You should have seen all those beautiful things!"

"But the snake! You were nearly killed, Kona! Those snakes have venom in their fangs, you should have known that! All the studies you have done, for naught?" Cika exclaimed incredulously.

But Kona just pushed herself up into a sitting position. "Cika, I am sorry. But I am still alive, and so are you. The snake did not bite me, and he did not bite you either. In fact, he stopped before he got to me and then was going to go away when you stepped in. Let him go Cika. We are all safe, and I have seen things I would never have dreamed of. I cannot wait to see more!"

Baffled but subdued, Cika sighed. "Alright. But we had better get moving again. Roniki is with the supply pack."

Once again, Kona retrieved her pack and Roniki and climbed up to Cika's broad back. Roniki nestled into Kona's arms and fell asleep, tired with all the play.

7.

That night, Kona built a fire in a small pit of stones that she and Cika gathered. Roniki even helped, hauling small rocks and pebbles. Over the trees and through a small clearing, the tall Selmar Mountains were slightly visible in the moonlight.

Kona looked at them for a long while, admiring their silent strength and glory. They were the guardians of the lands, Kona thought to herself. A faint smile touched her lips.

Sleeping soundly, Cika was snoring on the other side of the crackling fire. Roniki crawled over to Kona and sat next to the princess.

"Notta good night sleep with bigga noise from elephant," commented the rat, looking a bit miffed. Kona chuckled and handed Roniki a small piece of bread from the supply pack. The rat accepted it gratefully and nibbled a small piece off.

"You needa eat too. Not starve."

Roniki had ceased eating to look up at Kona, her expression of expectancy confirming her observation. Kona smiled and withdrew a piece of bread for herself as well. Nodding in approval, Roniki went back to eating her own meal.

"So what is your family like, Roniki?" asked Kona. The rat paused eating once more and looked deeply thoughtful.

"Roniki rat tribe biggest of all rat tribes. Much rats, hmmm," she began, adding a strange and wistful little hum to her last sentence. "Roniki has mamaratta and a pappyratta."

"Is that your mother and father?" asked Kona, confused by the rat's thickly accented dialect.

Nodding, Roniki continued, "And has four brotherrattas...only one sistaratta though. Others all growed up and gone to new rat tribes. Two brotherrattas killed by snake tribes."

"How awful!" exclaimed Kona. "I have never had siblings, but I can imagine how painful that would be."

Roniki shrugged. "Brotherrattas die, someday Roniki die too. This is way life always been, cannot change. So Roniki be happy while alive, worry later. Big Creator in Sky makes everything happen...so why worry?"

The simple comments of the young rat surprised and touched Kona. "Yes, I suppose you are right. I am so glad that you are with us, Roniki. You are a wonderful companion."

Embarrassed, Roniki looked down and studied her food intently. "Nice human too," she said.

Kona giggled. "Thank you, Roniki. Goodnight, try and get some sleep even though Cika is being louder than an army of boars."

The two of them chuckled together as they bedded down for the night. Kona rolled onto her side and closed her eyes, still smiling.

. . . . .

Cika was the first to wake the next morning. She lifted her head, and glanced across the last remaining embers in the fire pit to see Kona and Roniki snuggled together, sleeping soundly. Raising her trunk slightly, Cika smelled the air. Something was amiss, although she could not identify it. There was a foul odor in the air.

Lurching to her feet, Cika shook Kona's shoulder with her trunk. The young princess awoke instantly.

"Cika, is it morning? What is wrong?" she asked groggily. Cika spoke very quietly, and her tone was urgent.

"Get your things together. We must leave here right away. There is something amiss in the jungle. There is something or someone out there that would do us harm if they found us."

Without any other questions, Kona gathered her things together and secured her pack, settling the sleeping Roniki on top. Climbing up to Cika's back, Kona clung with her legs as the elephant began moving quickly away. Looking back, Kona searched the trees with her eyes, trying to see if anything followed them, but she could not spot anything out of the ordinary.

Cika began moving faster, her feet crunching through the underbrush. She stopped, and they paused to listen. Far in the distance they heard a spine-tingling, horrible sound. It was the wild cry of a hunting wolf pack.

Now Kona knew that many of the wolf tribes were loyal to the throne of Utomia. However, she also knew that there were many who were not. And with the famine... chills ran up and down Kona's spine.

"Hurry, Cika!" she said.

Roniki woke up and sensed right away that they were in danger. "Wolf pack follows," she commented softly. Kona did not respond.

Soon, the howling was louder, and sounded much closer than before. Cika tried to move as fast as she could, but she could not go very fast without making a lot of noise, cracking through the brush and plants that were everywhere. And they could not hide, because the wolves' superior sense of smell would easily track them.

Finally, when the howls were very close, and the sounds of the wolves crashing through the brush were quite audible, Cika stopped.

"Kona, get off my back and up in that tree. I will help you climb it. Hurry now. We do not have much time!"

Fear began creeping up into Kona's heart. "What about you, Cika?" she asked, her eyes wide as she began climbing up the tree laboriously. Cika did not respond, but pushed Kona up toward the tree with her trunk. Roniki scurried up the tree ahead of Kona, and looked out over the jungle from a high branch.

"Bad wolves verra close!" she exclaimed with a squeak of fright. "Elephant run far away now."

Cika shook her head. "No. I will not leave you two behind. I will fight. Maybe there are not many of them."

Frantic with worry, Kona gasped out, "But Cika you cannot! You do not know anything about fighting wolves, or fighting anything for that matter! They will kill you! You *cannot!*"

But Cika turned her back to the tree and faced the sounds that were drawing closer and closer. "Stay in that tree, Kona," she warned firmly.

There was a loud crashing of brush, and six wolves appeared from the trees. Kona noticed right away that they were skinny and looked as though they had not had a full meal for weeks. Saliva dripped from their fangs, and their eyes were sunken.

Cika lowered her tusks, and shook them threateningly. "Go on your way, rogues," she said darkly. The wolves did not respond, but growled and flattened their ears.

Kona bit back a scream as the largest wolf leapt into the air, teeth bared. Cika raised her head and the wolf landed perfectly in place for her tusks to make a wide sweep and throw him into a nearby tree.

At the swift defeat of their leader, the other five leapt in all at once, snarling and snapping their teeth. Cika blew a long trumpet-blast from her trunk and then went to work with her tusks and feet.

But with five wolves against one elephant, the odds were not in Cika's favor. Blood was soon mingling in the dirt from a dozen gashes that she had sustained. The wolves were merciless.

Cika made a thrust with her tusks that left her right side vulnerable. One of the wolves leapt for the opening and sank his teeth into the hide behind her ear.

Trumpeting in pain, Cika swung her head back and forth, trying to dislodge his hold. Another wolf jumped for her back, and dug in with his jaws. Blood flowed from Cika's now numerous wounds. The elephant crashed to the ground, prey to the wolves' fangs.

"CIKA!"

Kona's scream was cut short by the arrival of someone quite unexpected. There was a savage yell, and a young boy jumped from the brush to Cika's left and barreled into the wolves, a curved dagger in each hand. With this new threat, the wolves backed off, breathing heavily. After a moment of watching the boy stand ready, daggers held easily in his hands, the wolves turned tail and ran off into the brush.

Still in shock, Kona forced herself down from the tree, and fell the last few feet to Cika's side. She put her hand on Cika's shoulder, and brought her hand away sticky with blood.

The strange boy surveyed the wounds for a moment and then looked up at Kona. His emerald green eyes were sharp, and he pointed toward the brush.

"Bring me *Trymn* plants, and hurry. I need to staunch the bleeding," he said urgently. Kona stood and limped into the brush. She did not see the boy watching her carefully.

He took several large leaves and pressed them against the wounds. When Kona returned with the plants, he tore them and crushed them in his hands before applying them to the gashes.

Kona knelt beside Cika and touched the large ear that was lying still against the elephant's head.

"Is she…"

Cika suddenly lifted her head. "Stop worrying, Kona. I am fine. They are just a few scratches."

The boy looked up at her with a smile. "Well met, elephant. You fought bravely today to protect your friends."

For the first time, Kona truly looked at their rescuer. He had light, sandy brown hair that was unkempt and raggedly cut. Part of it fell over his eyes…which were the greenest color Kona had ever seen. His tunic was sleeveless and made from worn buckskins, revealing darkly bronzed arms. His hands were dirty and looked strong, yet they were gentle as he administered to Cika's wounds.

His breeches were cut off at his knees, and had pockets in the front. His brown boots were worn, as though they had seen many years of use. His leather thong belt held his two curved daggers, a perfectly matched pair. The weapons looked far too fancy to be carried by such a common looking person.

There was one other piece of finery that the boy had, and that was an etched bronze bracelet that circled his upper left arm, imprisoning the taut muscles.

Kona tore her gaze from the boy and returned it to Cika, who was also surveying their rescuer with great interest. "You have my thanks, young sir. How is it that you happened upon us at such a perfect time?" asked the elephant.

The young man smiled. "I heard the ruckus in the woods. I was on my way to Terar, actually."

This perked Kona's interest. "So are we!" she exclaimed, ignoring the warning look that Cika gave her. "Are you traveling alone then?"

The boy looked at her with his piercing green eyes again. Kona felt an unexpected tingle in her fingertips.

"I am traveling alone, yes. But it is peaceful that way," replied the boy. "I have always traveled on my own."

Silently tucking that bit of information away, Kona spoke again. "We do not even know your name to properly thank you," she offered. The boy looked at her for a long moment before responding.

"My name is Aren."

"Well then Aren…" Kona looked at him with a smile. "You have my thanks for the life of my best friend and companion."

Aren gave her a short nod and then stood up, walking into the brush and disappearing from view. Kona was completely baffled. The boy had not even acknowledged her gratitude.

Cika slowly lurched to her feet, and gave a sigh.

"Oh well, perhaps it is best he is gone. I am well enough to walk. We had best be on our way. For all we know, that boy could go and tell someone he has seen us and I am sure your father has hundreds of trackers out looking for us by now."

Kona suddenly realized something. "Cika, where's Roniki?" she asked in concern. The elephant looked up at the tree, where the small rat was peering over a branch, clinging to it.

"Roniki is here in tree!"

Kona looked up and let out a sigh of relief. "Good. Come down now, Roniki, the wolves are gone and we need to leave. Cika are you well enough to walk? I will walk beside you until you are healed completely."

Her trunk swaying back and forth, Cika looked proud. "Nonsense. My injuries are not serious. I have a thick hide. It will take more than a few wolf bites to bring me down."

"Cika stop being such a stubborn beast! You just barely got away with your life. If that boy had not shown up..."

Refusing to admit the fact that Aren had saved her, Cika huffed. "I could have defeated them," she said. Kona gave her an unconvinced look. Roniki scurried down from the tree and jumped up on top of Kona's pack.

"We go away now before bad wolves follow again," said the rat. Cika and Kona agreed, and the three of them set off through the jungle.

. . . . .

The moon was considerably brighter that night, for which Kona was thankful. Cika had fallen asleep soon after they'd found a suitable place to camp for the night, leaving the young princess with the task of finding firewood. Roniki had stayed behind to keep an eye on the supply pack and the sleeping elephant.

The ache in Kona's leg began to worsen as she tried to make her way through the twisted underbrush of the jungle. She bit back a cry of pain as she made a misstep over a protruding rock, and she fell to the ground. The wood in her arms scattered.

Covering her face in her hands, Kona took a deep breath to calm herself, ignoring the rushing pain through her leg. Reaching out, she began to pull the wood back into her arms, when a cool voice spoke behind her.

"Let me help you."

Looking up in surprise, Kona saw Aren standing behind her, a pack slung over one shoulder. She quickly stood up and smoothed her hair back out of her face.

"Thank you," she said, at a loss for what else to say. She watched as Aren swiftly gathered the branches that she had dropped in his arms.

"I realized that I never asked your name," he said.

"My name is…Tira," Kona replied. She prayed fervently for forgiveness, but she could not tell the boy her real name. Aren changed the subject.

"You have a crippled leg," he commented. "There must be a painful story to explain its existence." His frankness surprised Kona, but she lifted her chin. She would not be ashamed of her imperfection.

"I was very young. I do not remember it very well. I fell under the wheel of a merchant's cart, and it crushed my leg," she explained quietly. Aren did not look up at her, but nodded.

"It is a true miracle then that you even walk."

Kona had to agree to that. "It is. I had the best physicians in the country." Kona realized suddenly that she had just given away something of her status, and she silently rebuked herself for letting the information slip.

Having gathered all the wood, Aren straightened up, and his green eyes bored into Kona's blue ones.

"Your parents must be very wealthy then, to afford such luxuries," he observed, his tone and expression giving away nothing.

"They...they are," Kona stumbled, trying to come up with an answer. She could think of none. Aren stepped closer to her, and Kona felt her heart skip a beat. Had she given away too much?

"Then may I ask why you are here with no escort or proper protection from the miscreants that roam this jungle?" asked Aren, his voice dangerously cool.

"It was my choice...I am studying the different cultures and tribes," Kona said in a rush. She had not lied, but she had not given away more of the truth either. The corner of Aren's mouth lifted in a smirk, but he said nothing.

"Very well then, keep your secrets. I suppose you are needed at your camp. I'll help you carry the wood." Aren looked away from her, and Kona let out her breath in relief. She felt smaller than an ant whenever Aren looked at her with those burning green eyes.

Kona murmured a response and led the way back to Cika and Roniki. When the rat saw them coming, she chattered nervously at Aren's reappearance.

"Finda strong boy inna woods?" she asked Kona curiously. Glancing at the still sleeping Cika, the young princess nodded.

Wasting no time, Aren scooped out a hole in the earth in the middle of the camp, and began breaking the sticks. He arranged them carefully in the hole with the practiced ease of someone who has done the task many times.

"I see you are no stranger to making fires," said Kona. Without answering her, Aren nodded, never taking his gaze from his work.

Finally, he reached into his pack and withdrew two stones. Striking them against each other with long swift strokes, sparks began to fly into the pile of branches. Soon, a tendril of smoke rose from the hole.

Putting the two stones away, Aren bent down and blew softly onto the tiny flame under the branches. A few seconds later, the fire had grown to engulf the entire pile, and the warmth spread to Kona where she sat watching. Satisfied, Aren laid back against a large boulder, setting his pack beside him.

Kona laid out her blanket and crawled in between the two pieces, rolling on her back away from Aren.

As she fell asleep, she was unaware of him watching her.

. . . . .

"Kona!"

Cika's urgent tone of voice brought Kona out of her sleep quite quickly. She opened her eyes and saw her best friend standing over her looking completely flustered.

"What is he doing here?" asked Cika. "I thought he left!"

Kona looked to the side and saw Aren sitting across from them, looking amused with the proceedings. Though she had seen him the night before, Kona was slightly surprised that she had not dreamed his appearance.

"He came back and helped me last night when I was gathering firewood. He built the fire for us," replied Kona. At this, Cika was at a loss of what to say. She grunted softly and moved away, going back to stand by Roniki, who was nibbling on a bit of fruit that Aren had given her.

"Since I am going to Terar, I might as well travel with you," said Aren. It was not a question, simply a statement that would not be argued. Except by Cika.

"I do not believe we need an escort, young sir," she said. Aren raised one eyebrow slightly.

"Of course you don't. But I am coming with you."

Kona was surprised at Aren's insistence, but she did not say anything in defense of either him or Cika. The truth was that she didn't mind the idea of Aren's companionship. After all, he was protection against all of the dangerous sorts that they could run into on their journey.

However, Kona admitted to herself, if he discovered her true identity, it could become a problem. He might try to take her back to Utomia. Besides, they did not know anything about him. He could be a thief. She shuddered, fervently hoping that was not the case.

Cika had dropped her argument, but she did not look pleased with the situation.

"Alright then. Let's get going. Daylight doesn't wait for anyone," said Aren. He moved off toward a less dense area of the jungle. Kona bit back a comment at his bossiness, and gathered up her things.

In a few minutes, the four of them were walking along a worn path that was obviously traveled by people who knew the jungle.

"What kind of a path is this?" asked Cika.

"It is a gypsy path," replied Aren. There was a gasp of surprise from Cika. Kona felt a rush of excitement. The gypsies of Leyowan were those that chose to wander from city to city, playing music and living off the land. They rarely had much money, but had heard they were a happy, carefree people.

"Aren, are you a gypsy? How do you know about this path?"

The only answer was the sound of their feet making soft thudding sounds on the dirt. Kona felt a prickle of anger in her mind.

"Keep your secrets. How can we trust you if we do not know anything about you?"

Aren stopped and turned around to face her, anger on his face. Cika placed her trunk protectively in front of Kona, but Aren did not seem to notice.

"I never asked you to trust me. I am helping you, because I felt generous. I can leave right now if you want me to, but I am not going to answer your questions. You have no right to know anything about me."

Kona was left speechless, completely surprised at Aren's outburst, and the anger and hurt that showed in his eyes. When she finally found her voice, it was unsteady.

"I am sorry..." she murmured. "Thank you for helping us."

The hurt expression left Aren's eyes as swiftly as it had come, and the neutral mask fell back over his face. He turned and continued down the path, his stride more decisive than before. Cika moved in front of Kona and walked after him, clearly upset about the way he had spoken to the princess.

Kona lowered her head. She could not understand why, but knowing that Aren was angry with her made her feel distressed. Why was it so hard for her to be friends with him?

8.

Terar was not a wealthy village. It was large, but most of the trading that went on within its wooden palisade walls was for cheap trinkets and food supplies. Terar's inhabitants were nearly all human, with a reputation for being greedy and gluttonous. Loyalty and compassion were not among their known traits.

Afraid of being recognized, Kona had agreed to Aren's plan to disguise her. Now, in the grubby work dress that Aren had bartered out of an old merchant, dirt smeared over her arms and face, and her golden hair released from ribbon and dressed in two ragged braids, Kona felt like a simple peasant girl.

She had to admit, she felt excited at the prospect of being able to mingle with these people and be one of them, which was something she had only ever dreamed about. Aren and Cika were ahead of Kona and Roniki slightly, walking down the main street of the village. The hustle and bustle of the villagers' everyday lives filled Kona's ears and heart. She marveled at the way they bartered and haggled over different items, and how simple their way of life was. To be honest, she even found that she envied them, however slightly.

In her supply pack was the necklace that Nobio had given her, as well as her simple chain bracelet that she had brought along, a birthday present from her uncle Jathren, long ago. Now she almost wished she had not brought it.

She noticed that Aren seemed completely at ease around all the people, even going so far as to greet some of them.

Kona was ignored save for the curious looks of a couple passersby. She surmised that they were curious about anyone who traveled into their little village from the outside world of Leyowan. Perhaps they did not have visitors other than the merchants very often.

Up ahead, Cika kept glancing over her shoulder to make sure that Kona was still safe and behind them. She had protested when Aren suggested that they go in pairs of two, but had finally seen the wisdom of it. After all, if Cika and Kona were recognized by anyone, they would have a very big problem.

Roniki was perched on Kona's shoulder, playing the part of a young girl's loyal pet. She took the role very seriously, chuckling and tugging on Kona's two loose braids.

Kona glanced to the side and saw Aren and Cika waiting for her outside a tavern. The noise that she heard coming from inside made her nervous… shouts, clinking glass and loud stomping. When she got close enough, Aren leaned down and spoke quietly for only her and Cika to hear.

"I'm going inside to see if I cannot find out some of the latest news about the famine and what's going on around these parts. It pays to know these things."

Dropping a few coins in Kona's hand, Aren added, "You might as well go over to that baker's stand and buy yourself some food. Get some for Cika and Roniki while you're there too."

Kona nodded silently as Aren turned and disappeared into the noisy tavern. Walking across the street, Kona smelled the air appreciatively as the wonderful aroma of the baker's wares reached her nose.

Chattering excitedly, Roniki pointed out a small sugar biscuit. Cika was interested in a fresh loaf of bread. Kona found several honey cakes that looked simply delicious. Paying for the items, the three companions retreated to the side of the street and ate, watching all that went on, waiting for Aren to return.

Biting into the honey cake, Kona felt a shudder of delight. It tasted wonderful, much better than the honey cakes that she had at the palace, and those were her favorite treat!

Beside her, Roniki was savoring the sugar biscuit with much relish. Every few nibbles, she would pause and chuckle with glee.

Kona rose and went back to the baker's stand. Holding out a few coins, she bought another sugar biscuit and another loaf of bread for the road. She smiled as she tucked them away in her pack, thinking of Roniki's joy when she was given another one of the delicious biscuits.

As the golden haired princess turned around, she felt a calloused hand on her shoulder.

"'Ello there, ain't you a pretty lass?"

Turning her head, Kona saw that the voice belonged to a middle aged man wearing grungy old clothes and holding a mug in his hand. His breath reeked of liquor, and Kona felt a shudder run up her spine.

"Please excuse me, sir," she said quietly, trying to pull away from his grip, but his fingers tightened. Fright shone in Kona's eyes as she once again tried in vain to release herself from this stranger's grasp.

"Let her go, you good for nothing drunk!" Aren's voice pierced through Kona's fear and she saw him standing next to the man, eyes narrowed and dark.

The drunken man muttered something about 'overprotective brothers' and let go of Kona's shoulder. Raising the mug to his lips, he stumbled away. Kona's knees buckled with relief, and Aren reached out just in time to catch her before she fell.

"You're fine. He's gone now," Aren soothed. His voice was surprisingly calm and soft. Much different than the tone he had used with her a few days ago.

"Thank you...for saving me."

Before Aren could respond, a horseman rode through the street. His lathered horse stopped in the marketplace square.

Raising his voice, he shouted, "People of Terar, hear a message from your king, Morgo of Utomia. The Royal Princess Kona has disappeared, and is feared to have been kidnapped. If you have any knowledge of her whereabouts, you are to report to me directly!"

Aren glanced sideways at the girl who was pressing back against his arm as though she was trying to disappear. He set his jaw, resolving to talk to her very seriously when they were out of the city.

The townspeople were gathered around the horseman, and Aren saw the opportunity to get out of the village unnoticed. He beckoned to Cika and Roniki who were waiting for them a few paces back.

Grasping Kona's arm, Aren pulled her through the crowd, following the path Cika was creating for them.

Following silently, Kona's eyes glanced from side to side, watching the villagers for any sign of recognition. But thankfully, there was not much chance of that. Few of them even knew what the king himself looked like, much less the princess.

And Kona did not feel much like a princess at the moment. She followed Aren meekly through the crowd on the street, and did not say a word, even when they had left the town and headed back out onto the forest path.

As soon as they were within cover of the trees, Aren turned to Kona, his eyes blazing.

"You'd better stop pretending you are something you are not. And I'd better start getting some answers. If you want me to keep protecting you, I want to know where you're going, Princess Kona."

Shock and then despair crossed Kona's face. Cika came over to stand beside her, glaring at Aren.

"Watch how you speak to her, commoner!" she said angrily. Kona visibly flinched at her best friend's harsh tone. But the expression on her face was now one of total defeat.

"Tonight I will tell you everything," she promised quietly. Cika grunted in protest, but Aren nodded in agreement, his eyes allowing no room for argument.

"Yes, tonight you *will* tell me everything."

. . . . .

Kona watched as Aren started the fire. They were sheltered for the night in a cave, just big enough for the four of them. Roniki had not moved from her place on Kona's shoulder, but the young princess was silently thankful. She appreciated the comfort of her little friend's companionship. Cika had been watching Aren with a hawk's eye ever since he had turned on Kona in the woods outside of Terar.

Finished with the fire, Aren came to sit beside Kona. "Well then?"

Kona sighed deeply, half dreading the conversation, and half relieved that she would not have to keep so many secrets from Aren. She glanced at him, and saw that he was watching her expectantly.

"You were right, I am the Princess Kona. Forgive me for telling you that my name was something else. I have left Utomia with the single purpose of finding help for this country. The famine has hit us and my father refuses to call for aid. Many of his advisors think that he is wrong, and I stand with them. If Leyowan does not find help from another country, we will lose many lives," she finished.

Aren looked thoughtful. "So where are you planning on finding this help?" he asked.

"I am going to Terikanha."

At Kona's answer, Aren looked up in surprise. "You do know what they say about that country and its queen?"

"I will make my own judgment of that," replied Kona. "Some people said things that were spiteful about my mother, but she was not anything like what they said she was."

"How do you know?" asked Aren. "She died right after you were born."

Anger filled Kona, and she glared at the boy next to her. "My mother is the reason this country is still free! If it were not for her courage and determination, we would be ruled by the Morbians, and I would probably be dead!"

Aren held up his hands. "I meant no offense," he amended. Kona leaned back against the cave wall.

"So now you know my story. What is yours?" she asked. Aren shook his head and tossed a pebble into the fire.

"My story is my own. I have shared it with no one."

Kona's curiosity became irritation. "Aren you cannot expect me to travel with *you* if I do not know anything about you. For all I know, you could be some sort of spy or a thief."

"I have been both," said Aren quietly, keeping his gaze away from Kona. She was surprised at his confession.

"You have been a spy?" This time Kona could not hide her fascination. Aren nodded, but said nothing else. Kona scooted to the side so she was facing him, and tried again.

"Aren please...tell me."

The boy looked at her for a long moment, his eyes searching hers. Kona was silent and waited for him to speak.

Looking back toward the fire, Aren said, "I cannot. My memories are better left unremembered."

Cika made a groaning noise of annoyance. "Young sir, I believe you owe the Princess the explanation that she gave to you. How is it that you expect her to tell you about herself when you refuse to return the favor?"

Scowling, Aren tossed a couple more pebbles into the fire, and added several branches to the glowing flames. Kona decided to try a different approach.

"Aren, your story cannot be as painful as mine. I have lost a mother. I never knew her. I will not condemn you, no matter what your story is."

Kona was surprised when the expression Aren faced her with was one of deep anger.

"Perhaps you should think before you speak, Princess. You know nothing of my story, so do not so lightly assume my pain is less than yours. You may have lost your mother, yes. I have lost two parents who were dear to me, in a way more gruesome than you could even imagine. I saw them die!"

Aren stood up, his green eyes flashing. He looked at her intensely for a long minute before turning and striding out of the cave.

Speechless, Kona stared after him. She realized that she had hurt him very deeply, and that she had been wrong to assume things about his past. Cika cleared her throat.

"Let him go. We can make our way without him."

Kona glanced at her best friend in surprise. "Cika, he has not left us for good. He did not take any of his belongings with him. I have to go find him."

"But Princess, you cannot be out alone in the forest with a strange young man," warned Cika.

"I must apologize…what I said was wrong." Before Cika could protest, Kona was gone, hurrying out into the jungle in her awkward, lurching run.

. . . . .

Kona did not know how long she ran. But soon, her leg began to ache painfully, and she slowed to a walk. Stopping beside a small creek, she sank down to the ground, letting her tears flow freely. Gripping handfuls of her grungy dress, Kona squeezed her fists tightly, trying to close out some of the pain that she felt in her heart.

. . . . .

Aren was leaned against a tree, chewing forcefully on a long, dry blade of grass. He was trying desperately to close away the painful memories that the princess' questions had aroused.

Why couldn't she just leave him alone? She had her own past to worry about, and she did not need to be pushing her way into his.

Aren was suddenly aware of a sound he had not heard earlier. And that sound was one of someone crying.

Moving toward the sound, which was quite close to him, Aren stopped. He could see the shape of a girl huddled against a tree by the creek. He knew that it was Kona.

Half of Aren wanted to turn around and walk away, but the other side of him did not want to leave her alone in the dark.

"What are you doing out here?"

Kona turned when she heard Aren's voice. The boy saw the telltale tear stains that glistened on the princess' cheeks. She quickly reached up and wiped them away, leaving her face flushed but tearless.

"I was looking for you," she confessed quietly. "I wanted to ask your forgiveness for what I said earlier. It was wrong of me."

Aren felt unsure of what to say. He did not want her to apologize, but since she had, he did not know what to do. Since his parents had died no one had ever apologized to him for anything.

"I...forgive you," he said quickly. Then he stepped back, glad that it was over with.

"Thank you," replied Kona. She reached out for a branch and pulled herself up from the ground. Aren watched her as she began limping painfully back in the direction of the cave.

After a moment of indecision, Aren went after her and lifted her up into his arms as though she weighed no more than a child.

"What are you doing?" she asked in surprise. "I can walk."

"Walking is obviously hard for you," was the only explanation that Aren gave. His eyes were expressionless.

Kona felt the heaviness of exhaustion descending on her, and tried to mutter a response. But she was asleep before the words passed her lips.

Aren glanced down and saw Kona's closed eyelids, and sighed. She was heavier than he was willing to admit. But he carried her dutifully back through the trees and into the cave.

Cika nearly had a heart attack when she saw Aren walk in with Kona limp in his arms. But the boy shushed her and laid Kona down on her blanket.

"All is well, elephant," he said quietly. "She is fine. She just fell asleep before we got back."

Biting back her sharp retort about Aren carrying the princess, Cika lowered herself to the ground beside her best friend, resolving to guard her through the night. From what, she was not sure, but she did not trust Aren.

Roniki, however, seemed to think that Aren was now a member of their little family, and she scurried over to curl up in his lap. Aren seemed surprised, but a pleased glint shone in his eye as he leaned back against the cave wall to sleep.

Cika watched him for a long while before she finally allowed her eyes to close.

9.

Kona awoke early the next morning. As her eyes adjusted to the light, she saw Aren preparing two plates of food. Cika and Roniki were both still sleeping.

"You are up early," Kona commented. Aren glanced back at her and nodded. He handed her a wooden plate. On it was a piece of bread, a small slice of an apple and an orange, and a few berries.

Kona pushed herself up higher so she could eat, and dug into the food with a voracious appetite. Aren situated himself against the opposite wall. He watched Kona for a few seconds, and then grinned.

"I marvel that for as many years as it can take to learn manners, only a moment is required to forget them," he said, a mischievous glint in his eyes.

Looking up at Aren in surprise, Kona frowned, and then her eyes widened. "Oh..." she said. "I suppose I do look the part of a ravenous rogue." She set down the piece of bread she had been biting off, and set her plate down in her lap.

Aren rolled his eyes. "I meant no offense Princess. Only to tease you," he said exasperatedly.

"Why do humans have to be such early risers?" Cika's groaning voice filled the cave as she rose to her feet. Aren and Kona looked up at the young elephant innocently.

"Because there is so much of the day to enjoy, that I want to see every minute of it that I can," the princess responded. She did not see Aren's look of approval.

. . . . .

Morgo wandered aimlessly through the palace hallways. His tormented mind was filled with grief. How could he have let his daughter disappear like that? Had he protected her enough?

No one knew where she was, or where she had gone. No one knew if someone had taken her, or if she was even still alive. Morgo had waited so long for news of her, but none had come. The palace seemed dead without the bright, happy personality of the princess.

Many people and animals had gone off in search of the princess. But no one had found her.

Fear crept into Morgo's heart as he walked outside into the garden, one of Kona's favorite places. Had he lost his daughter as well as his beloved wife? Could God really have punished him further?

No. She had to be alive. She just couldn't be dead.

Morgo impatiently forced down the lump in his throat. Looking up, he saw the Council Hall in front of him. Suddenly, like a broken child, Morgo ran toward the building. He burst through the door, leaving it open behind him, and kept his pace through the golden statues that lined the hall.

Reaching the farthest door, he stopped. He had never gone into the Chamber of Heroes. He had never gathered the courage to face the likeness of…

Setting his hand on the door, Morgo pushed it open. As his eyes adjusted to the dim lighting of the candles, he glanced to the right and saw the stoic golden bull, its majestic face set looking toward the woman he had protected and been a loyal companion to for so many years.

Forcing himself to walk forward, Morgo looked up into the face of the golden statue to his left. When he saw her face, he could not hold back the tears any longer. With a grievous cry of pain, Morgo fell to his knees at the feet of the statue.

"Kikpona…" he whispered. He had not spoken her name for so many years. And now, he felt his heart break as it passed his lips. Would he never heal? He had suffered the scars of many wounds throughout his life, but the one that laced across his heart was the most painful of them all.

"I…I have lost our daughter," Morgo said brokenly. "I do not even know if she still lives."

The statue's only answer was a deep silence. Rising to his feet, Morgo gently placed a forefinger upon the red painted lips of the likeness. Tears ran down his face.

"If only I could speak to you. If only you were here with me. You were supposed to rule this country, not I. It is your city, not mine. Why did you have to die?" Morgo's voice was filled with pain and longing.

Again, silence filled the chamber. Morgo bent forward and rested his head against the statue's shoulder.

Footsteps from the hallway sounded in Morgo's ears, but he didn't look to see who it was. A moment later, a familiar voice reached him.

"Morgo? What are you doing here?"

Looking to the side, Morgo saw his sister in the doorway; three or four scrolls nestled into her arms, and a shocked expression on her face. Morgo turned toward her, a torrent of emotions racing through his mind.

"I just wanted to see her," he said quietly.

Vanddai glanced at the statue, and nodded. She still looked confused, but unwilling to ask any more questions of her easily irritated brother.

"I will leave you alone then," she said, and turned to go. But Morgo reached out and grasped her arm.

"No...stay. Please?"

Vanddai looked at him, now completely baffled. "Of course, if you wish it." Her tone clearly stated that she was wary of the situation, but she did not voice her apprehension.

Part of her wanted to reach out to her brother. She had never seen him with an expression of such utter sorrow. He looked lost, just as he had when they were young children alone in the forest for the first time without their parents.

But it was not the last time Vanddai was to be surprised that night, for at that moment, Morgo reached out and pulled her into an embrace.

"Forgive me, sister."

Relief flowed through Vanddai's heart. She silently breathed grateful thanks, and returned her brother's embrace.

"You are forgiven."

. . . . .

Kona watched Aren as he led their small group through the last bit of jungle that remained between them and the border of Leyowan and Sumeria. He seemed so confident, so sure of where he was going and what lay ahead.

Glancing back over her shoulder, Kona frowned as she surveyed the surrounding trees. She thought she heard rustling, but she was not sure.

"Roniki, do you hear that?" she whispered to the rodent perched on her shoulder. The rat chuckled softly.

"Roniki hears...something following."

"That is what I thought," whispered Kona. She glanced down at Cika, but debated on whether or not to say anything.

Aren turned and looked at the three following him. "We're not far from the Sumerian border. We should reach it in two or three days," he said. Cika frowned.

"Have you ever been to Sumeria?" she asked him. Aren glanced back over his shoulder at the inquisitive elephant before shaking his head. Cika huffed.

"Well, how is that! Our confident guide has never even traveled these forsaken paths! How are we supposed to find anything if we do not know where we are going? Answer me that!" the young elephant exclaimed exasperatedly.

Kona patted Cika's head. "Stop for a minute. We should eat."

The group paused at a small pool of water to eat and refresh themselves. While Kona was dividing up the food, Aren refilled the water bags from the pool. Roniki took the small chunk of bread and the few berries that Kona handed her solemnly.

"Roniki think maybe more food we need," she said. The golden haired princess nodded.

"Yes, you are right. We need to get more food at the next town, Aren."

The boy did not respond, but nodded. Cika lowered herself to the ground beside Kona, wolfing down the food she was given. Kona took a bite of her own food, and forced the dry bread down her throat. Wistfully she thought of the luscious feasts that her father's cook prepared. Forcing the memory of the delicious food from her mind, she finished her meager serving.

Roniki paused in her nibbling to listen carefully, her head turned in the direction of the woods where they had come from.

After a moment, she looked at Kona and whispered. "Not following anymore. Maybe gone now."

Curiosity sparked in Kona's mind. What had been following them earlier? Was it a wanderer, or a thief? Was it a lonely animal hoping to find companionship? Or could it be a spy from Utomia?

Fearful that her question could be a reality, Kona glanced around at the trees suspiciously. No matter what, she would not return to Utomia until she had accomplished her self-assigned mission.

. . . . .

Morgo slammed his fist into the table. The cheetah messenger in front of him cowered slightly, and the rest of the dinner guests cringed.

"What do you mean she has not been found?" Morgo raged. "I have sent scouts to every corner of this country, how is it that you cannot find her?"

The flustered cheetah frantically stumbled over his words as he tried to explain the situation to his king. "Your Majesty, please forgive us...I... we... one of the scouts did mention that someone had seen a golden-haired girl in Terar who left in rather a hurry, and she was with an elephant about the size of Lady Cika. But they were accompanied by a rat and a boy, about Her Highness's age."

A spark of confusion lit Morgo's eye. "Terar? What on earth would my daughter be doing in Terar?"

He sank back into his chair, and looked across the table to his sister. "Vanddai, why did she leave? What on earth would she be doing in Terar?" he asked helplessly, knowing that though he had asked, Vanddai could no more answer his questions than anyone else.

The king looked back at the cheetah messenger, who was fidgeting anxiously. "Forgive me, young one. I should not have shouted at you. Please inform your scouts to search the territory around Terar very thoroughly. If she is in that area, she cannot have gone far."

The cheetah bowed and raced from the room. Morgo glanced down at his platter of food. His appetite had completely deserted him.

Pushing back his chair, he rose and headed toward the door of the dining hall. After a moment, Jathren followed him. No one noticed Nobio's downcast expression as he struggled with the immensity of the secret he kept.

. . . . .

The withered leaves of the jungle trees provided little shade from the hot midday sun as the four companions went on their way. Not much was said, each of the three kept to their own thoughts. Aren was setting a very brusque pace through the jungle.

After a few hours of silence, Roniki decided to start conversation. She poked Kona's neck with a front toe.

"Roniki think that big mudpig walk slow."

Below them, Cika grumbled. "A *mudpig*? I beg your pardon, you little *rodent*, but I am not a mudpig! How positively rude! If you are going to make insulting comments then you will walk on your own four paws!"

Kona could not suppress a giggle at Cika's offended tone. Roniki chuckled merrily, and looked at Kona through her bright eyes.

"Roniki think big mudpig be angry. What you think?" she asked. Kona laughed aloud as Cika stopped dead in her tracks and flattened her ears. The young elephant simmered silently. Kona decided to make peace.

"It is alright, Cika. She is just trying to make us laugh."

With a sigh, Cika started walking again. "Well she may be making you laugh, Kona, but I am far from amused," she said, but Kona could tell that her friend was trying not to smile.

Aren glanced back over his shoulder. "Keep up, Cika."

Suddenly, Roniki made a low chattering sound, nearly inaudible. Kona glanced at the little rodent in concern. "What is wrong, Roniki?" she asked.

"Bad smell in air…" replied the rat quietly, her nose twitching. Kona frowned, and Cika stopped again. Neither of them questioned Roniki's keen sense of smell. If the rat was alerting them to danger, they were both going to take note of it. Aren stopped walking as well and came back to stand with Cika.

A rustling sound came from the tree above them. Looking up, Kona saw a large branch, and nearly gasped in shock as she saw a python snake wrapped around it, its eyes staring unflinchingly at the three travelers. Cika and Roniki saw it too, and both went rigid.

Aren whipped a dagger out of his belt and moved between the snake and the trembling elephant behind him.

Narrowing its black eyes, the snake spoke in a low tone. "Make no move, outlanderthh,"

Kona raised an eyebrow, for the snake's hiss came out with a very discernable lisp. Even with the severity of the situation, she still barely suppressed a smile. But she knew that snakes were notorious for being unpredictable in their loyalty, and none of them could be fully trusted.

"We mean you no harm if you return the favor," Cika said, her tusks raised slightly, prepared for any move the snake might make. Kona realized that the python was not fully grown, and in human years would have been about the same age as she was.

"Thhnakes thhouldn't truthht anyone but thhnakes," replied the python, its voice cracking slightly. Kona cocked an eyebrow, but Cika quickly translated.

"He says that snakes should not trust anyone but snakes," she said. Kona couldn't keep back a chuckle at that. The very idea of a snake with a lisp struck her as intensely funny.

The python was obviously surprised at her mirthful response, and swayed precariously on his tree perch. Trying to regain his balance, he only jeopardized his position more, and with a hiss of panic, he fell out of the tree with a loud thud.

The travelers could not hold their laughter any longer. Kona held her sides and laughed until there were tears in her eyes. Roniki chortled, and Cika curled up her trunk, as she always did when she was laughing. Even Aren was grinning from ear to ear.

Half-heartedly glowering at them from the ground, the python turned and darted under a large bush. Kona dismounted from Cika's back and followed, despite the elephant's whispered warning. Reaching out, Kona drew back the branches, and exposed the python. He was tightly coiled, his tail covering his eyes.

"Thhtay away," he mumbled.

Kona smiled. "We mean you no harm. My name is Kona, and my friends are Cika, Aren and Roniki. We are traveling to find food for our people, for there is a famine in our land."

The snake's tail was pulled clear of his eyes momentarily. "Famine? My family thhent me to find food too. My name is Thhedgewik."

"Nice to meet you, Thedgewik," said Kona kindly. But the young python shook his head side to side vehemently.

"No, not Thhedgewik. My name is Thhedgewik."

Kona frowned in confusion. "That is what I called you. Thedgwik."

Cika spoke from behind them. "You forget that our snake has a lisp, Kona. His name is Sedgewik. Am I right?"

The snake smiled and nodded. "Yethh, you are right," he replied. Then his expression became more sorrowful. "None of my family wanted to come with me. Can I travel with you?" he asked.

Cika began to reject the plea, but Kona patted Sedgwik's head. "Of course you can! We must help each other if we are all to survive this famine."

Aren shook his head, and low sound of disapproval came from Cika. The young elephant voiced her apprehension. "But Kona, how do we know that we can trust him?"

The young python recoiled slightly under her stern gaze, but Kona stepped between him and her best friend with a reassuring smile. "I believe that we can trust him, Cika. If he does not prove trustworthy, we will make him leave. But he is innocent until proven otherwise."

Sedgwik looked relieved and grateful that Kona had answered for him. "Yethh! I will be very helpful, I promithh…"

Although Cika still looked doubtful, she did not say anything. Roniki piped up from her perch on Cika's head. "Roniki think snake be naughty, then Roniki give snake big hurt on head."

With a smirk, Cika nodded. "Aye, I think I will not be stopping you, rat."

Kona glared at her two friends. "Do not be so hard on him. We need all the help we can get on this journey. Besides, now Sedgwik can speak to any snakes we come across, if they are hostile. Maybe he can convince them to leave us alone."

Neither the rat nor the elephant answered, but Kona could still sense their skepticism. She ignored it and climbed up onto Cika's back again.

"There is no way I am letting him up on my back," Cika stated. Kona rolled her eyes but looked apologetically down at Sedgewik.

"Can you keep up Sedgewik? We will not travel very fast."

The python nodded, and settled his whole length down on the jungle floor. "Yethh. I thhlither fathht."

Cika groaned. "He said that he can slither fast," she translated. Kona smiled at the young python as Cika began moving forward again. Sedgwik slid easily along the ground, having no trouble keeping up with Cika's slow, steady gait. Aren took the lead again, keeping his feet a good distance from the python.

10.

The five travelers came out of the Sidasor Jungle and reached a wide, open plain. Kona looked out over the massive expanse of rocky wasteland and saw hazy mountains standing like sentinels in the distance. Beyond the wasteland was another forest.

"Sumeria..." whispered Kona. Aren glanced back at her and nodded silently. Sedgewik raised himself up slightly for a better view.

"There isn't going to be a town until we get past this wasteland," said Aren. "The next place we can buy food is Nevor, and that's past the forest up ahead."

Cika regarded him dolefully. "I thought you said you had never been here."

"I haven't."

Aren offered no other explanation as he began the descent down the steep hill toward the wasteland. Sedgewik followed him. Cika stood still for a moment, and glanced over her shoulder at Kona.

"Are you sure you want to do this, Kona? We have never left our own country before."

The princess set her jaw firmly and nodded. "Yes, Cika. We are going to save Leyowan. I do not care how far we have to go," she replied. Cika sighed and moved forward down the slope.

. . . . .

The plains were hot and dry. And there were huge rocks everywhere. Kona eyed them nervously, expecting thieves to jump out at any moment. Cika's ears were flapping, and Roniki peered out from the top of Kona's supply pack. Sedgewik and Aren were the only two that seemed undaunted by the heat or the terrain.

"The thhand is warm!" exclaimed Sedgewik happily as he slithered along next to Aren. The snake seemed to be settling in well with his companions. He kept up with their pace easily, and appeared to have taken a liking to Aren.

Cika plodded along wearily. The trip was beginning to take its toll on her, as well as the heat and the burden she carried. Kona worried about her, but there wasn't much the young princess could do until they reached Nevor.

The sun had finally started sinking below the tops of the forest's trees when the five companions reached its shade. Aren removed his pack in a small clearing, canopied by overhanging branches. Dropping it next to a small boulder, he looked around at the dry foliage that surrounded them.

"The famine has already been here," observed Kona sadly, touching a brown leaf with a gentle forefinger.

Sedgewik stretched his long body out along the ground, and murmured a goodnight to his companions before falling asleep.

Cika sank to the ground with a low grunt of weariness. Kona held her water flask out.

"Here, Cika. Drink some of my water. There is enough left for us to share," she said. The young elephant did not argue as Kona had expected, but took a mouthful of the refreshing water.

"Kona, may I see the map?" asked Aren. The young princess reached inside her pack, removed the deeply sleeping Roniki, and then brought out the map that the little rat had been lying on.

Aren spread out the map on the ground and gazed at it intently. "We're about a day's journey from Nevor, and then it's another two days out of the forest and into Goraphel's Desert. I suggest we cross it instead of trying to go over the mountains."

"To try and cross that desert would be a fool's errand. We must go around it," replied Cika.

Aren glanced up at the elephant. "It's not as though we have a better route going around it. We will have to go past the Lake of Secrets, and over the Welkali range. It is a long path and it will be very cold up in the mountain passes."

With a shudder, Cika glared at him. "Wonderful. It sounds like a glorious expedition. We can either freeze to death on top of a mountain pass or die of thirst in this endless dessert."

Kona laughed. "You are such an enthusiastic companion, Cika. We are not going to freeze to death and we are not going to die of thirst." Cika huffed in exasperation but didn't respond.

"It is very dry here. We'll have to be careful and watch for predators or fires," said Aren.

Completely at a loss for words, Cika groaned and let her head drop to the ground in defeat. Roniki pointed at a small dot on the map.

"What is dot?"

"That's the Lake of Secrets," replied Aren. "A place we will fortunately avoid by going through Goraphel's desert."

Kona frowned. "Why? What is wrong with it?" she asked. Aren looked up at her in surprise.

"Surely you know the stories about the Lake of Secrets?" the boy said. But Kona just shook her head and looked at him expectantly. Aren did not look as though he particularly wanted to share the story.

"Many, many years ago, the Lake of Secrets was the place where the first followers of our religion in Sumeria worshipped. There are ruins of the old temple there. They were in hiding because the king of Sumeria was of the old religion, following pagan gods. One of the followers betrayed his kinsmen and told the king of their whereabouts in exchange for his life."

Kona gasped in horror. "How could anyone do such a wicked thing?" she said, her eyes filled with sorrow.

"Because men are sinful, and often follow their own weakness," replied Aren simply. "The king sent a hundred mounted men, and had all of the followers murdered. Men, women, children, male, female and young animals alike were killed without mercy. The leaders were burned alive at the stake. Ever since then, no one lingers long by the Lake of Secrets. It is a dark place."

"Well, I suppose it makes sense not to travel through it. It is farther if we go that way. But what is so evil about it now?"

Aren looked down at the map again. "I...I don't know. I've heard stories..."

"From superstitious people, no doubt, who have never been there themselves, I would wager," said Kona.

"You're very opinionated, for a girl." Aren's voice was teasing, but his eyes did not sparkle.

"Of course I am opinionated. I am going to be queen someday, you know," replied Kona matter-of-factly. She could not help but be slightly irritated. Aren shrugged and did not respond to her last comment. Instead, he folded the map and tucked it safely within his own pack.

"I think I will keep the map, since I am leading," he said.

Roniki had kept silent through the entire discussion, and was looking back and forth between Aren and Kona.

"Eat?"

The rat's quiet plea snapped Kona out of her irritation. "Of course, Roniki! I am sorry. You must be hungry."

Rummaging in her pack, the princess handed Roniki a piece of dried fruit. The rat accepted it gratefully and began devouring it without further comment. Kona tossed a chunk of the last bread loaf to Aren.

"That is the last of the food. We only have a few pieces of the fruit left," said Kona. She did not mention the little sugar biscuit she was saving for Roniki.

"When we get to Nevor, we will stock up on provisions again," replied Aren. "There isn't much we can do until then."

Kona laid out her blanket and crawled into it. "I think we should all get some rest. We have a long way to go if we are going to reach Nevor by tomorrow night."

Roniki scurried over and climbed into the blanket with Kona, snuggling into the crook of the princess' arm. Kona smiled and scratched behind Roniki's ear affectionately. The little rodent sighed blissfully and closed her eyes, resting her head on Kona's hand.

. . . . .

Aren roused them early the next morning, and soon had the weary group on their way through the forest. Cika plodded along as though she was asleep, and Kona cradled a droopy-eyed Roniki in her lap.

But Aren set a brisk pace through the dry trees. He knew that with as little food as they had, reaching Nevor as soon as possible was critical.

Glancing back over his shoulder, Aren saw that Kona was slumped on Cika's back, her chin resting on her collarbone. He felt a small twinge of regret in having to keep such a quick pace, but it was necessary.

Aren turned back to face forward again, and frowned. He still had not provided himself with a reason for his enthusiasm in this journey. The famine was not his problem necessarily. He could get through it by himself. But Aren did admit that he felt a strong sense of duty toward the journey's success and the survival of his countrymen.

"Aren...what is that smell?"

The weary voice of the princess alerted Aren to the danger. He stopped, and frowned as the faint scent of smoke reached his nose.

"Stay here," he said quietly, and handed his pack up to Kona. She held it as he raced away from them into the trees, disappearing from view.

Sedgewik raised his head, and then looked up at Kona. "Thhmoke..." he said, eyes wide.

"Do you....do you think a fire..." began Cika. But she never got to finish her sentence, because a moment later Aren burst back out of the trees, looking frantic. Kona gripped the pack she held.

"Aren?"

"A fire, we've got to get out of here!" he shouted. Kona could hear a roaring sound in the distance. Cika began to panic and dashed off into the trees away from the noise. Aren leapt after her, his strides easily keeping up with the elephant's run.

Roniki buried her face in Kona's dress, obviously as frightened as the rest of them. Sedgewik was slithering along the ground at a surprisingly fast rate, but he was having trouble keeping up with Cika.

"Turn right, elephant!" shouted Aren. "If we can make it to the wastelands we might be safe!"

The roar was getting louder. Kona glanced over her shoulder, and saw black smoke curling up above the trees, staining the beautiful blue sky a charcoal gray color. A tight fist closed around the princess' heart and squeezed painfully.

Cika's big feet seemed to shake the ground as she lumbered on, but her run was too slow. Sedgewik was now ahead of them, leading the way in the mad rush to escape the fire.

Kona saw Aren look over his shoulder and go pale at whatever it was he saw. The princess could now hear the distinct sound of the fire, the roaring and crackling.

Glancing to the side, Kona saw tiny flames racing along the dry underbrush, and knew that the fire had almost caught them. Cika stumbled, and Kona felt herself slipping. She tried to shout to Cika, but her voice was lost in the roaring sound of the flames.

Kona knew that she was not going to stay on Cika's back much longer. Grabbing hold of Roniki, the princess pushed the little rat up toward Cika's head. Roniki gripped the ridge of Cika's right ear, hanging on tightly. She glanced back at Kona in confusion. The princess tried to hang on to Cika, but the jolting movement of the elephant's run was impossible to defeat.

The panicked elephant was far too frightened and too focused on escaping the growing heat of the fire to notice the princess's plight. Roniki tried to alert Cika by nipping on the ear she was holding onto. Aren saw Kona's dangerous situation as well, but he was too far behind Cika to help.

Finally, Kona's fingers slipped, and she let out a cry as she fell to the ground. Aren was next to her in a flash, and pulling her to her feet. He yelled something to her but she could not hear the words. Ahead of them, Cika kept running. Aren pulled Kona along in the direction Cika had taken.

A bright wall of flame shot up from the ground directly in front of them. Kona screamed and grabbed onto Aren's arm.

The boy reached down and took Kona's hand, pulling her after him as he ran to the left. The roar of the fire was deafening, and sweat ran down the faces of the two humans desperately trying to save their lives.

Kona could not even feel her legs. She kept them moving, but she was not sure how. All she could feel was the heat, the sweat, the fear of dying. Was this really the end?

Aren's yell brought Kona out of her fearful trance. She looked ahead and saw the edge of a cliff. Briefly, she tried to struggle as Aren kept running straight for the drop off. But he kept a tight hold of her hand.

"Hang on to me!" Aren shouted into her ear. Kona threw her arms around his neck and held tight. Without hesitating, Aren carried her the last few yards toward the cliff's edge. Kona looked down and saw water below them. A long ways down.

She screamed as Aren's last few strides carried them over the edge.

. . . . .

Kona gasped for breath. The swirling water filled her nose and mouth. Her eyes sought the surface...but it was so far above her. She feebly kicked her legs and tried to move her arms, but she was so weak. She felt strong arms around her waist, and then she was being pulled to the surface.

. . . . .

"Kona..."

The crimson-cloaked figure reached out and took Kona's hand gently, her red hair falling in a scarlet river over her shoulders. "My daughter, you must rise. Your friends need you."

Kona wanted to throw her arms around the figure and never let go. "Mother...I need you. I do not know why I thought I was strong enough for this on my own. I cannot save Leyowan like you did."

The red haired woman smiled. "Yes you can. I believe in you. And so do your faithful companions. They have followed you this far."

"Mother..."

Kikpona's figure began to fade. "You are in a dream, Kona. Rise now, you must go on."

. . . . .

Aren watched the princess anxiously. Ever since he had pulled her from the water, she had gone unconscious, and had not awakened. He looked up at the small ledge that was sheltering them, and then out across the canyon to the fire charred forest on the other side.

He silently prayed that Cika and the others were alive. They'd had so little time to escape...

"Mother..."

Aren's attention returned to the princess at the sound of her voice. She was murmuring quietly, her eyes shifting back and forth beneath the closed lids. Aren reached out and shook her gently.

"Kona."

The blue eyes opened and stayed on him. "Aren...what happened? Where are we? Where are the others?"

The boy's eyes studied his worn boots. "We jumped from the cliff, and I carried you here. I do not know where the others are... you fell and they kept going. I don't know if they are still alive."

Tears filled Kona's eyes. "They must be alive. They have to be," she whispered. "What do we do now?"

"Well, we cannot go back to the other side. I've looked for a crossing and could not find one anywhere close to us. I think we have to keep going. The others will probably know that if we survived we would go on. If they are still alive, they will find us," Aren finished.

"Thank you."

Aren looked surprised at Kona's sudden gratitude. "For what?" he asked. The princess looked up at him.

"For saving me. You could have left me there."

"Don't be ridiculous," Aren retorted. "I am not that much of an uncivilized rogue. I'm not going to run away and leave a girl alone to die in a forest fire, no matter what you may think me capable of."

Kona shook her head and sat up. "I do not think you are an uncivilized rogue."

Raising one eyebrow, Aren smirked. "Not at all?" he asked. Kona noticed a tiny hint of a sparkle in his eyes.

She decided to play along. "Well…maybe a little bit. I suppose you could be mistaken for one if someone did not know you."

Aren laughed. Kona could not help but smile. She had not heard Aren laugh before, and it warmed her.

"Here, Royal Highness. I will let you choose the fruit you desire, so my uncivilized hands do not dirty your food," Aren teased her, handing over the pack. Kona laughed and took it.

"At least we have both of the packs," commented Aren gratefully. Kona nodded her agreement, but her face fell slightly.

"You do think they are alive?"

Aren looked up at her. She looked so downcast and miserable, he wanted to give her a tiny shred of hope that she could hold to. But he could not lie to her.

"I don't know, Kona," he said, and flinched when he saw her shoulders drop slightly in defeat. He quickly continued,

"But you know that if that elephant has anything to say about it, they will be fine. If they are together, they have a good chance of making it."

Kona looked up at him, and smiled again. "Cika will take care of them. But she will be so worried about me. I hope she does not panic."

. . . . .

Cika paced back and forth over the sandy ground. Roniki sat perched on top of Sedgewik's head, and they watched her anxiously.

"I cannot believe I was so stupid! How could I have not noticed her falling off? I was so caught up in my own ridiculous fear that I completely ignored everything else! I have failed her! How could I ever call myself her friend!" wailed Cika in despair.

Roniki tried comforting her. "Bigga elephant worry much again. Strong human boy with Kona. Take good care. She safe with him."

But Cika was inconsolable. "That is just it! I cannot bear to think of that ruffian alone with her! She will be kidnapped, or held for ransom! I just knew he was a scoundrel!"

With a sigh, Roniki sat down and patted the head of the python. "Bigga snake, she notta good listener."

Sedgewik full heartedly agreed. "The little rat ithh right. Kona is thhafe with the boy," he said, his lisp pronounced in his sentence. Cika stopped pacing and looked at them angrily.

"We do not know anything about him! He could be an assassin sent from that Terikanha place! Or a Morbian spy!"

Roniki rolled her eyes. "Or he be bigga evil elephant sent from sky," she said saucily. Cika grunted in frustration at the little rat's sarcasm.

"Wonderful. I am stranded in a forsaken wasteland with a cowardly snake and a sarcastic rat. My best friend is either dead or wandering Sumeria with a boy we know nothing about and who could very well kidnap her. Forgive me if I panic!"

. . . . .

Aren slowed the pace down considerably, pretending his own weariness so he could let Kona rest a bit. She was not about to admit it, but she was exhausted. He could see it in the way she shuffled her feet instead of picking them up to walk, and the way her shoulders drooped lower than usual. Aren had slung both packs over his shoulder so she would not have to carry one.

"Do you want some water?" he asked her. She nodded wordlessly, so he handed her the flask.

"Don't drink it all. You will need some again later," Aren cautioned. Kona took a small drink, and then handed it back. Aren closed the flask's top and slung it over his shoulder again.

"What about you?" asked Kona suspiciously.

"I am not thirsty," Aren lied. He was, but he did not know how much longer the water would hold out. And he could do without it better than Kona could. He could tell that she was not convinced, but she did not comment.

The rest of the forest looked much like the other half had before the fire. Dry, deserted, and completely uninhabitable.

"How much farther until we get to Nevor?" asked Kona. Aren looked back at her, and noticed that she was flushed and pale.

"I'm not really sure," he said truthfully. "I tried to figure out where we are, but I'm still not completely certain. I hope we can reach it by tomorrow, because we need food supplies. Besides, we will be able to find out if anyone has seen the others."

"I hope we get there."

Aren frowned at the princess' abnormally negative sentence. He glanced back again, and saw her slowing down.

"Are you alright, Kona?" he asked. She looked up at him through hazy eyes, and nodded mutely. Aren walked back to her, and hesitantly touched her forehead. It was very warm.

"You are sick," commented Aren. "We'd better get you to a shelter."

Kona tried to mutter a protest, but Aren gripped her hand and led her toward a dense cove of trees, where the sun was blocked by the dry branches. Spots of shade welcomed the two weary travelers. Kona did not protest when Aren led her to a large tree and made her sit down.

Removing the packs from his shoulders, Aren rifled through them and found the sugar biscuit. He reached out, offering it to Kona.

The princess stared at the proffered item, and felt a pang of sorrow through her haze of fever. She thought of Roniki, and wondered how the little rat was, and if she was safe. Or even alive.

"No… save that," she said.

Aren looked at her quizzically. "But Kona, we need to eat. Take it," he replied, once again offering her the biscuit. The princess shook her head.

"No. It is for Roniki. I need to save it so I can give it to Roniki. She likes those. They are her favorite," whispered Kona hopelessly. Her emotions felt completely foreign to her, as if she were in someone else's body. She felt sicker than she ever had in her life, both physically and mentally. Not knowing if her friends were safe was a horrible burden.

Aren looked at her for a long moment, but did not say anything. He put the sugar biscuit back in the pack, and brought out a piece of dried fruit instead.

"Alright. Eat this then," he said. Kona obediently took it and forced it down her painfully sore throat. Then she leaned back against the tree. A fit of coughing gripped her, and she clenched her fists as she gasped for breath.

Aren moved closer to her and handed her the water flask. "Drink."

Again, Kona followed his soft command without a word. The cool water felt soothing to her mouth and throat.

"Thank you," she said quietly. Aren nodded and took the flask back from her. He saw her looking at him expectantly and quickly raised the water to his lips, taking a small sip. Kona looked pleased, and closed her eyes.

"Good…" she murmured.

Aren watched her for several minutes while her breathing deepened and she fell asleep.

Reaching again for Kona's pack, Aren looked inside for the object he had felt while searching for food earlier. His hand came into contact with something smooth and cold. Pulling it out, he saw the silver medallion that Nobio had given to Kona before she left Utomia.

Staring at the necklace, Aren felt a strange ache in his heart. This medallion was the kind of gift that a young man would give to his sweetheart. Putting the piece back in the pack, Aren sat back against a tree. Of course he should have known that Kona would have an admirer.

Aren allowed his eyes to gaze at the sleeping girl across from him. Her hair ran down like streaming golden rivers to pool across her shoulders. Her long eyelashes swept down to rest delicately on her high cheekbones. Her lips seemed too dark a contrast from her pale face.

Forcing himself to look away, Aren glanced up at the sky. He made a silent promise to get Kona to her destination, no matter what.

11.

Cika pushed through the underbrush with renewed ferocity. Roniki sat perched on her head, while Sedgewik slithered along behind. The three travelers all had a unified purpose: finding Kona. So far, all they had seen was dry underbrush, after they had gotten away from the charred forest ruins that the fire had left behind.

If Aren and Kona's disappearance had done one good thing, it was that now Cika, Roniki and Sedgewik found a common companionship in the search for their friends.

"How far until town, bigga elephant?" asked Roniki. All three of them were suffering from severe hunger. The little food they had left had disappeared with Aren and Kona.

"I do not know, Roniki. I really do not know where we are," said Cika. She was trying so hard to be determined and constructive about their situation, but she could not help feeling despair.

Sedgewik glanced up at the elephant. "Thithh way," he said as he slithered off toward a denser section of brush.

"How on earth can you know where we are?" asked Cika. But Sedgewik did not answer, so Cika sighed and plodded off after him. Roniki crossed her little arms and looked down at the Cika's head.

"Roniki think maybe snake lead us into bad place," she commented. Cika did not disagree with her at all. But what other choice was there besides wandering around and getting even more lost?

"Come thithh way, friendthh!" came Sedgewik's excited voice from the brush. Cika let out a grunt, and prepared herself for whatever might be waiting for them. She pushed through the tangled bushes and branches, and was greeted by a sight that nearly brought her to happy tears. There at the edge of a slight drop, Cika saw a town below them.

"Sedgewik you were right!" she exclaimed. The snake looked very pleased with himself.

"Now to find Kona," said Cika. Her eyes were narrowed in determination. The three companions made their way carefully down the path toward the quiet village. Almost immediately, however, they sensed that something was wrong.

A lone figure came out toward them, dressed in shabby, grungy rags. It was a very old woman, bent over a gnarled walking stick. Wispy silver hair was visible around the edges of her cloak hood.

"Who's there?" she called out in a thin, wavering voice. Cika walked up closer and inclined her head respectfully.

"Please, madam, we are simply seeking food and shelter, and our friends. We were separated in the forest fire two days ago. A boy and a girl... have you seen them?"

The old woman shook her head. "I've nary seen a live soul for two months aside from my Pickins. He and I are the last ones ...everyone else died or left."

Despair squeezed Cika's heart like a fist. "I am terribly sorry, madam. Would it be possible for us to stay here with you until our friends come? We were all heading for this town, I believe. Are we in Nevor?"

"What's left of it, I'm afraid," said the old woman sadly. Turning around, she began walking back toward the houses.

"No food here."

Roniki's observation was echoed in the minds of all three travelers. There was no food. They could not expect the old woman to feed them when she no doubt had barely enough for herself, and whoever Pickins was. And worst of all, Kona and Aren had not been here. Which meant that they were most likely still lost...or dead.

. . . . .

Kona was getting worse. She coughed more now, a horrible, retching sound that ripped through Aren's heart every time he heard it. They had only traveled a few more miles from their previous position, and Aren was beginning to feel despair. He could not help Kona; he had no means by which to prepare any sort of remedy that could make her better. He could not find Nevor, or any other town or village.

Today was much like the last two. Aren woke up early in the morning and secured both of their nearly empty packs to Kona's back, and then carried her as far as he could manage.

137

She was limp in his arms, not even having the strength to hold onto his neck.

Aren gritted his teeth as he trudged through the dry woods. His whole body felt numb, as though it was trying to shut off the hunger and the ache that throbbed through every limb.

Looking down at the pale face of the sleeping girl he carried, Aren whispered, "Don't worry, Kona. We'll make it through. I promise."

There was no response from Kona, but Aren felt more hopeful having made his promise again.

"Aren?"

Looking down at the princess, Aren saw that her eyes were slightly open, though fever-glazed.

"Can we please rest awhile?" she asked quietly. Aren felt a strange sense that she was requesting the respite more for him than herself, but he nodded and carried her over to a grove of young trees.

The sun beat down upon them mercilessly, for few dry leaves of the surrounding forest did not offer much protection from the heat.

Kona sighed deeply as Aren set her down in the dry grass. "Do not...worry. He is watching...over us," she said breathlessly. She took long, deep breaths, and closed her eyes again.

. . . . .

The old woman led Cika and the others to an old, rundown hut on the edge of the former town. A bit of smoke curled up from the chimney, and the rickety wooden door was tilted slightly, giving it a lopsided appearance. Lounging in the doorway was a huge old black dog. He raised his head at the sight of them, and perked up his ears.

"Well, what have we here? I see you've brought visitors, Noora. Did the villagers give them any trouble?"

The old woman glanced back at the three travelers apologetically. "I'm sorry, you'll have to be patient with Pickins... he's a bit deaf, and not quite himself. He still thinks the villagers are in Nevor."

Rising shakily to his feet, the dog surveyed the newcomers carefully. "I see, we have a horse, a rabbit and a crocodile. No, no...an elephant, a snake, and a mouse."

Roniki bristled slightly on top of Cika's head. "Roniki is *not* mouse. Is rat."

The dog ignored her and padded silently into the hut, leaving Roniki quite miffed. The old woman, whom the travelers now knew was named Noora, shrugged and gestured them in. The hut was not large, but spacious enough for all of them to fit comfortably inside.

"Now then, a bit to eat," muttered Noora. She bustled around the cooking pit for several minutes, stirring something in a big pot hung over the flames. Finally, she removed five small wooden bowls from a box on the floor, and set them on the three legged table that took over the middle of the home.

Bringing the pot over to the table, Noora reached in with a ladle, and spooned out a very watery substance into the five bowls. The soup, if it could be called that, was mostly broth, and a few old vegetables. The mixture barely filled half of each bowl.

Noora wiped her hands on her ratty shawl. "I'm terribly sorry that I've not more to offer you poor souls. I've not much food left, Pickins and I have to scrounge around the forest for our meals."

"It ithh very generouthh of you to thhare anything," commented Sedgewik quietly. He did his best to imitate a smile for the old woman.

Noora stared at him for a moment, and then laughed brightly. It was more of a cackle, but the merriment was clear. "Well I never!" she said. "A snake with a lisp, what on earth will I find next?"

Looking up from his bowl, Pickins narrowed his eyes. "What's that about a mist? It hasn't rained here for a very long time, Noora."

Ignoring the dog, Noora set the bowls in front of her guests, and observed with a small smile as they dug in voraciously. Sitting down at the table, she picked up a spoon and began eating her own meal.

"So how long will you be staying, then?" she asked. Cika looked up from her soup, which she was trying to figure out how to eat with her trunk.

"Oh…I am not sure, actually. You see, our friends are still lost, and we cannot go on until we have found them. We

140

are on a journey to find supplies for Leyowan; the famine is taking a horrible toll there as well as here."

"I say; speak up!" said Pickins irritably. Cika repeated her comment more loudly so he could hear.

Noora looked thoughtful. "I'm afraid you'll have to go farther than Sumeria, dears. There's no food here either. What little we have we must save for ourselves, or else there won't be anyone in Sumeria left."

Roniki piped up, "We going Terikanha! Lotsa food there."

"Hush, Roniki!" exclaimed Cika. But Noora was already looking at them with an alarmed expression.

"Surely you cannot be journeying there! You must understand, there are dangerous and uncivilized broods that inhabit those forests!" Noora warned, shaking a wrinkled forefinger at her guests.

"Please, Noora…tell us?" asked Cika. She was curious, and besides, anything the old woman could tell her might be enough to convince Kona and Aren to turn back.

"Their way of life is so different from ours. They are carefree, and live every day for the pleasure of themselves. Their king died several years ago, leaving his wife to rule the country on her own. She has no heir, so it's quite possible that the Council will take the throne when she passes on."

Cika was intrigued. "The Council?"

Pickins groaned and let out a little growl. "Aye, the Council. A group of selfish fancy dressin' Terikhanians who think they're above the rest of life. Besides, anyone who lives in that country will tell you that the laws passed in the last few months surely were not the work of the queen."

"How does big black dog know much about other place?" asked Roniki suspiciously. But Pickins just gave a doggy grin, letting his tongue loll from the side of his mouth.

"Pickins has traveled all over the world, dear. He just lives here with me because both of us are getting on in years. His traveling days are over."

The dog muttered something about still being young, but the old woman shook her head and fondly stroked his ear.

"I suppose if this famine is going to leave anyone alive, there's no other choice for you young'ns. Just be careful there, y'hear? Keep your wits about you. And don't let them cheat you out of your money. Those greedy merchants prey on people from other lands who don't know any better."

Cika nodded. "Thank you, madam. I will make sure we are all very careful."

Noora smiled and leaned back in her chair. "Good. My, my… I'm getting rather tired with all this excitement. Pickins dear, will you show our guests where they'll be sleeping tonight?"

The old woman closed her eyes as Pickins led the way out of the hut and onto the main street of Nevor.

There was a larger abandoned home not far from Noora's hut that Pickins brought them to. The door was ajar, and the inside looked bare and empty, but spacious. Sedgewik slithered inside and promptly curled up in a corner. Cika barely fit through the doorway, even though it was large.

"Thank you, Pickins. This will be perfect," said Cika. The old dog bobbed his head and trotted back outside.

Roniki jumped down from Cika as the young elephant lowered herself down to the dirt floor. The little rat ran across the room and hopped up onto a window ledge. Looking outside, she sighed.

"Roniki keep watch for human boy and Kona."

Cika nodded. "Thank you, Roniki. Wake me if you see them." The elephant stretched out across the floor and closed her eyes.

. . . . .

Aren poked at the coals with a long stick. The glowing embers were all that remained of the fire he had made hours earlier. Once again, he had been forced to make camp early, because of Kona. She was getting worse, and was only awake for short amounts of time now.

At the moment, Kona was sleeping again, her chest moving slightly up and down as she breathed. It was those small movements, that sign of life, that kept Aren hopeful. But if he did not get her to a town or to someone who had healing knowledge soon, he was not sure how much longer she would be alive.

Suddenly, Kona's eyes flew open, and her fingers darted out to curl around Aren's hand. The boy jumped at the sudden movement. The hazy, fever-filled eyes of the princess fixated on him for a moment, and then closed again. But the hand that held Aren's did not loosen its grasp. The boy looked down at his captive hand, a mixture of uncertainty and discomfort on his face. He struggled within himself, he wanted to free himself from her grasp, but he did not want to move away from her touch.

After a torturous moment of indecision, Aren hesitantly curled his fingers around Kona's hand, and let out a deep breath he had been holding in.

She was so strong. He would never have made it this far, even with a sense of duty. But Kona did not give up for anything. She was so confident of her goal, and would stop at nothing to save her country. She had such loyalty.

To Aren's surprise, when he returned his gaze to the princess' face, he saw her watching him. Her flushed, pale cheeks belied her illness, but her eyes were bright.

"Why are you helping me?" she asked, her voice soft. Aren looked away from her, unable to meet her gaze.

"I don't know."

Kona smiled. "Yes you do. But whatever the reason, I thank you."

Looking back down at their entwined hands, Aren spoke quietly. "My parents were killed by rogue raiders when I was nine. I was gone, off playing in the woods. I usually stayed out all day when I could…I loved the forest. But that day something felt different. I saw the smoke long before I reached home."

There was a brief pause as Aren lowered his head, silently fighting the pain of the memories he was allowing to resurface. "When I finally came to the house, all that was left was burning ruins. They had set fire to everything. The barn was on fire as well, and the animals gone. My parents..." Aren clenched his fist. "My parents did not get out in time. I thought I saw my mother's face in a window..."

Kona closed her eyes tightly in sorrow. "I am so sorry, Aren."

Aren's voice broke as he continued. "I wandered from town to town, having no living relatives. I was a beggar on the streets for many years. I barely got enough to eat, but I made it through until I met an old man who took pity on me. He offered to take me in if I would help him with chores around his home.

I lived with him for three years, and he was very kind to me. He gave me my daggers as a gift, and taught me how to use them. I even allowed myself to hope that a better life was now mine. But he died, suddenly and without warning one night, leaving me alone again."

"What did you do?" asked Kona.

"I traveled again, some on my own. Some places I traveled with the gypsies. I was finally hired as a spy for an army outpost near the border of Morbia and Leyowan. But after a while, I grew tired of that life, and set out on my own again. I was a good many other things before I met you as well," Aren finished.

There was a long moment of silence. Aren finally willed himself to look back at the princess. He was surprised to see that she was sitting up, and she was looking at him with an expression of deep sadness.

"I cannot imagine what a horrible thing it must have been for you. To see your parents die like that. Do you think you will ever go back? Your home could be rebuilt."

Aren shook his head. "No. I will never return to that place. My parents' blood still stains the earth. Their killers were never found."

"Then…what will you do once we have returned to our homeland?" asked the princess. Aren looked down again, and shrugged.

"I don't know. I suppose I'll travel again. To where or with whom, I don't know. It has been so long since I've known any other life but travel and being free to do as I choose," he replied.

"As long as you still bear hatred for your parents' death, you will never be free, Aren."

The princess' voice was quiet, but her words were like thorns struck into the boy's heart. He pulled his hand away from hers and looked back to the fire. Kona realized that he was not going to say any more, so she lay back down. But talking with Aren had given her hope. Perhaps he was not as lost as she had supposed.

. . . . .

Pickins woke up the three travelers late the next morning. His insistent bark finally brought the other animals out of their deep sleep.

"Noora said to let y'all sleep in late today, but I say yer just being lazy!" called Pickins through the door. Cika lurched unsteadily to her feet and shook her head to clear the grogginess of sleep from her mind. Lifting her trunk, she answered the dog's accusation.

"You would be too if you had traveled as much as we have the last couple of days," she called back.

Pickins pushed open the rickety door of the shack and glared at the elephant. "Well get your shufflers a'movin because we're going hunting. You've all gotta earn your keep, see."

Roniki rubbed the sleep from her eyes with her paws. "Dog make not much sense."

The dog groaned. "I know this ain't a tent, rat!"

Although Cika knew that the dog's deafness was nothing to be laughed about, she could not help suppress a small snort at his translation of Roniki's sentence.

Raising her voice, Cika said, "We do not hunt. You should know that, sir."

"Of course not, we're looking for greens, not other animals. Goodness, what do you take me for?" replied the dog indignantly.

Sedgewik let out a long hiss of relief. "Thatthh good... I do not hunt either," he said sheepishly.

Pickins seemed to widen his eyes. "Goodness me, a snake that doesn't hunt? I've never heard of such a thing. No matter, I'm sure you'll be just as useful searching for greens."

Perking up a bit, Sedgewik nodded his head, and his eyes glittered slightly, which Cika found a bit disconcerting, but she chose to pass it off as one of his "snake traits". Without another word, Pickins turned around and trotted out the door. Cika gathered that they were expected to follow him.

"Come, Roniki," the elephant said, reaching out her trunk to the little rodent, who was still perched on the window sill. The rat scurried up to the top of Cika's head.

The three companions emerged from the dim shelter and out into the bright morning sunlight. Pickins was a little ways ahead of them, trotting stiffly down the street between the deserted buildings. Cika lumbered after him, her big feet stirring up dust clouds on the ground.

There were no sounds from the jungle surrounding the city. All the animals were gone, and the people had left long before them.

Cika heard the dry crunching of the brush and dead grass that she walked over, and cringed slightly. This famine was destroying the land, and there was nothing anyone could do about it.

As soon as they were in a denser part of the jungle, Pickins began nosing around in the brush. Roniki walked alongside him, pointing out anything that looked helpful. Sedgewik glanced up at Cika, and saw her staring off into nothingness, her eyes wistful.

"They will come back," the young python comforted. Cika looked down at him and sighed despairingly, but followed him farther into the jungle after Roniki and Pickins.

12.

Aren stumbled, barely catching himself before he collapsed to the ground. Sweat trickled down his neck, face and back as he strained his body to the limit. The water supply was gone. His tongue felt swollen and dry, and his lips were cracked. The limp figure in his arms was oblivious to the perilous situation they were in.

Looking down at the flushed, pale face of the princess in his arms, Aren felt like letting loose the tears held at bay behind his eyes. He had not cried for so long, but now it seemed as though his life and Kona's were both about to end.

He could not bear it. After coming all this way, for such a noble cause, this was the end? Was this really the outcome of all their work and hopes?

His legs and arms shook with exertion. The princess was getting harder and harder to carry. Aren knew that he could not keep going like this much longer. Their chances of survival were getting smaller and smaller.

All of Aren's dreams were flashing before his eyes, followed by memories. He saw his parents again, their laughter, their smiles. He saw the charred ruins of the estate, and his lifeless parents...

Aren let out a cry as his knees buckled underneath him. He barely managed to keep Kona in his arms. He let her slide to the ground, cushioning her head with his hand.

"WHY?" Aren shouted to the sky. His hands balled into fists, and the first tears began to run down his face, creating little rivers in the dirt and dust that covered his skin.

His head bowed, Aren reached up with a finger to touch his cheek. Looking at his hand, he saw the tiny splotch of water. Tears…

Reaching out to him, Aren's mother wiped the tears away from his face, just as she had wiped the blood away from his scraped arm.

"You must be more careful, my son," she rebuked the five year old boy, but her tone was light and loving. Aren sniffed, and wiped away the rest of the tears with his chubby hands. He looked up at his mother with wide green eyes.

She smiled. "You mustn't cry, Aren. You must be strong, and save your tears for times when they are needed the most."

Tears… yes, this was a time when they were needed. Aren stared down at his hands, now so much bigger than they had been all those years ago. These hands had seen much hardship. Hard calluses covered his knuckles and palms, a silent tribute to past fights, brawls, training. They were a man's hands.

Aren looked back down to the angelic face of the girl he had carried so many miles. Her fevered face still held an expression of majesty. Even close to death, she was still every bit a princess.

"Forgive me…Kona," Aren whispered to her. A light breeze ran over them, ruffling golden wisps of the girl's hair.

Aren raised his eyes to the sky once more, and saw the clouds wandering lazily across its blue expanse. Kona talked about God as though he could hear a person speak. Aren remembered vaguely his mother teaching him about prayers.

"Help me…" his first words were small, and he felt like a young boy again. "I cannot save us on my own. We cannot die now. We've come so far… please help us."

Aren felt strangely peaceful. He sighed and stretched out next to Kona, laying his head down in the warm dirt. He looked across at her. A strange urge filled him, and he reached out hesitantly to her face. His callused finger trailed tenderly down her cheekbone in a soft caress.

Protectiveness surged through him. He would not let her die.

. . . . .

The next morning found Aren in much the same state. He was completely exhausted, but still he pushed himself on, forcing one leg forward at a time. His boots had worn through, leaving his feet completely at the mercy of the rough, hot ground.

Aren frowned… perhaps he was weaker than he had thought, but … were those buildings? He blinked twice, trying to clear his vision. But everything was becoming so fuzzy…he could barely see.

God, help us…

The thought raced through Aren's mind as he laid Kona gently down on the ground. He was sure those were buildings…

Running ahead a few paces, Aren's vision faded in and out as he frantically tried to reach what he thought was a village. His arms were numb, and his legs felt as though they were stuck in mud. Blackness began to creep into his eyes. He opened his mouth to scream for help, but no sound came.

He collapsed heavily to the ground. But as his eyes closed…were those voices?

. . . . .

Aren's right eyelid was forced open. He saw was a pair of beady black eyes staring at him intently. They looked so much like…

"Roniki!"

Aren jerked up to a sitting position, and caught the rodent as she went flying through the air. She chuckled loudly as he held her in his hand.

"Roniki was bird! Can fly now!" she said, still chuckling. Aren all but crushed the rat against him as he did his best to hug her. She squirmed a bit and kicked out with her paws until he dropped her to his lap.

"How did you…where are we? How did you find us?" Aren began asking a flood of questions. Roniki sat up and brushed off her fur.

"You appear out of desert, we find, bring here. We in Nevor!" she answered each of his questions in turn, and then turned around in a little circle to show her excitement.

"Ah, I see someone finally decided to grace us with his presence," said Cika as she walked into the shelter. Her tone was sarcastic, but her eyes sparkled happily. Aren inclined his head to her.

"I never thought we would find you again," he said. "Kona…where's Kona?"

Cika curled her trunk. "She is safe. Noora is taking care of her. The fever is gone now. She will wake up soon." The elephant looked at Aren closely. "And *her highness* should be addressed with respect."

Ignoring the elephant, Aren swung his legs over the side of the rickety bed and attempted to stand. He began falling, but felt a warm trunk wrap around his middle and hold him up.

"You should not be getting out of bed yet. You are still very weak, young man." Cika's voice was softer now, and less severe. But Aren shook his head.

"I want to see her."

The possessiveness in his voice surprised and annoyed Cika, but she did not reply or refuse his request. Step by slow step, she led him out of the shelter, and down the street.

Aren looked around at the abandoned homes with a sense of sad wistfulness. Someday perhaps, they would be filled with laughing, happy families again.

The lonely shack at the end of the street had a thin line of smoke rising up from the old chimney. He shuffled a little faster until he was at the door of the small home. The door was propped open, and Aren saw an old woman walk across the small room inside. The old woman inside smiled at him when she saw him at the doorway.

"Well, well, well. I see that you're recovering quickly."

Aren's eyes adjusted to the dim lighting, and he immediately spied Kona lying on a rickety cot in the back of the room. She was very still.

"Is she…going to be alright?" asked Aren softly. The old woman glanced at him curiously, noting the concern in his voice. She gestured to the small pot that hung over the fire.

"I'm brewing some tea with the last of my herbs… she'll wake up soon, and she'll be fine. Rest is the best thing for her now."

"I will stay with her."

Aren's voice was firm. Noora looked over at him from where she was stirring the tea, prepared to remind him of his own recovery. But when she saw him looking anxiously at the sleeping girl on the bed, she changed her mind.

"Alright, but don't you be movin' around too much. You need your rest too, you hear?"

There was no answer. Aren moved over to sit on the small stool next to the bed. He leaned his elbows on his knees, his eyes never leaving the girl in front of him.

. . . . .

Aren was dozing, his head leaning back against the wall. He had watched Kona sleep for six hours. The others had gone out to hunt for food. His chest rose and fell as he breathed deeply. He was unaware of the pair of deep blue eyes that were watching him.

"Where…are we?"

The voice from the bed jerked Aren from his sleep, and his bleary eyes tried desperately to focus on the source of the sound. When he looked to the bed, he saw Kona awake, looking at him intently.

"You are awake!" Aren exclaimed. He reached out and took her hand in his. Her eyes looked down to their intertwined fingers in surprise. Aren's first thought was to take his hand away, but he decided against it.

"We're in Nevor. We came here yesterday, and the others found us. They have been here for a while, and were waiting for us."

A happy light appeared in Kona's eyes. "I knew they would be here, I told you that we would find them." There was a brief pause before she locked her gaze with his again. "Aren… when we were in the desert… you asked me for forgiveness."

The boy felt a lump in his throat. She did remember. "That…that I did," he replied honestly. "I did not think we were going to make it to help in time."

Kona offered him a smile. "And then you touched my cheek. And it made me feel safe. That is when I knew."

Barely able to speak, Aren managed, "Knew what?"

"That we would live."

Aren let his breath out slowly. He had been sure Kona was going to say something else. But of course not, he was being ridiculous. He could not have expected anything else. He felt Kona squeeze his hand lightly, and he looked back at her hesitantly. She was still smiling.

"Thank you," she said softly. Aren didn't respond, but leaned down and pressed his forehead to her hand.

There was a loud squeak, and Aren pulled back quickly, looking toward the doorway. He saw Cika standing there with Sedgewik coiled beside her. There was a flash of black and white fur, and Kona found herself bombarded by a wildly excited young rat.

"Always knew Kona come! Told bigga elephant all time. Now we go find lotsa food in Terikanha!" Roniki rattled off, chuckling in between sentences to show her merriment.

Kona laughed brightly. "I have missed you so much, Roniki," she said. The little rat covered her eyes with one paw, clearly pleased and slightly embarrassed. The princess glanced to the side and saw Sedgewik and Cika.

"Hello Sedgewik." The princess' eyes were misty at the sight of her friends. "I am so glad you are all safe. I was so worried about you."

Cika spoke up, though her voice was strained. "We worried about you too. Thanks to the boy, you are safe." The elephant looked at Aren, and a silent truce passed between them. Kona saw this and smiled.

"How soon can we leave?" she asked, surprising everyone in the room. Aren looked at her sternly.

"You are in no condition to travel anywhere. The soonest I will consider leaving is in a week. You need your strength," he replied. Kona's eyes narrowed and a determined glint entered them.

"Tomorrow. Cika can carry me and I will be recovered in no time."

"Absolutely out of the question," put in Cika. "You have been horribly ill. I will not take you anywhere. A week is not even enough time."

Kona squeezed her hand into a fist. "No. Three days. That is the most I'll allow. We must carry on, Cika. If we do not find help soon…"

"It is not worth it to me if you end up sick again or worse." Cika's voice was firm. But Kona wasn't backing down either.

"Then I will walk myself."

Utter disbelief showed on every face in the room. Aren was the first to answer the princess' incredible statement.

"Kona think about this rationally. You are sick. You've been very sick for days. You can't go anywhere right away or you will be sick again. And you are not walking anywhere."

"Three days."

There was no arguing when Kona had made up her mind. Cika sighed and shook her head before leaving the hut. Sedgewik followed her. Roniki perched on Kona's stomach and looked at her unblinkingly.

"Do not stare at me like that, Roniki. I will not risk the lives of my people because I was sick for a few days," stated Kona. Aren leaned back against the wall in amazement.

"You have made it sound as though you had a slight headache, Kona. You almost died!"

Kona gave him a bright smile. "But I am still alive, am I not?"

Closing his eyes, Aren gave up.

. . . . .

The three days passed quickly enough. The added help of Cika, Roniki, Sedgewik and Aren made the food searches much more profitable. Though meals were still small, there was enough to feed everyone. Still, Kona did notice the lines of worry that creased Noora's face every time she checked the food supply.

Finally, the day came for the travelers to continue on their way. Noora and Pickins said goodbye to them on the outskirts of Nevor.

Aren embraced the old woman. "Noora, I owe you a great debt for Kona's life. I will return and repay you someday."

Pulling back, Noora shook her head with a small chuckle, and placed her hands on Aren's shoulders. "The way you can repay me, young man, is by protecting that girl. And you're already doin' a fine job of that."

There was a low snort from Pickins. "Didn't say nothin' about no cat," he muttered irritably, before turning and disappearing back among the silent houses. Noora smiled.

"Don't you pay him any mind. He may seem like a tough old boy, but he's really a tender hearted soul."

Kona laughed from her seat on Cika's broad back. "Like someone else I know," she said, looking at Aren.

"Now, I've packed a few days rations into your packs," said Noora. "It's not much, but it should last until you can get to the next village."

Walking up to the elephant, Noora reached for Kona's hand. When she spoke, it was in a hushed tone. "You keep him close now. That young man has a good heart, and that's hard to find." Without another word, Noora patted Kona's hand and left, trudging back toward her hut.

Aren walked past Cika and started heading away from the village, but Kona saw the small grin that he tried to hide.

· · · · ·

The slow swaying of Cika's steady gait made Kona feel sleepy. She ignored the urge to close her eyes. She felt soft paws on her hand and looked down to see Roniki sitting on her palm.

"Glad to be together," said Roniki quietly. She curled her paws around Kona's finger. "Afraid you maybe die."

Kona smiled. "Well, I did not die. Aren took good care of me." The princess suddenly remembered something, and reached behind her for her pack. Opening it, she removed the crumbled sugar biscuit that she'd saved.

"Here, I saved this for you, Roniki," said Kona, offering the biscuit to the small rat. Roniki's eyes grew big as she took it, and then looked up at Kona.

161

"You save this… in desert?"

Kona nodded. Roniki looked down at the biscuit, holding it carefully in her small paws.

"Greatest gift Roniki ever given," the little rat said sincerely. When she met Kona's gaze, there were tiny tears welling up in her black eyes. "Next time Kona eat. Need food in desert."

"I needed something to remind me of you. I wanted to be sure that I could give it to you. It helped keep me alive," replied Kona.

Roniki curled up in Kona's palm, still holding onto her finger.

·····

Four days passed in an endless monotony of traveling. The food was running very low, even though Aren and Sedgewik went out every night to look for whatever might be available.

They'd had hopes that the next town might have inhabitants, but they were wrong. Two days after leaving Nevor, the companions had come upon the village of Omra, and discovered that it looked much the same as Nevor. Abandoned, and lifeless.

They pressed on, traveling for two more days until they were very close to a larger town called Kordaba. On the fourth night, Aren said that he believed they'd reach the town the next day.

Stars created dim light around the camp. Cika, Sedgewik and Roniki all lay sound asleep. But Kona sat on the edge of the circle, her knees up to her chest. There was a slight breeze, which flowed through her hair, gracefully lifting the golden tresses.

Kona heard a rustling, and then saw Aren sit down next to her out of the corner of her eye.

"You should sleep, Kona," he said quietly.

"Do you really think we can save it?"

The question surprised Aren immensely. Instinctively he knew what Kona was referring to, but she'd always been so determined and optimistic about their chances of success.

He looked out over the dry meadow that lay before them, his green eyes sweeping over the dead grass.

"It is unwise to think of it that way now. We set out to save Leyowan and the people that call her home. We can, and we must continue, until there is nothing left for us to accomplish."

There was a brief silence, and Aren felt rather than saw Kona's gaze shift to him. He waited for her to respond.

"I would have never made it this far without you, Aren."

Aren felt his chest tighten. That was not the answer that he had expected her to give. But he felt a sense of pride, knowing that he had helped her.

Kona spoke again. "All of you have helped me get this far. You, Sedgewik, Cika, and Roniki. I can never thank you enough for what you have done. When we return to Leyowan, I will see to it that my father rewards you richly."

"I haven't come all this way for gold and jewels, Kona." Aren's voice was gruff, and he avoided her gaze.

"Then why did you come all this way?" asked Kona, watching him carefully. Aren reached down and began to draw random patterns in the dirt with his thumb. There was a long pause before he spoke again.

"For you."

Kona felt her heart warm. She could not think of anything to say, and it didn't feel right to speak. So she just looked out over the meadow, silently hugging Aren's words to herself.

Feeling slightly embarrassed, Aren wondered if he had said it wrong... he had never been good at expressing his emotions. Especially with Kona. Before he had met her, his world had been comfortable. He could handle anything in his way; stand up to any force that stood between him and his destinations. But with Kona, it was different. He felt as vulnerable and as giddy as a love struck child.

Aren found himself studying Kona. There was a sense of fragility about her, but it was concealed beneath the immense strength of heart and will that seemed to hover around her at all times.

She always seemed so majestic, so much a princess. Even in rags and dirt, she still held herself like royalty. Her eyes were like sapphire pools, too deep to see the end of them, yet filled with so much hope and the love of life.

Aren pulled his gaze away reluctantly. Keeping his gaze on the meadow in front of them, he spoke.

"Though I gaze upon these heavenly stars,
They are but false gold to her beauty
For she is more radiant than the morning sun,
More celestial than the canopy of night,
Lovelier than any who walk the halls of earth."

Aren finished, and then dared himself to look at Kona. She was gazing at him intensely, her eyes shining.

"That was beautiful, Aren. I did not know you read poetry," she said. Aren shrugged and managed a small smile as he chose his next words carefully.

"I used to... my mother loved poetry, and she taught me to appreciate it and... to write it," he replied softly, memories of his mother flooding through his mind. Kona's eyes widened.

"You wrote that?" she asked.

Aren nodded. "I think of poetry whenever there is true inspiration near me. When I see something that I find beautiful, I compose a poem about it."

"So your poem... was it for your mother?" Kona asked. "Hearing you talk about her, she must have been beautiful, as you say."

But she was surprised to see Aren shake his head. "No. It was for you." He turned to her, and Kona saw fear and love mixed in his eyes. Aren leaned forward slightly, keeping his gaze locked with hers.

Kona felt as though her breath was failing her. Was he really going to... her heart leapt at the very thought.

"Kona, you should get some rest!"

Cika's voice came from the circle around the fire. Aren jerked backwards, and a red flush colored his face. Kona moved back also, keeping her eyes away from him.

They both returned to the firelight, and crawled into their blankets. Kona pointedly ignored the glare she was receiving from Cika, and rolled onto her side away from her best friend.

From that very moment, Kona knew that she and Aren would never be the same again.

13.

The next day was rather uneventful. Aren predicted that they would arrive in Kordaba late in the afternoon. Kona managed to avoid any conversation with either Aren or Cika as they went on their way. Roniki kept up a steady flow of chattering, which Kona was grateful for.

Once in a while Aren would glance back over his shoulder at her, but he did not smile, and he did not say anything. Kona wondered what he might be thinking about.

However, Kona had more than enough of her own thoughts to keep her busy. The preceding night's events had her completely baffled. She had never been in love before, so she did not know if what she was feeling was true or false. No one had ever really talked about those kinds of things at the palace. Especially not around her father.

The princess' thoughts were interrupted when she realized that Roniki had fallen asleep, and Cika had noticed.

"So...Kona. Would you mind enlightening me about that little talk you had with Aren last night?"

Biting her lip, Kona did not answer for a long moment. "We talked." she said. From the low grunt of exasperation she heard below her, it was obvious that her answer was not appreciated by Cika.

"Kona, I am not blind. He was going to…" there was a slight pause. "kiss you." Cika's voice was harsh at the end, the words having been forced out.

"I do not understand why you have such a grudge against Aren," said Kona, feeling slightly angry. "He is a wonderful person and he has been a huge help to us. You would probably be dead if he had not shown up to fight those wolves. I think, if nothing else, you owe him some gratitude."

"Kona, I do not want you to fall in love with him. What would your father say? He is a peasant!" Cika exclaimed.

Sorrow filled Kona's heart. She knew that her best friend was right, but she could not help feeling an ache at the words. As a royal, she was expected by her family and her country to marry well. And Aren was not a suitable match. But Kona realized that she had feelings for him in spite of his background.

"My family should want me to marry for love. My mother did, and she could have found a much nobler man than my father to marry. But she did not, because she loved him. As I love Aren," Kona finished. She bit back a small gasp at her own words. She had not planned on admitting her feelings so soon.

Cika stopped. Aren and Sedgewik noticed her movement and copied it, turning back to see what was the matter. Kona kept her gaze carefully away from Aren.

"Why have we thhtopped?" asked Sedgewik curiously. "We muthht keep traveling to the next town."

The young elephant stared at Aren for a long moment. The boy stood tall, waiting for someone to speak, unflinching under Cika's hard gaze. Finally, Cika's eyes softened and she sighed.

"Continue," she said quietly. Aren and Sedgewik turned and began moving forward again, and Cika followed. Kona held her breath as she waited for her best friend to explain her actions.

"If you love him, then I will not stand between you," Cika said, her voice soft. Kona smiled.

"Thank you."

. . . . .

The travelers stood before the heavy wood palisade wall around Kordaba. The pointed tops of the wall beams were fearsome and sharp. The gates were bolted, and there was no sign of anyone inside.

"Hello!" Aren called out. His voice echoed, but there was no answer. Sedgewik slithered up to the gates and tried to peer inside.

"I thheee no one," he observed. Aren frowned and shouted out again. Kona sat on Cika's back, feeling more and more despairing as the moments passed with no sign of an answer.

"Get out! We don't want your kind here!"

The gruff voice that came from inside the wall startled all five of the travelers. Aren walked up to the gate.

"Please! We are travelers seeking only rest and whatever food you can spare!" he said pleadingly. The gruff voice came again.

"Ha! You and every other nobody that comes our way. Kordaba looks out for her own, and you aren't one of us, so get gone before I send arrows over this wall!"

Cika curled her trunk and shook her tusks threateningly, obviously annoyed by the mysterious voice's rudeness.

"We can pay you for your trouble," offered Aren. "We ask only that we can stay here for a night and any food you can spare. We are journeying to another country to find food to send back to Sumeria and Leyowan."

There was a brief pause. "How much?"

Aren breathed a sigh of relief. "Would five gold pieces be satisfactory?" he offered generously. The gruff voice sounded a bit less harsh.

"Aye. But any trouble from you and you'll be cast out of this village like vermin, you hear?"

The gates creaked loudly as the bolt was drawn back and they were pushed outwards. Aren led the way through the opening. Glancing to the left, Kona saw the owner of the gruff voice. He was a middle aged man, bald and fierce of expression. A scar ran across his nose. What surprised Kona the most about him was his height. He barely came to Aren's collarbone.

"I'm Kern," he said. "You'll be stayin' there." He pointed to a rundown hut next to the wall on the left.

"Down the street there's the tavern, and I'll have my wife bring you some food later," Kern continued. He glanced at Aren, warily scrutinizing the youth's size and the two menacing looking daggers lodged in his belt.

"I'll be needin' those knives, young sir." Kern's voice was firm. But Kona saw the spark of anger in Aren's eyes.

"I think not. I have no hidden evil intentions towards anyone in this village, and these daggers were a gift from a very close friend. I will not allow anyone else to handle them," countered Aren.

Kern's expression hardened. "Then I'll be askin' you to leave. We don't allow armed guests in Kordaba. Not after the rabble we took in a few months ago."

Interested piqued, Kona asked, "What rabble? What happened?"

Kern turned to face her. "A group of Sumerian soldiers came here looking for shelter and food, much the same as you lot. Being a loyal village to the Lord and Lady of Sumeria, we took in these soldiers and let them stay here. The first night they were here, they plundered our houses, taking food and anything of value that we had. Naturally, we fought. Many of us were killed, including many of our women and children. The soldiers were merciless. So forgive me for bein' a bit uneasy about your friend here's frog stickers."

"That is horrible!" exclaimed Kona.

Kern looked at her in surprise, obviously not expecting sympathy. He frowned and looked back at Aren.

"Your daggers, please."

Aren rested his hands on the hilts of his weapons protectively. "I must respectfully decline, sir. You have my word that I will cause no harm to come to your people."

"I can't take the chance. You'll hand in your weapons or I will have you removed from this village," threatened Kern. He gave a short whistle, and several armed men stepped out from huts and behind the tavern.

Kona slipped down from Cika's back. The elephant grunted a warning and held out her trunk in front of the princess.

"Please sir, I realize your hesitation to allow us in. But we only wish to stay the night, not to cause any trouble for you and your people."

Kern looked undecided. "I don't know…" he kept looking at Aren intensely, as though he was trying to decipher the boy's true intentions. "Alright, you can keep your pretty little knives, boy. But if they leave your belt even once while you're staying here, I'll have a sword in your gut faster than you can call for help."

It was obvious that Aren was angered by the way Kern had spoken, but he inclined his head slightly and said nothing.

There was a lift in the tense atmosphere as everyone present relaxed. Kern bobbed his head in the direction of the tavern.

"We'll leave you to settle in, but feel free to come and get something to eat and drink when you're ready." The tone of his voice indicated that he wanted them where he could see them to make sure they did not cause trouble.

. . . . .

The hut was smaller than the one that Noora had given them in Nevor, but it was cozy. Aren pulled Kona aside while the others were putting away the packs.

"Keep your eyes and ears open. I know the types of these men. They're not to be trusted for a moment. If they feel threatened in any way, they'd rather strike you down and be wrong than have you get the upper hand and strike them first. And another thing... don't leave my side."

Kona saw genuine concern for her radiating from Aren's eyes. She smiled and put a hand on his arm. "Do not worry. Everything is going to be fine."

Aren led the way out of the hut toward the tavern. Cika followed closely behind Kona, her eyes sweeping from one side of the street to another. Sedgewik and Roniki seemed less nervous, and they chatted back and forth amiably.

The tavern was noisy, and filled with people. There were quite a few women and children in the room, but only a few animals. It was almost as if this town had escaped the nightmarish famine that had destroyed so many of their neighboring villages.

Kona leaned in to Aren's ear. "Strange, I wonder how they are surviving in such pleasant conditions here while their fellow Sumerians struggle to eat each day." Aren didn't respond but Kona saw the faint look of disgust in his expression, and knew that he agreed with her.

A large man with a full mug of some dark liquid came up to Kona and looked at her with bleary eyes. Remembering her experience in Terar, Kona shrank back behind Aren.

"'m goin' outside," the man slurred, before stumbling to the door. Aren shook his head and went up to the tavern keeper.

"May we request five glasses of water and some food?" he asked courteously. The man looked at him with an expression that was a cross between perplexity and amusement, but shrugged and headed toward the back room.

"Well ain't this a pretty thing... the sissy boy and 'is friends want some water and vittles!" came a nasally, unpleasant voice.

Aren looked down to see a thin, rough looking man with a scraggly beard staring up at him over a foaming mug. The man's eyes were cold, and there was a dark glint in them that warned of danger.

"I have no quarrel with you, sir. Who are you?" Aren asked quietly, though inwardly he was panicking. He knew this man. Memories of younger years flooded back to his mind.

The man grinned, revealing yellowed, broken teeth. "Name's Arnolf. Thems some mighty fancy daggers you got there. Can't fer the life of me figger why you'd be carryin' them around though. Those are a man's weapons."

Aren shrugged. "They are. Which is why I carry them. Good day," he finished, ending the conversation and leading Kona over to a table in the back corner of the room. Kona had noticed the panicked expression on Aren's face, but when she asked him about it, he simply shook his head.

It wasn't long before their food and water arrived. The tavern keeper set it down in front of them with an air of tolerance, and then left.

Sedgewik coiled up on the chair and reached out his mouth for a bite of the green leaves that were in front of him. Roniki sat on the table and devoured the piece of bread she held in her paws. Aren kept glancing over to where the strange man sat.

Kona ate her soup in silence, a bittersweet feeling racing through her. It was good to eat real food again, but she could not help feeling guilty when she thought of all the people and animals with nothing to eat.

"Are you alright, Kona?" asked Cika quietly. Kona looked up to see her friends watching her carefully. She immediately offered them a small smile and nodded.

"Of course," she replied. The others went back to eating their food. Except for Cika. She moved closer to Kona and spoke in a low voice.

"That man who spoke to the boy earlier, he is staring at us again." Cika's eyes focused on Aren for a moment. "The one who talked about the daggers…"

It took Kona a moment to realize that Cika was referring to Aren as 'the boy'. Then she could not help the slight twinge of annoyance she felt, but she said nothing. She knew that both Cika and Aren still didn't trust or like each other.

She stole a glance to the side and saw the man sitting lazily in his chair, sipping from the mug he held. His narrowed eyes were fixed on Aren, as if he had seen the boy before.

If Aren noticed the man's blatant stare, he didn't acknowledge it. He simply continued eating his food.

After a short while, the man stood up and left the tavern. Kona let out a slow breath, a sense of relief washing over her. She pushed back her empty bowl and folded her hands in her lap. She still felt a little weak from her bout of illness in the desert, and suddenly she was very tired.

"Aren, I think we should go. It is getting late and we should leave tomorrow morning," she said. Aren glanced at her for a moment, studying the deep circles under her eyes and her flushed cheeks.

He nodded and stood up from his chair to take her hand as she followed his movement. Cika came around the side and let Kona lean on her from the other side. Together, the five friends made their way back out to the quiet street, and toward the abandoned home they were staying in.

Kona managed to get out her blanket and crawl into it before falling fast asleep. Cika gently pulled the soft fabric up to Kona's neck with her trunk.

"She needs to rest. This will be good for her," said the elephant quietly. Roniki scurried across the floor and into the blanket with Kona. Her tiny head peeked out from under it, and she sighed as she settled down to sleep as well.

Aren waited until Sedgewik and Cika had settled in to sleep, and then ducked outside, closing the door quietly behind him.

The cool night air hit his face as he walked into the street, and glanced down the long row of homes. The noise from the tavern had quieted a bit, but Aren wasn't interested in that.

He frowned and bit his lip... years ago, when his life had been at its lowest point, he had been a beggar in the town of Avorak in Leyowan. He had been about fourteen years old, alone and desperately seeking any form of work to feed himself.

Arnolf had come up to him and offered him a job. A simple one, he had said, that required secrecy. Desperate, Aren had agreed eagerly.

That night, when Arnolf came to get Aren for the job, it had turned out that the "work" involved thievery of weapons from a blacksmith. When Aren had realized what the man was doing, he had refused to help and made a run for the home of the blacksmith.

When the burly blacksmith came out and saw Arnolf stealing from his shop, he immediately went to drive the thief away, brandishing a heavy sword. Aren hadn't stayed around to find out what happened, but he had always known that meeting up with the thief again could be dangerous.

And with Kona here... Aren sighed. He knew that the man had recognized him, even though he was now four years older. And it was not because of the face...it was the daggers. They were the same weapons that Arnolf had tried to coax out of him four years ago. Aren was so absorbed in his thoughts that he didn't see the shadow moving up behind him.

"I thought I recognized you, boy," said a grating, unpleasant voice. Aren spun around to see Arnolf standing behind him. The man spit into the dirt street, his eyes glinting coldly.

Aren straightened his shoulders, but did not answer Arnolf. The thief frowned and studied Aren closely.

"Huh…you've grown. Not the little waif you were all those years ago, are ya?" asked Arnolf with a short, barking laugh. "I see you've still got them daggers… and I still want em. Too fancy for the likes of you."

Aren shook his head. "You'll never learn. I am not selling them."

There was another short laugh from Arnolf. "I ain't plannin' on buying them from ya. You nearly got me killed four years ago, and I haven't forgotten it."

"I'm afraid I cannot give them to you, sir," Aren said, his patience wearing thin, and his fingers twitching as he rested them on the hilts of the daggers. He did not know what Arnolf was going to do next, and he was not going to be caught unprepared.

Arnolf grinned, showing his yellowed, broken teeth. "Would ya care to make a wager, then? I'd be willin' to duel you for 'em. Winner takes all."

Surprise flashed across Aren's face. And then suspicion. "You have nothing to offer me, Arnolf. Nothing that you have would interest me."

The thief shrugged. "Perhaps not... but I was under the impression that you and yer little group of misfits were goin' somewhere... yer gonna get awful hungry with no food."

Aren raised one eyebrow. "And you have rations?" he asked.

Nodding, Arnolf pointed to one of the houses. "That I do. Enough to feed all five of you fer near a week or more."

The offer was tempting. Aren knew that finding food outside of Kordaba would be difficult. The next village, Torgir, was many days journey. It would take nearly a week to reach it. But Arnolf was not the type to simply offer the food and then relinquish it if he was defeated in a fair fight.

"And how do I know that you will give me the rations if I win?" asked Aren, his eyes watching Arnolf's expression.

The thief laughed. "I can't rightly get anywhere fast with 'em, now can I?" he responded.

Aren thought over this for a moment. He was confident in his skills with the weapons he had, but on the off chance that Arnolf would cheat... he was not willing to surrender his beloved daggers. Besides that, Aren was more interested in keeping Kona safe, and he was not sure what Arnolf could be capable of.

"I tell you what, boy. Even have one of your little friends come out here and be a witness that the fight's fair," suggested Arnolf. Aren instantly glanced at him in confusion. Why was Arnolf making such a point to show good morals?

"Alright, I'll do it. But make one false move, thief, and you will pay dearly for it," said Aren, his eyes showing that he was completely serious about his threat. Arnolf nodded, looking pleased.

Aren jogged back to the house where his companions were staying. Glancing inside, he debated on who to choose. Cika looked very much asleep, and Roniki was laying on her back next to Kona, all four paws up in the air, an occasional kick of a back foot her only movement.

"Aren?"

The boy looked down to see Sedgewik coiled loosely by the door, his black eyes looking up worriedly.

"Sedgewik, I need you to come outside with me for a few minutes. I'm going to be in a duel. If I win, we have food enough until the next village."

The python looked confused. "Very thhtrange...you humanthh," he said, shaking his head to and fro. But he uncoiled his long body and followed Aren out the door. Arnolf was waiting for them out in the street, holding two small hand axes.

The thief glanced at the fifteen foot python and his expression changed slightly from silent gloating to unease. But he simply said, "First one of us unable to keep fighting is the loser."

Aren shrugged. "So be it."

Sedgewik retreated to a dark shadow under the roof of one of the houses to watch and stay out of the way.

Pulling his daggers from his belt, Aren flipped them around in his hands. An adrenaline rush ripped through him. He had not dueled in so long, and he'd forgotten how thrilling it could be.

Arnolf's face twisted into a vicious scowl as he advanced toward the boy in front of him. He made a thrust to Aren's chest, which the boy side stepped easily. With a growl of frustration, the thief brought his axes together and shoved Aren backwards toward the tavern.

Setting his jaw in determination, Aren retaliated by using the corner of the water trough to launch himself into the air, bringing his daggers in from opposite sides, aiming for Arnolf's arms.

Arnolf met his blades with the two axes, and the two of them strained against each other's strength, each trying to gain the advantage. The thief was surprised by the strength that Aren possessed. The boy's arm muscles bulged as he pushed against the axes that held his daggers at bay.

With a shove, Aren managed to knock Arnolf backwards into the dirt street. The thief jumped back to his feet instantly, and swung his left axe wide. The weapon sliced through the air just as Aren stepped back to avoid it. It missed his stomach by a fraction of an inch.

With a growl of anger, Arnolf lunged, both axes held out in front of him. One of the blades sliced across Aren's lower thigh, leaving a small but painful wound. Aren grunted as he

181

tried to ignore the bleeding cut and retaliate before Arnolf could make a second strike.

It was obvious that Arnolf was getting impatient, and Aren knew that the thief would soon make a mistake, trying to finish the match quickly and defeat Aren. He was right.

Arnolf whirled and brought his axes down toward Aren's right shoulder. The boy ducked under the swing and brought his dagger up into the thief's left arm. Arnolf roared with pain and fell backwards, Aren on top of him. They both let go of their weapons, trying to punch each other.

They rolled over and over in the dirt, fists flying, and dust clouds rising from their scuffling. Stopping with Aren on top, the two opponents grappled with each other. Aren pinned Arnolf's arms and raised his fist above the thief's face. Arnolf flinched and braced himself for the blow. But Aren never struck.

"I win," the boy said quietly. "But I won't harm you any more than I already have. You owe me the rations you promised."

Arnolf's eyes darted to something behind Aren and he instantly began to call out, "Thief! Rogue! Robber!"

Aren moved back in surprise, and looked over his shoulder. He saw men from the tavern stepping out toward him, brandishing weapons. Out of their midst came the little man who had opened the gate of Kordaba for the travelers earlier, Kern.

The small gatekeeper looked very angry. His face was red, and he held a short sword in his hand. He glared at Aren.

"You! I knew it was a mistake to let you lot in 'ere! I knew you was bad folk from the beginnin', I did. Get out of Kordaba, or we'll 'ave your 'eads on a spike!" the little man shouted.

Aren raised his hands. "You don't understand! This was a fair fight. This man," he explained, gesturing to Arnolf, "this man challenged me to a duel, and he promised to give me food and rations for our journey if I won. I have just defeated him fairly, and I intend to see that he keeps his word."

Kern glanced toward Arnolf expectantly. "Well? Is this true?"

The thief looked at Aren, and the boy was sure he saw a glint in the thief's eyes. "No sir. This boy attacked me when I was walkin' home from the tavern. He told me to give him my money and provisions."

Shaking his head, Aren protested, "That's not true. I have a witness!"

He gestured to the shadows, and Sedgewik slithered into view. There were murmurs of unrest from the crowd as the python stopped beside Aren.

Kern looked impatient. "Well?"

Sedgewik lifted his head and looked at the little man solemnly. "It is true athh he thhaid. I am a witnethh."

Raucous laughter rippled through the men standing by. Sedgewik drew back slightly as Kern nearly fell to the ground, his laughter loud and grating. The little man shook his head.

"This is your witness, boy? A dumb snake who ain't even able to talk right?" he said, still chuckling mirthfully. "Alright you've had your fun, now get out of Kordaba before I take a belt to ya, boy!"

Anger ripped through Aren, and he had to fight to keep himself from launching a dagger right into Kern's gloating face. He stood tall and turned away from the jeering crowd, with Sedgewik at his heels, ignoring the crass comments that were hurled after him. The python beside him was silent, but when Aren glanced down, he saw a tiny tear escape from the snake's eye.

"It's not your fault, Sedgewik. Don't blame yourself," said Aren. But Sedgewik simply slithered faster toward the hut, and didn't respond.

Aren sighed and felt dread creep into his mind. How was he going to explain this to that fussy elephant?

14.

"I can't believe you were so foolish, boy!"

Aren raised his eyes to the skies and bit his lip to keep from making a remark he would regret. Cika had been berating him ever since he had awoken her in the early hours of the morning, saying that they were being forced to leave.

Kona and Roniki had not said much, not wanting to test Cika's raw irritation and get more of the anger she was giving Aren. Sedgewik had been silent since last night's happenings, ignoring everyone's concerned comments to him.

And now as they walked away from the palisade walls of Kordaba, Cika was making sure that Aren knew just how mad she really was.

"We finally get to a place where we might have had provisions given to us for the rest of this journey, and you just had to go and show off how manly you are. If you had not gotten into a fight, we might still be sleeping in a comfortable shelter right now!"

Aren made a low growling sound as he fought back his annoyance. But Cika did not seem to notice his growing irritation.

"Maybe you should start thinking about what is best for all of us, and stop being so selfish," commented Cika with a huff.

At that, Aren stopped short and turned to face her, anger etched into every part of his face. "Maybe you should stop talking, elephant. Did you ever consider that? You do not know anything about what happened last night, so maybe you should leave well enough alone!"

Surprised, Cika had to think for a moment before she could respond. "Well then…please enlighten me," she retorted finally.

"I was challenged by Arnolf to a duel. I had a brief meeting with him many years ago, and it was not a pleasant one. He wanted my daggers, and I refused. So he offered to duel me for them. If I won, he promised me enough provisions to last us a whole week. And more importantly I was trying to keep Kona safe!"

Aren's voice had risen to a shout by the last sentence, and he turned abruptly around and began marching forward without waiting for Cika's reply.

Flabbergasted, Cika followed him quietly. She felt Kona slide off her back and glanced over at the princess. Kona's eyes caught those of her best friend carefully and she gave Cika a very calculated look.

The elephant avoided her gaze. "Maybe I was a bit harsh on the boy," she admitted, not loud enough for Aren to hear.

Kona did not answer, but smiled and nodded slightly. Cika sighed, but Kona did not avert her gaze. She kept up with Cika's lumbering walk in her awkward, limping stride.

Finally, Cika huffed. "Fine. I will apologize. But not until we stop tonight."

Satisfied, Kona smiled again and limped a little faster until she caught up with Aren. Reaching out, she put a hand on his arm.

"She did not mean to come down on you so hard, Aren. We are all a little tense. We need to stick together in this," Kona said reassuringly.

Aren moved his arm, and Kona thought he was going to ignore her. But after a long moment, she felt his warm hand touch hers. Gently, their fingers intertwined, and they continued on hand in hand.

. . . . .

That night, Cika did apologize to Aren. She still did not use his name, but Aren did not use hers either. The tense atmosphere lifted slightly, giving the whole group a little more relief.

The companions formed a sleeping circle around their small fire. Sedgewik, Cika and Roniki had fallen asleep, but Kona lay awake, gazing up at the sparkling stars that adorned the velvet midnight sky. She made out several constellations, and felt a rush of homesickness pass over her. She missed Quetoro's patient lessons, Vanddai's storytelling, and Makkiu's gentle purr when Kona sang for him.

An image of Nobio's face entered Kona's mind. A soft smile came to her lips as she thought of her faithful friend.

"Kona...are you awake?"

Aren's voice was quiet, but Kona rolled over on her stomach to see him. He was lying on his stomach too, his head resting on his arms, which were folded in front of him.

Kona smiled. "Does that answer your question?" she asked. Aren grinned at her, and then a slight flush stained his cheeks.

"...about the other night."

Kona's heart skipped a beat. They were finally going to talk about 'that night', and their almost kiss. She was not sure if she was glad or terrified. But she could not show either.

There was a long pause before Aren continued. "I am sorry that I... you know... I should not have done that."

Unable to suppress a smile, Kona replied, "Aren, you did not do anything."

Surprised, the boy lifted his head and met her gaze, his brown hair falling haphazardly over one eye. Kona tried to fight the urge to tell him just how wonderful he looked at that moment.

"I know that you must have someone special to you...back home. I don't know what I was thinking, but it was wrong of me," Aren said softly, his eyes dropping to his hands. He pulled a blade of dry grass from the ground and began fiddling with it.

Confusion filled Kona. "Someone special?" she asked. Aren nodded, still not meeting her eyes.

"I do not have anyone special back home, Aren."

The boy looked up at that, and gestured to the medallion that Kona wore around her neck. "He must have been someone close to give you a gift like that. That's a *regna* medallion, something that someone gives to the person they love."

Kona's eyebrows lifted. "I did not know you were familiar with noble traditions, Aren."

The boy shrugged. "I keep myself informed. So... who is he?" he asked, although in his heart, he really did not want to know.

"This medallion was given to me by a very dear friend named Nobio. He was supposed to be my betrothed, but he already loved someone else. So when I left on this journey, the betrothal had to be broken. I left not only to save Leyowan, but so Nobio could marry the girl he loves. He gave me this medallion to ensure that I would return. He was afraid for me," Kona explained softly.

Aren's green eyes lifted. "Nobio..." he said, rolling the name on his tongue. "He sounds like a very... noble person."

With a smile, Kona poked Aren's arm lightly. "He is... he reminds me a lot of you."

Looking up quickly, Aren's eyes filled with surprise. He did not really know what to say. He suddenly felt hope returning to his troubled mind. He had never imagined that Kona would not already have someone.

"Do you... do you want to go for a walk?" he asked, not really sure what else to say. He wanted to be alone with Kona, to talk to her out of range of prying ears.

The princess nodded and crawled out of her blankets. Once they were several feet away from their sleeping companions, Aren reached for her hand. Kona intertwined their fingers, loving the feel of it. She had never felt so protected and cared for in her life.

Her limp was less pronounced, and she felt as though she were walking through clouds. Aren looked over and smiled at her.

The moon shone down brightly over the two young people as they made their way through the stands of birch trees. The light filtered through the trees, creating halos around Kona and Aren's bodies. They finally stopped in a wide meadow. Barely visible in the distance were the Welkali mountain monarchs, reaching high up into the sky with rigid peaks. The twinkling stars reminded Kona of diamonds in a royal's necklace, gracing the dark velvet neck of the sky.

"They are so beautiful," Kona whispered, looking up at the thousands of tiny bright lights. Aren nodded his agreement.

"So you really... do not have anyone special?" he asked her. Kona looked at him and smiled.

"Well... actually I do. There is a boy that I know," she paused to see Aren's gaze fall. Reaching out, she touched his cheek tenderly and continued, "I met him not long ago... and he is the most wonderful, caring person I have ever known."

Green eyes met blue as Aren processed her words. "And... do you love this boy, as he loves you?" he asked, his voice low and rough with emotion.

Kona's breath froze in the cold night air as she opened her mouth to speak. "I love him with all my heart and soul. And I always will," she said. She tilted her head back slightly, and Aren leaned forward.

Their lips met in the gentlest of kisses. Aren wrapped his arms around Kona as if she were a fragile doll that could break if he let her fall. Kona lifted her arms and placed her hands tenderly on each side of Aren's face.

Kona felt weightless, as though she were a feather. In Aren's arms, she was safe and whole. There was no fear, no worry, only peace and happiness.

They pulled apart breathlessly, still holding on to each other as though the world would crumble beneath them if they let go. Kona buried her face in Aren's shoulder like a small child seeking solace.

"I love you, Aren."

Aren closed his eyes and rested his cheek on the top of Kona's head, breathing in the soft scent of her. She smelled of woodland flowers.

"Your father…" he said softly. He did not have to finish his sentence. Kona knew full well what was implied in it.

"My father cannot force me to marry someone I do not love. Besides, my mother married him when she could have married someone of more noble blood. I will never let you go. You are mine."

There was a sweet possessiveness in Kona's voice that made Aren's heart falter. Her mumbled words were a balm to his still healing heart. After all the pain and suffering he had sustained in his life, he now found comfort in the love of this beautiful girl. He could not remember a time when he had been happier.

Kona sighed, and turned her face to look up at Aren. "It is my birthday tomorrow," she said. "I am going to be seventeen years old."

A smile came to Aren's face. "Such a young one," he teased her good naturedly. Kona rolled her eyes dramatically and shook her head.

"Not so young. You only think I am young because of your old age," she chided, returning his teasing. Aren chuckled and kissed the top of her head.

"Eighteen is hardly enough to be considered old age. I will not be nineteen for nearly a year yet," he responded in protest. But Kona simply shrugged and wiggled her eyebrows.

Aren laughed, and pulled her after him farther into the meadow. He waded through the sea of tall grasses. Kona followed him, but her limp kept them from walking too fast. Aren did not seem to notice.

He turned to face Kona, a new light of joy on his face. "Dance with me."

Taken aback, Kona frowned. "Dance? Aren do not be silly, I cannot dance... my leg will not... I cannot."

"You can. Trust me. I won't let you fall."

Kona felt herself swept into a gentle embrace against Aren, his arms around her waist. She lifted trembling hands to his shoulders. His eyes found hers, and unspoken reassurance passed between them.

Very slowly, they began to move back and forth, swaying to silent music that came from their hearts.

Aren held her gently, keeping his promise. Kona began to relax as they danced silently in the green ocean of meadow grass.

They stayed in the meadow for a long time, wordlessly dancing, before they finally began to make their way back toward their companions.

. . . . .

Kona was nearly asleep, lulled by the side to side motion of Cika's lumbering gait. She had not had much sleep last night, and the dancing with Aren had made her completely exhausted. Roniki was perched on Cika's back in front of the princess, watching Kona with her black eyes.

"Kona not sleep much," observed the rat dryly. She poked at Kona's hand with her paw as she spoke.

"I am sorry Roniki. I was awake most of the night. I did not feel like sleeping." Kona smiled down at the little rodent, hoping that her words sounded convincing. After all... they were true.

She heard a chuckle from Aren up ahead, and could help but smile. Roniki heard him too, and looked expectantly at Kona. The princess could not stop the smile that spread across her lips, and she shrugged. Roniki shook her head in exasperation, and turned around to face forward again, since she obviously wasn't going to get any answers from Kona.

Aren jogged up ahead around a bend of trees, disappearing from view. He soon reappeared with a wide grin, waving at them to follow him. Cika lumbered forward a little more quickly, rounding the bend of trees where Aren had gone.

She stopped as she saw Aren up ahead, standing on the bank of a wide river. Kona's eyes widened as she saw the powerful rushing water racing downstream, following the same path it had for thousands of years. She slipped down off of Cika's back and limped over to join Aren.

"The Rihannor River," Aren said. "The bridge is not far, only a few more miles, I would guess."

Kona frowned. "You know, for never having been here, you certainly know a lot about this land, Aren. One could get suspicious that you *have* been here before when you talk like that."

Aren chuckled and shook his head. "I read the map."

They both laughed. Roniki came scurrying across the rocks of the riverbank and climbed up Aren's leg and arm until she reached his shoulder.

"Bigga river…we swim?" she asked hopefully. Aren grinned and tickled the little rat's belly. Roniki made a giggling sound and ducked her head.

"I don't think thho, Roniki," commented Sedgewik. "River flowthh too fathht to thhwim, right Aren?"

The boy nodded. "Yes, it does flow too fast. A little rat like you would not have a chance of making it across, and neither would we," he said, looking pointedly at Roniki. She sat up and crossed her front legs.

194

"Humpfh. Roniki good swimmer," she countered huffily. Aren laughed and shrugged, nearly causing the little rat to topple off his shoulder.

"I'm sure you are, but this river is not safe for any of us, even a champion swimmer such as yourself," he responded. Kona bit back a smile at Roniki's proud expression.

Kona took the map from Aren's hand and opened it. After a long moment, she looked up at him.

"If we wait to cross the river until we are closer to Terikanha, then we will be much closer to their capitol city, Talda. We would only have to skirt the very edge of Goraphel's Desert, so it would not be as hazardous as taking the Welkali Mountain passes."

Aren glanced down to where Kona was pointing on the map. "I suppose we could. It would be a shorter distance."

There was a loud grunt from behind them. "I think we have company, and from the sound of things... lots of it," observed Cika quietly. All five companions stilled, and felt a slow rumble in the ground.

Silently Aren slipped one of his daggers out of his belt, and stepped in front of Kona protectively. The rumbling grew louder...

. . . . .

Vanddai found Morgo in the Chamber of Heroes. Her brother was gazing up at the face of Kikpona's likeness, his hands clasped behind his back.

"Morgo… we will find her. I have sent out two more horse scouts and four cheetah messengers. There will not be a village in Leyowan or Sumeria that we will not have interrogated."

The king of Leyowan turned to face his sister. "You really believe we will find her? Vanddai, it's been over a month since Kona disappeared. She might have been abducted or worse. We are not getting any information back from any of the villages. Only the story from Terar about a girl who was traveling with a boy. That could have been anyone."

Vanddai sighed. "I have sent couriers to all of the monarchs in our neighbor countries to alert them."

As she finished her sentence, they were alerted to the sound of hooves clopping against the stone floor. Vanddai and Morgo turned to see Quetoro standing in the doorway with Nobio at his side. The old horse shook his mane.

"I believe this young man knows where Kona has gone."

Surprise was expressed on both Vanddai and Morgo's faces as they looked at the boy. Nobio was fidgeting uneasily.

"I cannot say, my lord. She made me promise…" said Nobio dejectedly. "I cannot go back on my word."

Morgo nearly lunged across the room, and gripped Nobio's shoulders tightly. "What you cannot do is remain silent, boy! You have known where she was all this time, and you never breathed a word? Insolent fool!"

Trembling under the king's wrath, Nobio remained silent. "Punish me in any way you wish, my lord. But I cannot betray Her Highness's trust in me."

Vanddai intervened before Morgo could do any damage. "Nobio, please. You must understand that we have to find her and bring her home. Kona cannot care for herself on her own, even if Cika is with her."

"I cannot believe you, boy. If you do not tell me where she is..." Morgo ran a hand through his hair to calm himself.

Nobio lifted his chin. "Princess Kona is stronger than any of you give her credit for. She has gone on a noble journey, and I will not betray her."

All occupants of the room were astounded by Nobio's declaration. The boy's hands clenched and unclenched at his sides, and his gaze remained on the opposite wall, but there was a fire in his eyes.

Quetoro stepped in. "Nobio, I respect your word to the Princess. Perhaps there is a way you can tell us without breaking your promise. If I bring a map, will you show me where she is?"

There was a long pause, and all eyes were glued to Nobio. He finally sighed. "I do not know where she is. But I will show you where she is going. And may I forever be held accountable if my word is broken."

Two servants brought in a map table and set it in the middle of the chamber. Morgo eagerly leaned over the map as Nobio reached out with a finger and pointed to a spot.

Shocked gasps filled the room. Vanddai spoke first. "Why in heaven's name would Kona go to Terikanha? Surely she knows the...nature of that country!"

Morgo looked up at Nobio. "Why has she gone there?"

The boy met the king's gaze, his eyes filled with pride. "Princess Kona is going to save Leyowan."

.....

The rumbling was very close now, and was escalating to a thunderous sound. Aren protectively encircled Kona's waist with his arm, ready to pull her out of the way if she should be in danger.

With a great cracking of the brush, huge elk suddenly began emerging from the trees, leaping over the path, their legs flying as they bounded past the travelers and down into the shallows of the river.

They kept coming, more and more elk were leaping out of the woods. They were mostly does, and there were a few fawns that stayed close to their mothers' sides.

A huge buck elk emerged from the forest. His antlers were gigantic, and they were very fearsome looking. Kona felt Aren pull her back against them as the buck saw them.

He snorted wildly and his eyes narrowed as they fixated on the outlanders. His chest heaving from the run, he came up to stand in front of them. Cika stepped up beside Aren, but even she would be no match for the buck if he chose to attack them.

There was a moment of extreme tension as the buck surveyed them all carefully. Kona held her breath.

"Who are you, and what are you doing in my territory?" asked the buck. His voice was very deep and husky. Kona liked him immediately. Pushing Aren's hand away, she moved forward and inclined her head.

"I pray for your forgiveness, Noble Elk, we never meant to intrude. We are passing through Sumeria, and we will not be here long."

The elk bellowed loudly. "I should very well hope not. This is my land, and you are trespassing without my permission!" he said fiercely, his antlers lowering slightly. Aren jerked Kona back against him, and one of his daggers came out of his belt.

"Ragul!"

A soft voice reprimanded the big elk monarch from behind him. A doe stepped forward, a young fawn at her side. She had wide, elegant eyes and a very gentle expression.

"Is that any way to treat guests? What must they think of us?" she asked the buck, looking at him meaningfully. Clearing his throat, the buck stepped back and raised his antlers.

"Yes, well...protecting the herd is a serious occupation, Sarra..." the buck appeared as though he were trying to regain his dignity.

The doe smiled slightly and shook her head, turning to the travelers. "Please forgive my mate's lack of graciousness," she said, glancing at the buck, who was thoroughly irked.

Kona bit back a giggle. "Thank you... we did not mean to intrude on your land. We are passing through."

Pulling back a bit of his composure, Ragul shook his head slightly and looked closely at Cika. "What, madam, are you?" he asked roughly. "Some relation to cattle, I would assume?"

Aren nearly choked on his laughter, and Kona chuckled. Cika, however, was less than amused.

"I surely am not, thank you!" she replied. "I am an elephant. Haven't you barbaric miscreants ever seen an elephant?"

Before anyone could respond, the fawn beside Sarra bounced forward. "I am not a harcaric isn'tcrant!" he exclaimed, looking pointedly at Cika.

The elephant was caught by surprise. "No no, it is barbaric miscreant."

"That. I'm not one," said the fawn. "I am Rigan, and Ragul's my papa! He is the leader of this herd." There was a lot of pride in the young one's voice.

"Well I never…" began Cika.

Kona stepped forward and dropped in an awkward curtsey. "Pleased to make your acquaintance, Rigan. My name is Kona. I am sure you must be very proud of your father. He is a very noble creature."

The fawn bobbed his head. "Nice to meetcher too, Kona. Oh look, a mouse, mama!" he exclaimed, looking at Roniki, who had perched on Kona's shoulder.

The little rat glowered for a moment and glanced down at Cika, who was smiling knowingly. "Roniki think bigga antler head cousin to mudpig," she said.

Sarra smiled again. "Well, in any case... it would be our honor if you would join us and stay the night. We do not have visitors very often."

After a moment of indecision, Aren nodded. "Thank you, that is very kind of you to offer. We would be honored to stay the night with your tribe."

15.

Aren built a fire in the wide meadow, and the five travelers shared the warm circle with Ragul and his family. Sarra and Rigan were huddled together, and Ragul stood behind them, watching over the sleeping elk tribe.

The elk were spread out over the whole meadow, small brown dots in a sea of the dry grass.

"It is so peaceful," commented Kona, who was lying next to Sarra. The elk mother lifted her head and nodded.

"It is. Long ago this meadow used to be green and beautiful, and the tree leaves were large and vibrant. The wildflowers would bloom amongst the grasses, in blues and purples and reds. Birds used to perch in the branches and sing to us as we grazed. We called it Prosper Valley."

Kona heard the sad note of wistfulness in Sarra's voice. "Someday it will be beautiful again," the princess comforted. "This famine cannot last forever."

"But it has already taken so much from us. Our herd has lost many elk. Some left to find food, but many were taken from us. My mother was among them, as was Ragul's brother," said Sarra. A tear made its way from her dark eye down to her smooth muzzle.

Kona surprised the doe by moving closer and leaning up against Sarra's warm side. The princess reached up and stroked Sarra's neck.

"My mother died too… I was only a few weeks old. She was killed in the war between Leyowan and Morbia sixteen years ago."

Sarra looked down at the young princess with a soft smile. "We share the same sorrow, then."

Kona watched the fire for a long while, until Sarra and the other travelers had fallen asleep. She looked around the circle at Sedgewik, Cika and Roniki…where was Aren? The boy was not anywhere to be seen. Slowly moving away from the sleeping Sarra, Kona stood up and looked around.

"He is in the woods," said Ragul quietly. He gave her a knowing look, and Kona felt a smile come to her face. The monarch of the elk tribe had warmed up to her considerably.

The princess limped off in the direction of the trees. Ragul watched her leave, and then turned his majestic gaze back to guarding his herd.

. . . . .

Kona picked her way through the underbrush carefully, holding onto tree branches to keep from falling.

"Aren?"

There was no answer. Kona sighed and continued over a log, carefully stepping over with her good leg first.

"Aren, where are you?" she called again.

"I'm here."

Kona tried to turn around, but lost her balance and fell forward. Strong arms caught her and pulled her back up to her feet. Kona looked up to see Aren grinning down at her.

"There you go again, falling into my arms," he teased her. Kona smiled and shook her head.

"You could have answered me right away and then I would not have fallen," she chided him in reply. Aren chuckled and pulled her close to him tenderly. Kona nestled her face into the crook of his neck, feeling safe and secure.

"Happy birthday, my love."

Kona's head came back up. She had completely forgotten about her own birthday. She glanced up at Aren, who was no longer smiling.

"You remembered," she said softly. It was not a question, simply a statement of gratitude. Aren shook his head at her, a smirk lifting the corner of his mouth.

"Of course I remembered. You don't actually think that I would forget the birthday of the woman I love?" he asked her in an exasperated tone. Kona laughed and thumped her fist against his chest playfully. Aren pulled her over until they were falling into the grass, landing on the soft ground.

Kona laughed aloud as Aren tickled her sides. After a few minutes, Aren finally let go of her and rolled away slightly.

"I made you something," he said. Kona rolled over to face him, her hair mussed and her face flushed from laughing. Aren removed something from the pocket in his tunic and pressed it into Kona's hand. The princess looked down and saw a tiny carved figurine of a warrior. She gasped. It was her mother.

Long hair flowed down over a carefully carved breastplate. The figure was holding a spear, and it felt as though the wooden eyes were staring into Kona's soul.

Tears filled Kona's eyes. It was her mother, every bit the warrior queen Kona had always known she was. Aren frowned and studied Kona's reaction carefully.

"Don't... don't you like it?" he asked.

Kona lifted her tear filled eyes to Aren's clear green ones. "No, Aren... it is perfect. It is exactly like her. She is beautiful."

Relief crossed Aren's face. "Good. I tried to make it as close as possible...from the stories you have told and the tales I heard back in Leyowan. I had to put the spear in... it was one of my favorite things about her story."

Kona touched the tiny wooden spear with a gentle finger. "Aren, when did you find the time to do this?"

"Mostly when you were asleep. The others knew about it, but I asked them to keep it a secret."

Kona smiled. "Thank you. It really is beautiful. You know... I have never actually seen my mother's spear. My father keeps it locked away somewhere in the palace, in a secret chamber, with her crown and scepter, and most of her things. He always told me that he would let me see them when I was older."

That surprised Aren. "You have never been allowed to see your mother's things? I cannot understand that."

"You do not know my father," said Kona wistfully. "His word is final. He has always been disappointed in me. I am a crippled girl, not the replica of my mother that he wanted."

Aren reached out and smoothed a finger down Kona's cheekbone gently. "I am sure he loves you, Kona. You're beautiful, and I am sure that if your mother was here, she would be very, very proud of you for what you are doing."

Long lashes swept over soft cheeks as Kona closed her eyes. "Your love is the best gift of all. Thank you for remembering my birthday."

Aren reached an arm around Kona's shoulders and pulled her close to him. Hugging her gently, he replied, "You are welcome. I will always think you are beautiful."

"How much farther until we reach Terikanha?" asked Kona.

"Only a day or two," replied Aren. "We should not have too much farther to travel. From the map, it looks like we will go through a border town in Terikanha called Togleby."

Kona frowned at Aren's look of worry. "What else did the elk say?" she asked, not sure if she really wanted to know.

Aren sighed. "Kona, I am not completely confident about going to this country. Sarra told me that the council has been ruling Terikanha for the past five years, and the queen has been just a public figure. I do not know if she is just a weak monarch, or if there is something going on that we don't know about, but I don't like the look of things regardless of what is going on."

"Well, we cannot turn back now. We have to go to Terikanha, because if we do not, Leyowan will be destroyed by the famine," Kona pointed out quietly.

"I don't want to put you in unnecessary danger, Kona." Aren's eyes were full of concern. "If what Sarra said was true, they may or may not be hostile to foreigners, and I'm not willing to take the risk. Perhaps you should stay here with the elk tribe and let the rest of us journey to Terikanha. That way if something goes wrong…"

"No, Aren. I am going with you. I have come this far. The queen is not likely to take you seriously unless I am with you," Kona said. "That is the reason I came. She will know that it is serious if the princess of Leyowan has come to plead for help."

Aren pulled his arm away from Kona and stood up. "The princess of Leyowan is a dangerous title when you are in a foreign country."

"Perhaps, but I cannot avoid what I must do, Aren. I have not come all this way just to sit here while you all cross into Terikanha without me. I will not have it!" she exclaimed. Aren glanced down at her in surprise. Kona never raised her voice. He immediately knelt down beside her and took her hand.

"I'm sorry; I am just worried for you, that's all."

Kona lowered her head. "I know, and I am sorry too. I should not have gotten angry. I suppose I am just worried about actually accomplishing the goal we set out to do."

"We will. And no matter what happens, I will always be there to protect you," Aren said softly. He leaned in and pressed a gentle kiss to Kona's forehead.

. . . . .

The next morning dawned swiftly over the sleeping elk tribe. Ragul of course was the first to awake, and he let out a loud bugle. Slowly, the brown dots that lay around the meadow began to rise.

Kona felt herself being shaken gently, and she opened her eyes to see Cika standing above her.

"Awake, my princess. It is time we were off," the elephant said. "We have a long journey to make if we want to make Togleby by tomorrow morning."

Grasping hold of one of Cika's tusks, Kona pulled herself up from the ground. She glanced around to see Roniki perched on Sedgewik's head next to Cika. But there was no sign of Aren.

"Where is Aren?" asked Kona worriedly.

"He went into the forest to see if he could scrounge up more edible plants for us to take. He wanted to make sure we had enough to eat," replied Cika.

Just then, Kona saw Aren himself walking out of the trees, her pack slung over his shoulder. He lifted a hand and waved jovially. Kona smiled and waved back. When she turned back to Cika, she saw a grim look of amusement on her best friend's face.

"I never dreamed it would be him," said the elephant wryly. "I knew eventually you would fall for someone, but I would much rather it had been Nobio."

Kona chuckled. "Oh Cika do not be silly. You know that Nobio is in love with another girl. I would never be able to live with myself if I were to take that affection away from him."

"I know, but I cannot help but feeling a bit of distaste for your choice. You could have easily found someone..." Cika paused, "more civilized."

"Am I not civilized, friend elephant?"

Aren spoke from behind Cika, having heard the last bit of the conversation as he had approached them. Kona bit back a smile as Cika turned her head to look at him.

"Hardly," Cika huffed. "Kona, we had better be going now."

Sarra, Rigan and Ragul came to stand in front of them. Sarra spoke first. "We were honored to have you with us, even if it was for a short time. Someday perhaps you shall come and visit us again."

"Roniki like bigga antler heads," piped up the little rat. "Maybe come back soon, eh Kona?"

Everyone laughed except for Ragul. But Kona thought she saw a small smile tugging at the corner of his mouth. The big elk stepped forward, and everyone fell silent.

"As my mate has said, you are welcome with our tribe. Now be on your way. It will be a long journey if you wish to reach the border of Terikanha soon."

Cika lowered herself to the ground, and Aren helped Kona get up to the elephant's back. Once Cika was standing again, Aren handed the food pack up to Kona, who strapped it to her back.

"Alright, let us be on our way then," said Cika. She nodded to Ragul and Sarra, and winked at Rigan. The little elk calf smiled brightly and tried to stand taller.

As the companions made their way back toward the river, Sarra looked up at her mate. "I fear for them."

. . . . .

Kona stared at the forest in front of her. Lush green spilled out over the ground in every direction. It was a paradise untouched by the famine, completely the same as it always had been.

They had finally reached the border of Terikanha, after traveling for nearly two days away from the elk tribe.

The famine had stretched to the very edges of Sumeria, but Terikanha was a different scene entirely.

"Thhomthing ithh not right here," commented Sedgewik in a barely audible whisper. The python was stretched flat on the ground, as if he were trying to be as invisible as possible.

"I have to agree with you, Sedgewik." Cika looked at Kona meaningfully. "Maybe this is not a good idea."

The princess felt a cool breeze coming from the forest, and frowned. "It does feel a little strange, but what other course do we have? We did not travel all this way for nothing. We must go on."

Aren gripped her wrist. "Kona...please, think about what I told you earlier. Stay in Sumeria. The elephant and I can go in your place."

There was a loud grunt from Cika. "Speak for yourself, boy. I never agreed to march on into that forest, and I certainly am not going to do so willingly. There is a darkness ahead that I have no wish to confront."

Raising his eyebrows, Aren looked at Cika. "So you are afraid, then?"

Another grunt. "Humpf. As if," Cika said defensively. "I am simply questioning your intelligence."

Kona sighed and began limping toward the trees. "While you two figure out the levels of your intelligence, I am going in that forest. I do not care who is coming with me."

Instantly, Roniki jumped off of Cika's head and went racing after the princess. Sedgewik slithered past Aren and followed the first two. The elephant and the boy glared at each other for a moment.

"Well I for one am not going to let her go in there without my protection," said Aren. He turned on his heel and stalked into the trees after Sedgewik.

Cika stood there alone. The elephant lifted her head and looked up at clouds rolling lazily through the sky. "I cannot believe this. All I have ever wanted was to live a quiet life in Leyowan, marry my betrothed, and raise a calf or two. Was that too much to ask?"

Getting no answer from the clouds, Cika sighed deeply and strode resignedly into the forest.

．．．．．

Kona picked her way carefully through the thick forest underbrush, holding on to Aren's arm for balance. She noticed that his other hand never strayed far from his belt, where his daggers were readily available should the need arise.

"Do you know how far it is to Togleby?" asked Kona, breaking the tense silence. Aren glanced at her.

"I don't know. Not too far. From the map, it looks like there is a ferry that we can take across the river, but we have to buy passage in Togleby. I am really not sure what to expect, but I think we should not use your real name."

"My name is Tira, remember?" asked Kona teasingly. Aren saw a small smile touching her lips. He chuckled.

"Ah yes… my elusive little forest waif. What a sight you were."

Kona pretended offense. "Well, I was not used to such lowly work. Picking up sticks for a fire! I might have gotten dirt on my dress!" she said dramatically, waving one of her hands for effect.

"What a horrible mess that would have been," replied Aren. "And you would never be able to live it down."

They both laughed, but were interrupted by Cika's voice behind them. "Laugh while you can, but I think we are being followed." The elephant's tone was low enough so that only Kona and Aren could hear her.

Roniki jumped from Cika's head to Aren's shoulder. "Roniki smells bad scent," she whispered, holding her paws to her nose and grimacing.

"What kind of a bad scent?" asked Aren. The little rat reluctantly removed her paws and sniffed the air, still grimacing.

"Wolf…no…not wolf…smells like wolf…but not wolf," she said, tilting her head slightly in confusion. "Bad smell…more than wolf. Roniki not smell this before."

Aren looked at Kona with a frown. "I don't know what she smells, but whatever it is, it doesn't sound good. Just keep your guard up, and stay close."

Cika moved closer to them, and Sedgewik slithered beside Kona on the opposite side of Aren. Roniki moved to Kona's shoulder, and resumed holding her nose with her paws.

"Bad smell now bigger bad smell!" she whispered, vigorously shaking her head.

Even Kona could now smell a strange, foul scent in the slight breeze. Aren looked worried, and his hand moved to the hilt of his right dagger.

A very faint cackling sound came from somewhere behind the travelers. Aren's dagger was instantly out of his belt and into his hand. "Come on, we've got to try and hide!" he said. Roniki jumped off of Kona's shoulder and scurried into the brush.

Cika snorted. "Hide? How on earth is an elephant supposed to *hide?*" she said, but Kona could hear the nervousness in her voice.

As they passed a large tree, Aren pushed Kona down toward a small cavity near the roots, a nook just big enough for her to hide in. She tried to protest, but he shushed her and then turned to join the others.

Kona crouched in among the large, twisted roots of the tree, and heard nothing but silence for what felt like an eternity of minutes.

"Kona?"

Aren's voice came over the tree roots. The princess looked up and saw Aren extending a hand down to her.

"I think they have gone."

Kona took Aren's hand and let him pull her up to him, and she sank into his arms, relieved. Cika was standing just beyond them with Sedgewik.

Suddenly there was loud and raucous laughter from the surrounding brush. Kona jumped. It was not human laughter, but a harsh, grating sound that made her very blood run cold.

"Nobody move or dis rat gonna get eated!" proclaimed a voice giddily. The companions whirled to see a full grown hyena fidgeting around, Roniki clenched carefully in her jaws. The little rat's eyes were huge, and she looked terrified.

"Roniki!" exclaimed Kona, her hands flying up to cover her mouth in horror. Another hyena joined the first, and then another, then another. The four hyenas cackled and laughed at the three horrified travelers. Finally, Aren grew angry.

215

"Put her down, you spineless rogues!" he said, his dagger clenched firmly in his hand.

The second hyena, who was the largest, chuckled a bit before replying. "Drop yer pretty knife there, human boy. Nobody crosses dis border without leave of the council," he said. "Yer haven't got any permission, cuz we'd know about it iffen yer did."

Aren scowled darkly. "That's no reason to threaten Roniki. Let her go, she has done nothing to you, and neither have we."

"Do yer hear dat, Brooz?" the third hyena cackled. "Mebbe we should let her go, or mebbe she'd be a nice lunch!"

The four hyenas laughed again. Aren flipped his dagger. "I'm warning you, let her go!"

Roniki squeaked in terror as the hyena holding her tossed his head. Kona felt helpless, what were they going to do?

Aren lunged for the hyena with Roniki, and in a flash, several things happened. Roniki was flung high into the air as all four hyenas leapt to meet Aren. Three black robed figures appeared from hiding places in the brush, and Aren was pinned to the ground.

One of the black robed warriors tied Aren's hands behind his back tightly with rope. Another of them drew the scimitar from the scabbard bound to his back and held it toward Cika. The third approached Kona, more rope in his hand.

"This is an outrage! What uncivilized barbarians would do such a thing!" exclaimed Cika, helpless to do anything to assist

Kona or Aren with the scimitar that was being held to her throat.

Kona shuddered as the black robed man roughly drew her arms together in front of her and tied them with the rope, which scraped mercilessly across the tender skin of Kona's wrists. The young princess felt tears come to her eyes. She had never been treated this roughly in her whole life.

Roniki was grabbed from the ground and secured in a wooden cage. The little rat huddled in the corner, shaking uncontrollably with fear.

"Who are you? What are you doing to us?" demanded Cika angrily. The warrior holding the scimitar to her throat did not reply, but the other two brought chains and began securing them to Cika's legs. The elephant let out a loud bellow and stomped her feet angrily.

"You will not treat me like a common criminal!" she bellowed. "What mercenaries of evil are you!?" The warrior with the scimitar moved to Kona and held the blade to her throat. Cika instantly quieted down, but Kona could feel the fury radiating from her best friend.

Quickly, Kona said, "I demand to be taken to the council of Terikanha!"

Surprise emanated from the warriors and the hyenas, and then annoyance. One of the warriors spat on the ground.

"We don't have a choice now. If they demand to be taken to the council, it is law that they must."

Brooz, the largest hyena, stepped forward, his tongue lolling carelessly from his mouth. He cocked his head to the side and looked at Kona, eyes sparkling with amusement.

"We'll just see about yer now. The council ain't gonna like yer, I kin tell yer that," he said with a lopsided grin.

Although the situation was not what she had expected, Kona realized that maybe it was not as bad as she thought. They were going to the council of Terikanha, exactly where they wanted to go!

"Who are you?" she asked. The hyena grinned again.

"Finest border patrol, we are. Finest in der whole country. Dat's why der council put us out here. My name's Brooz, and this is Nork, Sneezenit, and Flunk, my pack mates. Der three human warriors is Getane, Rilding, and Aliano."

One of the black robed warriors turned to glare at Brooz angrily. The hyena cackled. "Don't yer give me dat look. No harm in her knowin' yer name, is there? She ain't gonna tell nobody."

Flunk, the hyena who had captured Roniki, strode forward and peered at the little rodent through the bars of her cage. Roniki shivered and cowered into the corner, her little black eyes wide.

"Hmmm… I loves rats…good eatin'," the hyena said in a low, ominous voice. Roniki flinched visibly, and Flunk laughed.

"Come on youz... we've gotta make Togleby by nightfall," observed Nork. Out of the four hyenas, he seemed the most solemn.

Rilding roughly pulled Aren to his feet, re-sheathing his scimitar. He pulled the daggers out of Aren's belt and put them into one of his cloak's dark folds. Kona saw Aren silently noting their placement, and then his dark glare that was turned upon the black robed warrior.

Getane stood behind Kona, a knife held to her back. "Move," he said. Kona found herself being pushed through the forest ahead of Getane, Aren beside her, similarly treated.

The final warrior, Aliano, tied a rope to the chain hanging from Cika's neck, which was attached to those about her massive feet. He led her along, the chains forcing her to shuffle uncomfortably through the underbrush. The four hyenas gamboled around the group, laughing and making jokes about the prisoners back and forth.

Kona saw a small cut running across Aren's brow, and a tiny trickle of blood was running down the side of his face. She wanted to reach out and wipe it away, but she could not because her hands were bound.

"*Hha kuneth ma'al,*" she whispered. She saw Aren glance at her, surprised by her use of the ancient Leyowan language. Kona smiled. She had told him she loved him, and meant every word sincerely. Though she didn't know if he knew the ancient language, Kona hoped that Aren could understand her message.

Getane shoved Kona lightly from behind. "No talking!" he commanded in a deep growl. Kona bowed her head and limped painfully on, ignoring the throb in her leg. She could sense Aren's worried gaze on her, but she did not say a word.

Silently, Kona sent a prayer heavenward that they would safely make it to their destination, because as it was... she was afraid for all of them.

Suddenly Kona realized something... Sedgewik was not with them.

16.

Kona was exhausted. They had been mercilessly driven through the forest by the three warriors, and had not paused for a moment since their capture. Kona's leg was growing numb with pain, and she was sure that she would collapse at any moment. Aren did not look much better. Kona could see sweat running down his face.

Nork came bounding back in the odd hyena gait, finished scouting up ahead. "Togleby is in sight!" he exclaimed.

Relieved, Kona shuffled on. Finally she could rest, and give her leg time to recover from the day's march. Cika grunted loudly behind the princess, not quite as silent with her relief.

Kona was worried about Roniki. The little rat's cage was tied to Cika's back, but Roniki was still huddled in the corner, her face hidden in her paws. She had held the same position for the entire trek.

And Sedgewik... Kona still had not figured out what had happened to the python. She was sure that their captors had not been aware of his presence, but how had he managed to hide from them so long? Kona sighed. He had probably left, fleeing for safety. She could hardly blame him. After all, he was not bound to the group in any way other than friendship... But would he really abandon them?

.....

Two beady black eyes followed every move of the warriors and their strange motley of prisoners.

The fifteen foot long python raised his head slightly, still hidden by the dense underbrush. Up ahead, he could see the walls of a large city. Even from here he could hear the deafening noise of hundreds of Terikanhians in the city, doing their daily business.

Sedgewik saw the warriors roughly shoving Aren and Kona ahead of them, now impatient to reach the city and be rid of their prisoners. The python's eyes narrowed as he saw dark lines of red around Kona's wrists where the rope had scraped against her skin.

Aren kept glancing into the woods, as if he expected someone to show up and rescue them. He also dared frequent looks at the robe of the warrior Rilding, where his daggers were snugly hidden.

As the warriors, hyenas and prisoners passed Sedgewik's hiding place and continued down the hill toward Togleby, the python slid out of the brush and followed them silently.

.....

Kona was overwhelmed by the city of Togleby. There was so much to see! Even as a prisoner, she could not help but feel excitement as they walked through the main streets. Tall stone buildings stretched up on either side of the road, and market vendors were everywhere, selling every imaginable ware and food.

There were many different kinds of animals as well. Most of them were animals that Kona had never seen before, and that she had only read about in stories. There were camels, gazelles, zebras, monkeys, and many more. A few were familiar species like horses, oxen, and panthers. And of course, there were many humans.

A group of small children gathered around Cika as she was led through the street, gawking and whispering amongst themselves. They had obviously never seen an elephant before.

Cika reached out her trunk to one of them in a gesture of friendship, and the little boy's eyes grew round as saucers. He touched the end of her trunk with a finger, and then squealed and ran into the crowd. Cika chuckled.

The warrior leading her tugged on the rope. "No more!" he warned her, obviously meaning for her to keep to herself.

Aren stared at all the merchants along the roadway. Some were haggling over prices with customers, some were yelling, and others were calling out the wares they were selling to the passersby.

Green vines grew over the buildings, and there were patches of grass and flowers along the street. There were many exotic ware merchants in Togleby. They were selling jewelry and precious stones. Some sold intricately woven rugs, and still others sold perfumes and veils.

Kona sniffed the air appreciatively as they passed the stand of a baker who was selling pastries, and realized how hungry she was. She pressed her bound hands to her stomach, which was growling.

A finely dressed woman came up to the warriors, her heavily painted eyes roving over Aren.

"New slaves? Hmmm… I like this one." She tilted Aren's chin with a long fingernail. He glared at her angrily, but could not move away. The woman smiled, but it was not warm. "How much?"

Rilding growled a response. "These are not slaves. Now go on your way, Amha, for there is nothing for you here."

Visible disappointment registered on the woman's face, but she obediently stepped away from Aren, still watching him. Kona felt a strange possessiveness come over her, and she was glad when they continued on their way. She could not stand the thought of that woman laying one of her fingers on Aren.

"What did she mean by slaves?" asked Aren. Behind him, Rilding chuckled in amusement.

Brooz trotted up to walk beside Aren as he answered. "Slave trade is legal in Terikanha. Der council issued the decree three years ago. Dese three warriors are slaves to der Council and Her Majesty der Queen. Me and my pack mates earned our freedom by servin' as city guards fer two years. Now we'z paid to work fer der Council as border patrol."

Kona was in disbelief over what she was hearing. "You still trade in slaves here? It is banned in every other country!"

But Brooz just cackled. "Terikanha ain't like every other country. Life is different here... sooner you unnerstand dat, the better for you. Slaves are der main trade here in Togleby. Dat's probably what yer and yer friends will become after der Council doesn't want yer."

"I will never be a slave," Aren said between clenched teeth. Brooz was taken aback by the anger and disgust in his tone and dropped back to walk with his pack.

. . . . .

The prisoners were roughly shoved down into dark cells in the guardhouse of Togleby. Aren was placed in a cell next to Kona, and Cika was placed in a barred stall across from them.

The warriors left the building, locking the door behind them. There was very little light, but Kona could make out the form of Cika behind the bars of her stall.

"I am so sorry, Kona."

The princess turned her head and saw Aren pressed against the bars between them, holding his hand through one of the slats. Kona sighed and reached out, placing her hand in his larger one.

"We are going to be alright, Aren. I know we are. As soon as we get to the council, all this will be straightened out, and we will be able to go home."

Even though it was dark, Kona saw the skeptical expression on Aren's face. "I don't know. Any council who approves a law legalizing slave trade is not to be trusted, especially since you are royalty. What if they hold you for ransom? These people seem very greedy, Kona. I would not expect much more from them."

"I will not assume anything until they have actually performed the deed, Aren," Kona replied softly.

Aren's eyes narrowed. "They have already taken you prisoner, tied your wrists, and treated you as if you were no more than a common thief! What more must they do to us before your trust is betrayed in them?"

Lowering his head, Aren tried to pull his hand away from Kona's. But she squeezed reassuringly.

"Aren...sometimes it is better to expect the better of people. If they understand that you expect more of them, sometimes they change. That is my hope."

Cika's voice came from across the room. "You obviously do not know Her Highness as well as me, boy. Her heart is as pure as a spring rose, and she never gives up on the fact that anyone can change for the better."

Shaking his head, Aren looked through the bars at the innocent blue eyes of the girl in the next cell. She smiled faintly.

"Trust, Aren... we are not alone in this," she said, her eyes glancing upwards. "He knows what will happen."

Aren sighed. "I hope so. I really hope so."

. . . . .

Cika's snores filled the building as she slept soundly. Aren and Kona were sleeping side by side, their hands still joined through the bars between them. Outside, the long grass around the guardhouse rustled slightly. Sedgewik peered through the dark doorway in toward the cells.

The guard was sleeping at his post, leaned against the building opposite the python. Sedgewik's eyes glimmered and he slithered from his hiding place quietly toward the guard.

Rearing up slightly, he drew back his head, being sure to keep his fangs carefully inside his mouth. In a movement as fast as lightning, he darted forward, the blunt end of his nose hitting the guard in the right temple. The man's eyes opened for an instant before he slumped down against the building.

Sedgewik let out a relieved sigh, and then slid on down the stairs and into the cell house, after relieving the guard of his keys.

He saw Cika sleeping through the slats of her stall, and he slipped between them with little difficulty.

"Thhika!"

The snake's whisper brought Cika out of her sleep. Groggily she swung her head around, narrowly missing Sedgewik, who immediately dropped his own head to the ground.

"Careful, thhilly!" he said. Cika carefully made out the form of the large python on the floor of her stall, and her eyes grew wide.

"Sedgewik? Oh my goodness! We thought you had left us!" she exclaimed in surprise. The python looked pleased with himself, and his head swung from side to side.

"I wouldn't leave. You're my friendthh… the only friendthh I have. I came to rethhcue you all," he proclaimed. "I made the guard outhhide go to thhleep for a while, but we thhtill don't have much time."

Cika smiled. "Not much time, got it." She paused. "Sedgewik, you are a true friend. I am sorry that I have been so hard on you all this time."

Embarrassed, Sedgewik did not reply, but grabbed the keys in his mouth and slithered back out of the stall toward the two sleeping humans. Unable to crawl into the cells, he called out their names quietly.

"Aren, Kona! Wake up, thhleepy humans!"

The two of them sat up, looking around for the owner of the familiar voice. Once they saw him, Kona moved to the front of her cell, her face alight with joy.

"Sedgewik! You came back! Oh I knew you would!"

The python tossed the keys through Aren's cell bars, and the boy immediately went to work on the lock. He soon had the door open, and then went to unlock Kona's door as well. As soon as it was free, the princess walked into his arms, and he held her for a long moment.

"You will never spend another night in a cell, Kona. Not as long as I live to prevent it," Aren said, his voice low and gruff.

"Time enough for making promises later," Cika said from her stall. "Get me out of here! We do not have much time."

Kona took the keys from Aren and opened the stall door. "Come on; we must get out of here... I am sure we will not have much time before the guard changes and we will be caught."

"Where'thh the little one?" asked Sedgewik, worry in his eyes. Kona looked around the room. There was no sign of Roniki's cage.

"Oh no... I bet they have her in the guardhouse with them," Cika said. "There is no way we will be able to get her out of there... they are sure to have someone awake."

Aren's face was grim but determined. "Don't worry about that. I have a score to settle with that big hoodlum who stole my daggers. I am not leaving without them. I'll go in there, get my weapons and find Roniki, then meet you at the edge of town."

The four of them exited the cell house and walked safely past the guard, who was still unconscious. Aren began to head toward the guardhouse, but he was stopped when Kona placed a gentle hand on his arm.

"Aren... do not do this alone. I will come with you," she said. Aren looked at her incredulously and shook his head.

"Absolutely not. I'm doing this to get you to safety, not put you in more danger. Cika and Sedgewik have to get you out of here if anything happens to me. And besides, with your leg, if something did go wrong..."

"I would hold you back," finished Kona. Her gaze was suddenly focused on the ground, and Aren thought he saw hurt in her eyes. He pulled her into an embrace.

"Kona, you know that I love you, and I want you to be safe. I'm doing this for you. Please understand that. Stay with Sedgewik and Cika. I'll get Roniki and then find you, I promise."

The princess stepped back, and Cika lowered herself down to the ground so that Kona could climb up. Once seated on the elephant's back, Kona looked down meaningfully at Aren.

"I hold you to that promise," she said. Aren nodded.

"Good. But you promise me something. If anything goes wrong, you do not come back for me. Keep going to Talda, and implore the queen. Don't look back for me," he said. Kona choked back tears, and nodded.

"I love…you," she said brokenly. Aren smiled and reached up, holding his gold medallion up to her.

"Take this… my mother gave it to me, and now it will remind you of me, just as it reminds me of her."

Kona accepted the gift and tied it around her neck carefully, gently touching the gold circle. Aren looked up at her lovingly, and squeezed her hand before turning toward the guardhouse.

Cika and Sedgewik hurried toward the outskirts of town without stopping to look back. Aren waited until they were safely out of sight, and then opened the door of the guardhouse.

Once inside, his eyes adjusted to the dim light, and he saw all three warriors and the hyena pack sleeping soundly. He looked around, and saw his two daggers peeking out from Rilding's belt. He bit back a growl of frustration. Getting his weapons back would be harder than he bargained for.

His eyes swept the room once more, this time for something else. At first he did not see her, but when he looked a second time, he saw the wooden cage sitting between Flunk and Brooz, guarded by the sleeping hyenas. Inside, Roniki was staring at him, wide-eyed. Aren held a finger to his lips to motion her to be quiet.

Leaning down, he reached over Brooz and unlatched the door to Roniki's cage. The little rat stayed cowered in the corner even when the door swung free. Aren motioned her out, but she stayed crouched down, staring at him with unblinking eyes.

Aren motioned again, and this time, Roniki crept out of the cage, still staring at Aren. She did not make any effort to speak, just walked up his proffered hand and perched on his shoulder, holding on to his shirt neck tightly with both paws.

Aren stepped carefully between the two warriors sleeping on the floor and stopped in front of Rilding, who was sleeping upright in the chair. Aren reached out a hand toward the warrior's belt.

Carefully, he eased his hand around the hilt of the first dagger, and slipped it slowly out of the belt. He waited, but there was no response from the sleeping warrior. Drawing a sigh of relief, Aren reached for the second weapon. As soon as his hand closed around the hilt, he began pulling it free.

Rilding's eyes snapped open, and with a cry of rage, he lunged out of the chair at Aren. The boy was pinned flat against the wall. Roniki jumped from his shoulder to the table, where the window was wide open.

Now the hyenas were awake as well, and the other two warriors. All of them began making an awful ruckus, snarling and shouting as they struggled with Aren. The boy looked at Roniki.

"Go, Roniki! Find the others! Run!" he yelled, just before Rilding stabbed Aren's side with his own dagger.

The rat leapt from the window and raced out over the grass, tiny tears running from her eyes as she heard Aren's cry of pain.

. . . . .

Kona heard the noise begin in the guardhouse, and agony closed its fist around her heart like a cold vise.

"NO!" she cried out, twisting around on Cika's back to see the guardhouse. She heard an anguished scream of pain, but could not tell whose it was. She closed her eyes tightly, a hard lump in her throat.

"Remember your promise, Kona," whispered Cika below her. But the elephant lowered her head in sorrow even as she spoke.

Sedgewik sniffled audibly from the ground, but Kona just stared into the darkness behind them as the noise faded into the night. Her arms gave way, and she dropped to Cika's broad back completely, her cheek resting against the warm hide. Her heart felt empty, her mind numb.

A loud squeaking sound came from behind them, and Cika stopped abruptly. Sedgewik slithered back into the darkness, and Kona heard his excited exclamation.

"Roniki!"

The next thing Kona knew, there was a trembling rat crouched under her arm, nestled in the fabric of her dress, tears running down her small face. Roniki's paws ran over Kona's arm, as if she were trying to reassure herself that the princess really was there.

"Human boy..." she whispered, her accent heavy in her sorrow. That was the breaking point for Kona. The tears came freely now, creating rivers down her cheeks. She held Roniki close, silently sobbing.

. . . . .

The four companions kept moving toward the river. Cika could hardly bear the agonizing silence that had fallen over the group ever since Roniki had found them. She could still hear Kona crying softly, and Sedgewik still slithered mutely beside her.

Even Cika herself felt a dull throbbing in her heart. It was as if somehow, Aren's absence and uncertain fate had stolen

233

the very life from the group, the will to go on. But Cika silently promised the boy that she would do whatever it took to get Kona to the queen.

What surprised Cika was the fact that thus far, they had not been followed. Surely the border patrol would know about the escape of their other prisoners once they had discovered Aren.

In the deepest corner of her heart, Cika knew the reason. Somehow, even in the situation he was in, Aren had still managed to protect them.

Cika let her head droop slightly. She had never given Aren the chance to prove himself. She had always just treated him like he had no right to love Kona. But now she could see the truth. There was no one in the world who loved the princess more than the boy in that guardhouse, the boy who had willingly sacrificed himself for the lives of his friends. Even friends so undeserving as Cika, who had distanced herself from him since the day they had met.

If she ever saw him again… she would set things right.

17.

The river's noise grew closer and closer. Kona lifted her head slightly and looked up ahead through the damp tendrils of hair that were stuck to her cheeks, held prisoner by the salty trails of her drying tears.

Dawn was breaking, spreading its golden fingers across the slowly brightening sky. But the sunrise held no joy or beauty for Kona as it usually did.

"There is a ferry up ahead, Kona. You must compose yourself. We have to convince the ferryman to take us across," said Cika beneath her quietly. The elephant trudged on toward the ferry, which was visible beyond the trees. The rush of the river was now very close, and Kona could see it lazily moving on its way ahead of them.

The ferryman was old, and had a snowy white beard that hung down to the belt that held up tattered breeches over his thin frame.

"Who's there?" he called out when he saw the elephant coming toward him through the trees. "My heavens and stars... be that an elephant?" he exclaimed excitedly.

Cika bowed her head towards him graciously. "Good sir, we implore you to take us across the river. Our errand is of the greatest importance."

The little old man smiled and shrugged. "Good thing ye came to me instead of that ferry down river a ways. That's the main one, most folks think it's safer than ol' Kia here," he said, patting the railing of his ferryboat. "Thet overgrown lout that runs the main ferry wouldn't take you across for less than ten gold pieces each! Ridiculous sum, that."

Kona pulled her money pouch from her pack, which she had retrieved from the cell house before they had escaped. "How much do we owe you, kind sir?" she asked.

The old man pulled on his shirt ties thoughtfully. "Well fer the pleasure it'd be to take an elephant across, I s'pose five gold pieces'll do just fine. I wouldn't charge ye that much, but I've got grandkids to feed, you know."

Handing the gold down to the ferryman, Kona managed to smile. "Thank you very much, sir. What is your name?"

The ferryman smiled back. "I'm called Nob. 'cept when my wife's mad, then I'm called an old riverdog," he said, shaking his head and chuckling. He motioned them on board, and the four companions got onto the ferry. Cika was afraid her weight and size might be too much for the rickety ferryboat to handle, but the wooden boards held.

Nob unwound the ropes from the ferry's corner posts, and lodged his long pole into the shore, pushing them out into the river. The water eased them across toward the opposite shore, which was a fair distance away. With Nob's expert ferrying, the companions soon reached the other side. As the ferryman secured the boat to the posts in the riverbank, the companions left the ferry and made their way up to the grassy bank.

"Thank you, Nob," said Kona from Cika's back. The old man nodded and waved with a smile.

"Don't mention it, missy. I haven't had to take this ferry across in nearly three years," he said, his eyes misting happily. Without another word, Nob released the ferry from the posts and began poling back across the river.

Kona watched him go wistfully. Roniki was still curled up in her arms, having not moved since the previous night when she had found the rest of the group.

"What happened to him, Roniki? Did you see anything?" asked Kona. The little rat raised her head and looked up at the princess. Roniki hesitated, not sure if she should tell what she saw.

"Bad things... very bad," said the little rat quietly. Cika grunted and began walking again.

"What bad things?" asked Kona. Her gaze was still riveted on the far off bank of the river where they had come from, as if she were searching for something, even knowing she would not find it.

Roniki shivered and burrowed deeper into Kona's arms. "Roniki not say."

Kona did not respond, and did not even show disappointment at Roniki's refusal to tell her exactly what had gone on in the guardhouse. She just kept watching the bank of the river until it faded from view.

. . . . .

Pain.

Agonizing pain...

What was this burning, aching, unbearable pain that he felt?

Kona!

Kona...she's safe...

. . . . .

Cika stopped in front of a wide road. It looked very well traveled, and there was a sign in the ground on the opposite side that read: Talda 12 miles. The elephant took a deep breath and took stock of their surroundings. There was not anyone on the road. It obviously was not the main road into Talda, or it would be teeming with all sorts of people and animals going to and from the city.

The elephant turned her head slightly to see Sedgewik watching her. The big snake had changed since their capture at the border. He seemed more alert, strong, and confident.

"Well, Sedgewik," said Cika. "How are the other two?"

The python raised himself up off the ground a bit so that he could see Kona and Roniki. Cika saw a sad look come to his eyes.

"They are thhtill the thhame," he said. Cika sighed, feeling despair creeping up to her heart. Kona and Roniki had clung to each other since escaping from Togleby, refusing either food or water, and had not said a word since the river.

"I think we will rest here," said the elephant, unsure of what else to do. After all, she was not supposed to be the leader... that had been Aren's task. And he had been much better at it than she.

Cika lowered herself to the ground, and Kona slipped off of her back, carrying Roniki in her arms. The princess walked to the nearest tree and sank down against its trunk. Cika looked at her, and felt angry.

"Kona, you need to get a hold of yourself. We are almost to Talda, the place we have gone through all this to get to. Do you really want Aren's sacrifice to have been in vain? Do you think he would approve of the way you are acting now?" asked Cika quietly. She hated to hit the raw nerve that Aren's name would grate against for the princess, but there was little else she could do.

The golden haired girl looked up at her best friend. "I have failed him," she whispered.

"No, Kona. You can change that. You will not fail him if you go to Talda and get the help for Leyowan that we came for. You will fail him if you continue to act this way. There is still hope. Not all is lost." Cika prayed that her words would bring the princess out of her lethargy.

"I do not even know if he is still alive, Cika," Kona responded. "Roniki will not tell me anything."

Sedgewik slithered over and tapped Roniki's head gently with the bottom of his jaw. The little rat lifted her head and looked at him through clouded eyes.

"Tell uthh what happened to the human boy, Roniki," pleaded Sedgewik. "Help Kona."

Roniki looked at the three faces that were watching her intently, and finally she spoke. "Roniki not see everything. Human boy open cage, then try to get pointy sticks…"

"Pointy sticks?" asked Cika.

"His daggerthh," explained Sedgewik softly. Roniki didn't seem to notice the interruption.

"Big black warrior jump out, and human boy tell Roniki to run… then Roniki run away, find Kona."

"Did they hurt him, Roniki? I heard a scream," said Kona.

Roniki nodded. "Get pointy stick in side, much blood," she said, holding one paw against her side to illustrate. After she finished talking, the little rodent buried her head in Kona's arms again.

Kona bit back a gasp, and her eyes shut tightly. "Cika I do not know if I can go on, knowing that he is still back there and hurt so badly…"

The elephant sighed. "We have no other course, Kona. To return to Togleby would be a mission of fools. The only way to save Aren is to find the queen and plead for his life. And who knows, perhaps the warriors will still take him to the council in Talda. Maybe we will see him there and be able to rescue him."

Though every bone in her body ached to return to Togleby and rescue Aren, Kona knew that Cika was right. They had no other choice… and she had made him a promise.

"Let us continue on, then," the princess said softly. "The sooner we reach Talda and the queen, the sooner we can save Aren."

. . . . .

The road curved around a bend of trees to the left and was lost from sight. Kona sighed. They had already turned so many corners that she was beginning to wonder if the road really did lead to Talda, or if it was just a maze to confuse weary travelers such as they were.

Cika trudged on, her massive feet creating small craters in the soft dirt. The trees rustled softly as the breeze blew through their leaves.

As they came around the bend, Kona automatically looked ahead, expecting to see more road and trees. But what she did see completely astounded her. Cika came to a complete stop.

They were on a hill overlooking the most magnificent city any of them had ever seen.

A limestone wall ran around the entire perimeter of the city. Iron gates were placed every quarter mile in the wall, opening to wide streets that led toward the center of the city.

Talda was built as a large circle, and all the roads led straight toward the central building in the city, which was a palace so grand that it took Kona's breath away.

Tall golden spires reached high up into the air, crowning round towers that anchored each corner of the massive palace. The domed roof of the palace was inlaid with gold, and shone brightly in the sun. The Terikanhian flag flew from each of the corner spires, proudly waving in the wind.

"It is so beautiful," said Kona breathlessly. "I cannot believe that we have finally made it to Talda."

Cika began moving again. "Well we do not have any time to waste. We must find the queen immediately, and plead our cause," she said. The four companions made their way down the hill, toward the beautiful city where they hoped to find what they were seeking.

.....

If Togleby was a busy, thriving trade town, Talda outmatched it by a clear mile. There were people and animals everywhere. Cika was having a difficult time making her way through the throngs of people. Talda was a huge city, and it was still a long ways to the palace from the busy market streets.

"A jewel for the beautiful lady?" a market vendor called out, lifting high a dark green pendant toward Kona, who politely shook her head. She kept her gaze focused on the looming palace up ahead, ignoring all the noise around her.

I am going to save you, Aren. I swear it.

The voices receded into silence, and Kona saw an image of Aren's face in her mind, his bright smile and loving expression turned toward her. His impish eyes sparkled as his hair fell haphazardly across his face.

Unbidden, another image came to view. The serene and noble face of a blue eyed woman gazed at Kona, her lips curved into a gentle smile.

Mother...I am going to make you proud of me, Kona promised. Even though her mother was not there, the

242

princess still felt love enveloping her. If Kikpona had lived to see her daughter's mission nearing success, Kona was sure she would have been proud.

The palace grew closer and closer and the homes that the four companions were passing grew more and more ornate and large. Well dressed women and children walked the streets, and the animals wore large gold chains around their necks.

Curious looks were cast over the odd foursome as they continued on toward the palace, and murmurs broke out among those on the streets.

"Obviously elephants are not common in this country," observed Cika wryly as a group of women pointed at her and spoke in hushed whispers among themselves. Sedgewik slithered alongside her quietly, not drawing as much attention from the onlookers.

Kona straightened her shoulders. She was the princess of Leyowan, and she had acted like a commoner long enough. These people would soon know that the daughter of Kikpona herself was in their city.

The four of them walked straight up to the guards that stood in front of the steps leading to one of the palace's main doorways. The guards were huge tigers who wore plated armor with spikes protruding from the shoulders.

"Who are you and what do you want here?" asked the left guard suspiciously. He could tell that the travelers were outlanders.

"I am Princess Kona of Leyowan, and I demand to be taken to your queen," answered Kona, her voice steady and commanding. The two tigers glanced at each other in surprise, and then looked at Kona again.

"I don't believe you," said the right guard. "No princess of anywhere would go around dressed like that. If you were the princess of Leyowan, you'd have an armed escort."

Kona slipped off of Cika's back and walked up to the guards, her shoulders straight and her chin held high. "I did not ask you if you believed me. I have told you who I am and I expect my demands to be obeyed."

Her confidence and commanding presence made the two guards nervous. The left guard's tail swept back and forth nervously.

"Very well, I will take you to the council, and they will decide if they wish to speak with you or not."

Kona's eyes narrowed, but she followed the guard up the steps, Cika, Sedgewik and Roniki right behind her. The palace doors were opened by heavily robed men who wore hoods to cover their faces. Kona found herself in a long, columned hallway. The floor was marble, and sculptures stood in regal silence between the columns.

Their footfalls echoed in the brightly lit chamber. Light streamed in from windows with carved wooden panes. Guards stood everywhere, some human, others animals, all wearing heavy robes.

Green vines grew over the columns, and plants were everywhere, some growing from open places in the floor, others in brightly painted pots.

"Wait here," said the tiger. The four companions stopped as the guard slipped inside a wooden door. Kona couldn't hear anything from inside, but she knew that she was about to meet the council of Terikanha, and the thought both excited and frightened her.

She looked down at her tattered dress, and sighed. The only thing she was wearing that was befitting of her royalty was the gold medallion that Aren had given her before their escape. Her fingers curled around the circular pendant and she held it, feeling a little of her confidence returning.

The door to the council chamber was thrown open, and the tiger guard returned.

"Come in, outlanders," he said. "The council will receive you now."

Kona led the way into the large chamber. Thirty council members sat in carved chairs that were placed in the shape of a circle. The floor was inlaid with a mosaic depicting Terikanha's forests. But what Kona noticed right away was that all the council members were human.

"Welcome, guests," said the council member farthest away from the four companions. He was middle aged, with a dark brown beard that was trimmed to a point. His robes were very well made and embroidered. Kona instantly felt uncomfortable in his presence.

He continued, "I am Lord Kazih, and I have been told that you are Princess Kona of Leyowan. Seeing your tattered clothes and unkempt appearance, I cannot say that I do not believe you."

Anger flared in Kona at the insult to her family and her country, but the council members laughed in amusement.

"I came to your country in good faith, Lord Kazih, as a princess who has come to plead for the lives of her people. Yet you would treat me so rudely?" she asked, her gaze unwavering from Lord Kazih's.

Another council member spoke. "We have no alliances with any other countries, nor do we wish to begin now. Why should we treat you any other way when all you have come to do is to take what is not yours?"

Lord Kazih spoke before Kona could respond. "Aye, we know what you have come for, Princess Kona. We know of the famine and the havoc it is wreaking upon your country. What else have you come for, if not to ask for our aid?"

"You are correct in assuming what my intentions here. But can this council truly be so coldhearted as to let the rest of the world starve in this famine, when you could be of help to them?" Kona countered, keeping her anger at bay.

Lord Kazih rose from his seat and came to stand in the middle of the chamber. "Our country has only ever looked after the best interests of its own. What can you offer us that we do not already have?"

"I can offer friendship, and a peaceful alliance with Leyowan. You are mistaken if you believe Leyowan will let such a refusal pass without reacting when the famine is over. Especially after I have been treated so brutally since the day I crossed your borders. I have been tied, treated roughly, and threatened with enslavement by members of your border patrol. Do not think that my father will take such shameful conduct lightly," Kona said.

Lord Kazih smiled and lifted his hands. "You assume much, Your Highness. The council will discuss the matter. For now, you will be escorted to private chambers where you will await our decision. I am sure you are weary from your travels. We will have the serving girl draw you a bath." Without another word, Kona followed the servant out of the council chamber, silently fuming with anger.

The other three companions walked after her, not daring to speak. None of them had ever seen the princess so angry. The servant led them up a flight of stairs and down a long hallway. She opened one of the doors and gestured them inside.

Kona entered the room and went directly to the window that stretched across the whole outer wall. It was a beautiful view of the city and the road leading up to the palace.

The princess heard Cika requiring food and drink from the servant, and then the woman left, closing the door firmly behind her.

Kona whirled. "How dare they!" she exclaimed. "How could they be so...so... heartless?" Her voice was high and sharp, and her eyes were snapping with blue sparks. Her small hands were balled into tight fists. "I do not understand."

She sank down onto a chair made out of cushions, and fiddled with the tassels on one of the pillows.

"I do not understand either, princess. But you conducted yourself wonderfully in the council chamber. Your father would have been proud of you," responded Cika truthfully. "And perhaps the council will decide in our favor."

Sedgewik coiled on top of another chair. "I don't think so. They are too proud," he said.

Kona stared at him. "Sedgewik... your lisp..." she said, a smile growing on her lips despite the situation they were in. The python looked at her in surprise.

"What of it, Your Highnethh?" he asked.

"Your lisp was gone when you spoke a moment ago..." Kona replied. Sedgewik lifted his head.

"It was? Really?"

Kona nodded. "And there it's gone again!"

The python blinked rapidly. "Well...so it is! I...I don't believe this, my mother said that I would never get rid of that awful thing."

There was a low grunt from Cika. "I guess she was wrong then. I must say I am feeling relieved. It will be much easier for everyone else to understand you now, and I will not have to translate. That was such a bother," she said, but she smiled, softening her words.

Roniki chattered nervously as the door was pushed open to reveal the serving girl with a tray of fruits and glasses. Another servant came in behind her with a large copper tub.

"Here you are, m'lady," the first servant said with a forced smile. "Now you can bathe and wash. I'll have Geria come back in with a dress for you shortly. Is there anything else I can bring you?"

Kona lifted one of the glasses from the tray and stared at the strange liquid inside. She'd never seen anything like it before. "Could you tell me what exactly...is this?" she asked the servant.

The woman smiled. "Oh! That's the juice pressed from oranges, grown right in the palace orchard, m'lady. It's a very popular drink among the rich folk here."

"Ah...thank you," Kona said, dismissing the servants. The two women hurried out the door. One of them soon returned with buckets of warm water. She filled the tub halfway, and then left several rags and some sweet smelling perfume, as well as a hairbrush.

When the servant was gone, Kona undressed and slipped into the tub with a deep sigh. The water felt so refreshing. She lay back against the hard side of the tub and closed her eyes.

"Feeling better, Your Highness?" asked Cika. "At least now we can get you looking and smelling more like a princess."

Kona reached over the side of the tub and picked up the rags. She dipped them in the perfume and then ran them over her arms and neck. Roniki perched on the edge of the tub precariously.

"Smella good," she observed, sniffing the air. Kona smiled.

"That's the perfume, Roniki. It smells like the perfume my Aunt Vanddai wears," the princess replied, a wistful look crossing her face. "I miss home."

No one responded, but Kona could tell that her three friends were thinking the same thing. "Once I am better dressed and more presentable, I will go back to the council and plead for Aren's life. I must find him. I will not rest until I have found him and know he is alive and safe."

Cika nodded, her ears flapping back and forth. "I fear for him," she admitted. "I do not like the thought of him being treated like scum by those barbaric, uncivilized, oafish, vulgar-"

"Neither do I, Cika. But it is useless to think on such things now. I believe the queen might be able to help us," said Kona hopefully.

"The council never even mentioned the queen. I think her reign is in greater danger than we were told." Cika paused. "I do not like it... we have not even seen her, and she is supposedly the monarch of this land, not the council."

Roniki stood up on her back feet. "Many bad men in council. Roniki not like them."

The little rat crossed her paws, attempting to look severe, but she lost her balance and with a shriek, plunged down into the tub of perfumed water. Cika's trunk darted in and lifted the wet rat free of the water as Kona and Sedgewik laughed.

Cika dropped the little rodent on a chair, chuckling mirthfully.

Roniki shook herself, making her fur stick out in every direction, and she chattered in irritation. "Evil smelly water," she grumbled.

Kona rose from the tub and took the linen sheet that Cika held out for her, wrapping it around herself.

"I do hope that servant comes with the dress soon," she said. "I do not want to waste any more time here. I have to find the queen and beg her to help me find Aren and save him before it is too late. If he is as badly wounded as Roniki says…we may already be running out of time."

As if the servant girl had read Kona's mind, the door to the chamber opened and Geria came in, a dress and undergarments hung carefully over her arm, several small jars in her hands. She bobbed into a curtsey and looked nervously at the princess.

"M'lady…my queen has requested a secret audience with you in her private chambers. The council is not to be informed of your meeting. Please hurry and dress, and then I will take you to her."

With the servant's help, Kona quickly drew on the undergarments, and then slid into the dress. It was a beautiful gown, royal blue, with gold thread embroidered in an intricate pattern over the bust. The skirt was long and flowed out to the floor in a regal train.

Kona sat down in front of the large mirror and closed her eyes while Geria applied a red color to her lips and blue paint to her eyelids.

Finally, all was ready. "Please follow me, m'lady," said Geria, leading the way out the door. The four companions followed her silently. Kona felt like a princess once again as she swept along the hallway in the beautiful gown, her hair brushed and tumbling in golden curls about her shoulders. Aren's medallion hung from her neck down to her chest, matching the gold embroidery on the dress.

Geria led them up to the third floor of the palace, where large double doors stood at the top of the stairs, leading into the queen's private level. The servant opened one of the doors and ushered the princess and her friends inside.

"Princess Kona of Leyowan has come at your request, Your Majesty," the woman said courteously, bowing to the figure seated on the large throne in the middle of the room.

Instantly Kona felt a kinship with the woman before her, and was amazed by the queen's commanding presence and beauty. The queen of Terikanha had piercing brown eyes and midnight black hair. Her black dress was plain, but accentuated the beauty of its wearer. A silver crown was nestled in her braided hair.

"I am Queen Naryana... welcome to Terikanha, my child."

18.

For a long moment, the two royal women gazed at each other silently. Then Queen Naryana came down from her throne and crossed the space between them.

"I am so very sorry, Kona," she said softly, and held out her arms. "I cannot begin to apologize for the way you have been treated here."

Kona felt her confidence and composure crumbling around her. Like a small child, she walked into the queen's embrace. Naryana closed her arms around the princess and rested her cheek against the golden curls.

"At long last I meet the daughter of Queen Kikpona herself," whispered the queen. "How I have longed for this moment."

Kona drew back slightly. "You know of my mother?"

"Of course! Her legend spreads farther than Terikanha. Your mother is famous throughout all the lands for her courage and wisdom. The earth wept for her when she was killed. I was not very old when she died... only a child of twelve," replied the queen.

"My queen... I am very troubled. We were captured by some of your border patrol when we crossed into Terikanha. We four escaped, but the fifth, a boy called Aren, sacrificed himself to allow us to escape. I believe he is still alive, but I must find him... I fear time is running short. If I cannot find him soon… he is terribly wounded, and…" Kona's voice faded as her eyes filled with tears.

Queen Naryana placed a hand on the princess' shoulder. "They will bring him here, for that is what they have been commanded to do. They must bring all intruders from outside countries to Talda for questioning. It will not be long before they arrive, I am sure of it."

"Will you help me, Your Majesty?" asked Kona. Her blue eyes searched the dark brown ones above her.

"Of course I will. The council may have passed the law restraining my rule, but they cannot refuse me a slave that I request, so we can use that as an excuse to bring him here," replied the queen thoughtfully. "I will provide you with anything I can to help him. You can be assured of his safe admittance to my palace."

Kona felt some of her fear melt away with the queen's reassurance. "Your Majesty, I came to Terikanha to ask you for-"

"Food for your people, yes I know," finished the queen. "The council's evil has spread so thickly over the land that I have little power left to do anything. They are greedy, self-centered men whose lust for power and wealth blinds them to the plight of others."

"Can you do nothing, my lady?" asked Kona. "How can they keep you so powerless to rule? You are the queen."

Queen Naryana smiled slightly. "I am queen in name, but they passed a law that restricts my rule to their command. I must seek their approval in nearly everything that I do. The past three years, I have been nothing but a puppet for their foul purposes. Yet I can do nothing."

"Why have you not asked for help? Surely Leyowan would have come to your aid had you asked for our assistance," said Kona in surprise.

The queen's shoulders lowered slightly, and her eyes gazed out the window into the city. "I tried to send couriers...five of them I sent out in secret, yet all five were intercepted and killed by the council. I could not get word out to any of the other countries. Finally the council imprisoned all of my loyal guards and servants except for five handmaidens. Geria is one of them."

The serving girl bowed her head quietly. "And thankful I am to be in your service, Majesty."

Queen Naryana smiled at the servant. "She has been my eyes and ears outside of these chambers. She told me all that went on in the council chamber today, and what was said to you by those miscreants."

"Is there no way you can repeal the law?" Kona wondered aloud. The queen shook her head.

"The only way that a council law can be repealed is if I marry, thus giving Terikanha a rightful king, negating all need for a council. The only reason that the council was formed was because they felt that a queen needed advisors to assist her in her rule. So when I became queen after my father died, they immediately formed the council in order to control the throne of Terikanha through me. It was not long after that they passed the law of restriction, judging me unfit to rule."

Kona frowned. "And is there no one you would marry, Your Majesty?"

The queen shook her head again. "None who are young enough and of royal blood. The king of Nenamene is nearly ninety years old, and his nephew and heir is already sixty-four. I am only twenty-eight years old. The council could wait until my husband passed on and then resume their control."

"Must your husband be a king before he marries you?" questioned Kona thoughtfully, her mind searching for any possible answer to the situation at hand.

"No, but he must be of royal blood. That is Terikanhian law. A king may marry a non-royal woman for his queen, but a queen must marry a man of royal blood in order to crown him king."

"What of the Crown Prince of Sumeria?" offered the princess. A sad look passed over the queen's face.

"I had also hoped that he might have me, but his mother betrothed him to another woman because she did not approve of me for her son. I do not believe there is anyone that I can marry. I even thought once of your father, but I could never ask him to fill Kikpona's place with someone like me."

Kona sighed. "He would never agree to it for exactly that reason. He would never marry another woman after my mother. And he would never want to be king of two countries. He struggles enough with Leyowan."

Having kept silence for a long while, Cika spoke up. "Forgive my intrusion, Your Majesty, but perhaps we could look at the law again…maybe we could find a loophole through which to overthrow the council."

The queen turned and looked at the elephant. "Ah, perhaps you are right, my friend. But I have looked over it many times. However, a new, fresh set of eyes may find something that I have been missing. Kona, you have not introduced me to your friends and loyal companions."

Kona stepped back toward her friends and smiled at them. "Of course, my lady. They are all native to Leyowan, as I am. This is Cika, my closest companion and best friend. She is the daughter of a great elephant chieftain in Leyowan. And this is Sedgewik, a very brave python. He was the one who rescued us from the guardhouse in Togleby when we were captured," the princess said, gesturing to each in turn.

"And this," she said, holding out her hand for Roniki to jump onto, "is Roniki, who is very courageous and kind."

The queen inclined her head slightly to the three companions of the princess. "It is with great pleasure that I make your acquaintances, friends of the princess. I hope that your stay in Terikanha will be more pleasurable from now on."

Sedgewik lifted his head up. "We thank you for your hospitality, noble queen," he said. Kona noticed a proud gleam in his eyes, and knew he was extremely grateful for the loss of his lisp.

"Your Majesty, forgive me, but I believe that we should return to our chambers. The council is sure to be sending their answer to us at any time, and I do not wish for them to discover our meeting," said Kona apologetically. "I will return to you when I can."

"Of course, my child. Go with my blessing, and do not worry about the boy you seek," the queen said compassionately.

Kona and her friends bowed deeply before leaving the room. As they walked out the door, Kona turned and gave the queen a grateful look.

. . . . .

The road up to the palace was crossed by many people during the next few hours, and Kona watched them all. She sat in a carved chair next to the window, her hands clenched in her lap, her eyes sweeping the road for any sign of the border patrol and Aren.

Her heart felt like it was breaking. She could not take this monotony of Aren's absence. It was as if her very life was being drained from her a little more every moment he was gone.

"Your Highness, please eat something." Sedgewik spoke from the floor next to her, his voice pleading.

"I cannot, Sedgewik. I will not rest until I know that Aren is alive and safe, and with me again. I have no appetite for food right now." She paused and looked down at him. "Please understand."

Cika sighed. "Kona, you are not going to help Aren by starving yourself. You need to eat something."

The elephant reached for the bowl of fruit and grasped a fresh apple from the mix with her trunk. She held it out to Kona silently, the expression in her eyes both reassuring and encouraging.

"Do it for me," she said.

Kona took the apple and bit into it reluctantly. Cika nodded and moved to stand beside the princess.

"There, you see? You do not want to be hungry when Aren arrives, do you?"

Before the princess had a chance to respond, the door to the chamber opened, revealing Lord Kazih himself. The tall council member closed the door behind him and crossed to the center of the room. Sedgewik and Cika stood protectively beside Kona. The princess rose from her chair.

"What is the decision of the council?" she asked, her eyes locked with the nobleman's. Lord Kazih finally spoke.

"The council has discussed the situation at great length, and we believe that it is unnecessary for us to send aid to your people. Your father, King Morgo, should have taken more care to store up for these difficult times and provide for his own nation. Why should we pay the price for his mistake?"

Fury mounted in Kona's heart. "That is your answer?" she forced out between clenched teeth. "How dare you insult my father!"

"Be careful, Your Highness. You are not in Leyowan anymore. Here you have no power, no title. You may stay here as long as you wish, but the council's decision will not change," replied Lord Kazih smoothly, a smug smile on his face.

"Be that as it may, a grave mistake you have made today, Lord Kazih," said Kona calmly, her anger hidden behind her cool words.

The man looked taken aback by her threat, but he bowed shortly and strode out of the room without another word. Kona sank back to her chair, attempting to control her mounting rage.

"We came all this way, made it this far... to the very council of Terikanha, only to be refused by a group of greedy, conniving traitors who care nothing for anyone but themselves!" she exclaimed.

Cika grunted. "There is nothing we can do, Kona. They have made their decision. Our only hope now is to find a way to free the queen from their control. She can help us, but not as she is now."

Nodding, Kona raised a trembling hand to her forehead. "I wish my mother was here instead of me... she would know what to do."

. . . . .

A white horse thundered through the depths of the shadowed Sumerian forests, its hooves flying through the dry, brittle underbrush. Its rider wore a long, hooded cloak and leather armor. A sword hung at his side.

His eyes remained straight ahead toward Terikanha, and there was a determined scowl on his face.

I'm coming, Kona. Only a few more days and I will finally see your face again. Wait for me, Kona, daughter of my sister.

. . . . .

Kona leaned against the window, her eyes growing heavy as the sun sank low into the western landscape. Her robe was gathered around her to keep out the evening chill. Her hands dropped to her lap as her eyes began to drift closed.

The others had already fallen asleep on the cushions and floor of the chamber, exhausted from the past days.

I'm here...

A tiny voice sprang unbidden to Kona's mind. She opened her eyes slightly and looked down to the road below. What she saw at first thrilled her, and then nearly broke her heart.

A small group of black robed warriors were walking up the road, leading a group of human prisoners behind them. Hyenas flanked the procession on both sides. There were four of them, and they all looked very familiar.

But what drew Kona's eyes immediately was the last prisoner in the line. His dirty brown hair was mussed and caked with mud. His shoeless feet shuffled painfully along the street. His hands were bound together tightly with ropes that had left his skin raw and scraped. His breeches were ripped and tattered, and a large bloodstain covered nearly the entire left side of his shirt.

261

"AREN!"

Kona leapt from her chair, knocking it over in her haste to reach the door. The others woke up groggily at her shout, and saw her race out the door. Kona ignored the pain that automatically shot up her leg as she ran down the stairs two at a time, barely managing not to fall.

Her blue train flew out behind her like a banner as she ran through the last hallway, her awkward gait forgotten as she called to the guards at the door.

"Open the doors! Now!"

The confused guards did as she asked, pulling the heavy wooden doors open to let her out. Kona brushed past them and flew down the remaining few steps to the pathway. The border patrol was still about a hundred yards away, and they stopped short when they saw Kona limping toward them as fast as she could.

Aren's knees gave out beneath him, and he fell to the road heavily, his hands raised high, still attached to the other prisoners' ropes.

"Release him!" Kona commanded as she rapidly closed the gap between herself and Aren.

Rilding, the closest warrior to Aren, quickly cut the boy's ropes free of the main line that all the prisoners were tied to. Aren's hands dropped to the ground. Kona fell to her knees beside him.

"Aren... it is me..." she whispered, tears falling from her eyes as she lifted his head to her lap, cradling him in her arms. "I knew you had come. I kept my promise..."

She raised her face to the darkening sky. "Thank you, Lord. Thank you." Her hands gently caressed Aren's grime covered face. His green eyes opened slightly, and then widened a little with recognition. They were fever glazed, but they gazed at Kona intensely.

"You...made it...you are safe," he murmured through parched lips. Kona bit back a sob and nodded, running her fingers through his dirty hair.

"Thanks to you, we are all safe. And now you are too," she told him firmly, lifting his hand to her cheek. She placed a tender kiss on his knuckles, and then pressed his hand once more to her face.

"I am...not afraid to die."

Aren's soft whisper struck a chord in Kona's heart. She squeezed his hand reassuringly. "No...you are not going to die. Do not talk like that. I am going to take care of you myself."

"I am...getting your dress dirty," mumbled Aren. His eyes closed, and his head rested gently in her lap. Kona glanced to the side at the bloodstain, and felt fearful. She was almost hesitant to look at the damage that had been done.

"If you please my lady...who are you?" asked the warrior Getane. The border patrol was in confusion over the strange happenings.

Kona looked up at him angrily. "I am Princess Kona of Leyowan, the girl you treated with such disrespect. And this is the man I love. Count your days carefully, warriors, for if he dies..."

Geria and several other servants brought a long board with poles attached to it out to the line of prisoners. They carefully eased Aren onto the stretcher and lifted him up on their shoulders. Kona lifted her skirts off the ground and followed them back into the palace.

. . . . .

The servants placed Aren on the lavish bed in Kona's guest chamber. Cika, Sedgewik and Roniki gathered around the bed worriedly as Kona quickly sent the servants scurrying for water, a fresh change of clothes, and bandages for Aren's wound.

Her hands worked quickly as she unlaced the ties of his shirt. She silently prayed that what she would find beneath it would still be fixable. Who knew how badly he had been treated after that night.

"Human boy live?" asked Roniki in concern. Kona did not pause in her work, but looked up at the little rodent.

"He will live, Roniki. I am not going to let anything happen to him," she replied determinedly. "Geria, bring that hot water over here!"

The servant hurried over with a bowl of steaming water, as well as several clean rags and some long bandage strips. Kona pulled what was left of Aren's shirt away from his body, and held a hand to her mouth in horror.

The wound was deep, and was oozing with infection. The edges were bright red and inflamed. Dried blood and dirt caked the perimeter of the wound, making it hard to see the extent of the damage. Kona pulled the rest of the shirt away and dropped it to the floor. She dipped one of the clean rags in the bowl of water and began gently dabbing it at the wound, clearing away some of the grime.

Aren moaned softly, still unconscious. Kona paused for a moment, her expression turning to one of worry.

"Best to do this now while he is asleep, Your Highness. It will be easier for both of you," observed Geria kindly. Kona took a deep breath and continued, wiping away the dried blood.

The wound was worse than she had hoped. Infection had already begun to set in due to the lack of care Aren had received. If the border patrol had taken care of it at all, he might be in a much better situation.

"How could they leave him like this?" asked Kona, biting back her anger. Cika moved toward the bed, looking over the still form of the boy who was laying on it. Kona watched her best friend out of the corner of her eye. Cika looked genuinely worried about Aren, and her ears were flapping nervously.

"I will pray for him," said the elephant shortly, before turning around and going to the other side of the room.

Kona leaned in close to Aren's face. "I believe you have made a friend this day, my love," she whispered low, so she would not be overheard by Cika. "I am so glad you are here with me again. Now we must focus on making you well."

Reaching back, Kona dipped the rag in the hot water again, and resumed her work cleaning out the wound.

Once she was finished, Geria helped her wind the long bandage strips around Aren's abdomen.

"Let him sleep. Rest is the best thing for him now," said the servant woman with a smile. "I'm glad that you found him. I will inform her Majesty of this. I'm sure she'll be very happy to hear of it."

"Of course, thank you for your help, Geria," replied Kona gratefully. "Inform the queen and tell her that I will try to see her later. I am sure Lord Kazih will have something to say about all this."

The serving woman bowed and turned to leave. As she was walking out the door, Lord Kazih himself entered the chamber, a scowl on his face.

"I trust you have a good explanation for this? The queen's servants are not to be used for your amusement, Princess. I never gave approval for this boy to given sanctuary here. Who is he?"

Kona turned rapidly, her eyes sparking angrily. "This *man* is with me, and you will let him stay here because he was wounded by *your* border patrol. Geria was giving me assistance with his injuries of her own free will; it was with no order from your queen that she came to me."

The nobleman looked at her skeptically, and then turned his attention to Aren. Walking up to the bed, he crossed his arms.

"I will expect you not to overstay your welcome, Princess Kona," he said venomously. "The council does not want you here much longer, so I suggest you pray that your friend heals quickly."

With that, Lord Kazih turned and left the room, closing the door firmly behind him. Kona resisted the urge to stomp her foot in frustration.

"I really do not understand why he hates me so much, Sedgewik," she told the python, who was coiled on the nearest chair. The snake lifted his head from the cushions.

"He hates us because we threaten him. We might be able to help the queen regain control, and he knows that. And that is the very thing he fears most."

19.

Aren opened his eyes slowly, squinting as he was met by the bright morning sunlight streaming through the window. He tried to push himself up, but stopped when he felt a sharp pain in his side. Looking down, he saw bandages wrapped around his bared torso. A thin line of blood was seeping through them.

The boy frowned. Where was he? Looking around, to his great amazement, he saw Cika, Sedgewik, and Roniki all sleeping in the room. And beside the bed, sleeping in a chair... was Kona.

The princess's chest rose and fell slightly as she breathed easily in her sleep. Her golden curls shone in the morning sunlight. And she wore a deep blue dress with embroidery on the front.

Aren leaned back against the wall and watched her. He was sure that he had never seen anything so beautiful in his life.

"I wish I could wake up to that sight every morning," he said quietly. Kona's eyes opened quickly and she groggily scanned the room before seeing that Aren was awake. A wide smile came to her face.

"Aren!" she exclaimed. She crawled up onto the bed and carefully hugged him. Aren wrapped his arms around her, and winced when the movement put strain on his wound. Kona immediately leaned back.

"Be careful! I spent two hours cleaning up that wound, and now look what you have done; you have started it bleeding again!"

Aren smiled and pulled her close to him, planting a firm kiss on her lips. She pushed against him for a moment, and then relaxed. Aren finally drew back, still holding on to her hand.

"I did not know if I was going to see you again," he said, tenderly stroking a finger down her cheek. Kona leaned into his hand, closing her eyes.

"I am here, and so are you," Kona replied. She sighed. "I want to go home, Aren. I want to see Leyowan when it is green and healthy, when the rivers flow to the top of the banks, and the trees grow tall. I want to get away from all this suffering and sorrow. I want to help the queen negate the council's law and resume the full control of the throne."

Aren placed his hands on either side of Kona's face as he spoke. "Council law? What's all this about?"

"The queen is being controlled by the council of Terikanha. They are evil, greedy men who do not care for anyone but themselves. They passed a law stating that the queen was unfit to rule, and the only way she can repeal it is by finding a loophole or marrying a man of royal blood," responded Kona dejectedly.

Aren dropped his hands to the bed sheets. "By the time either of those happen, it will be too late to save Leyowan."

. . . . .

Later that morning, the queen came to pay a visit to her guests. The door opened to reveal Queen Naryana and two of her handmaidens. She went immediately to the bed where Aren was sitting with Kona. The princess paused in her task of feeding him some soup.

"I am glad to see you are making a recovery, young Aren," said the queen. "You have a very talented healer."

Kona blushed slightly. "Your Majesty, how is it that you have come to visit us? I thought you said the council was not to know of our meetings. Is anything wrong?" she asked worriedly. But the queen simply laughed and shook her head.

"No no, dear one. There is nothing wrong. I simply wanted to go where I pleased in my own palace. There is nothing in their law that says I cannot visit my guests."

"Is there any possible way that we could have a look at the law?" asked Aren. He took the bowl of soup from Kona and resumed eating it himself. The queen tilted her head slightly.

"I suppose there is no harm in it, as long as the council does not know. If they were to discover that you are trying to help me, they would force you to leave this very day."

Kona shook her head. "I cannot believe that they have so much control over a royal. In Leyowan, something like this would never be permitted unless the king or queen truly was evil. The people would never stand for it."

"The people here are too afraid of the council to act against the law, even though they may be on my side," said the queen. "I will leave you now, but I will have Geria bring you a copy of the law later. Just remember, keep it out of sight of Lord Kazih, or things could get much worse."

"We will look it over thoroughly, Your Majesty. You have my word on that," said Aren.

The queen gave him a grateful smile and then turned to leave, her servants following close behind her. Aren looked at Kona meaningfully.

"I am hoping that we will find something that will help the queen, but we should be a little realistic, Kona. We need to start thinking about the journey home. We did the best we could, but maybe it just wasn't meant to be," he said softly.

Cika offered her own thoughts. "And your father will be worried enough as it is..."

Kona's gaze dropped to her folded hands. "He will be very worried. And he will be angry too. I just wish I would have been able to make him proud of me," she said. "And my mother..."

A warm hand gripped the hands of the princess gently. She looked up to see Aren gazing at her with an expression of regret.

"I am so sorry, Kona. But I just want you to know that no matter what happens, you have made me proud. And if you had never come on this journey, I would not have you. I would still be alone in the forest, chasing a pack of wolves around," he said with a grin.

Kona had to chuckle. "What a terror you were then. But you could not have arrived at a better time."

They both fell silent as Cika came up toward the bed, looking very solemn. Her dark eyes stared at Aren for a long moment. "I have waited long enough to say this. I just wanted you to know that I am grateful for everything you have done for us. I have not been fair to you. I am sorry, Aren."

Both Kona and Aren's expressions turned to surprise. Cika had never called Aren by his real name until now.

"I don't know what to say," Aren responded, at a loss for words. "Thank you, but I am sorry too...Cika. You are a good friend to Kona, a friend she is going to need for the rest of her life."

Kona smiled. "I am glad you two have finally decided to be friends," she teased. The door to the chamber opened, and Geria came in with several scrolls in her arms. She deposited them on the bed and then left the room. Kona and Aren both reached for a scroll, and Cika, Sedgewik and Roniki crowded around the bed to see.

"Alright...now let's see if we can free a queen," said Aren.

. . . . .

Hours later, the five companions were still bent over the scrolls, reading every line carefully. Kona pushed back the parchment she was reading with a sigh.

"I cannot find anything, Aren. There is nothing here that negates this law, or makes it invalid in any way," she said. She put the scroll back in the pile with the others that she had already looked over. Aren placed his with the others as well.

"I am going to try and convince the council one more time… and then, maybe it is time to go home," said the princess wearily.

Aren shook his head. "Kona, you cannot expect them to change their minds. You said yourself that they are greedy and think only of themselves. The only way to get the queen out of this is to find someone for her to marry. And we cannot expect that to just happen tomorrow."

"Human boy speak wisdom," offered Roniki. "Not much good to wait."

"I know… but I just cannot bear to face my father like this. He will be angry that I left, and if I return with nothing, I cannot imagine what he will do. More importantly, I have failed our country." Kona's voice trailed off. Aren reached out and lifted her chin with his finger.

"No matter what your father says, I will be there. I am going to ask him for your hand in marriage the moment we return."

Cika grunted wryly. "You might want to let him get to know you a bit first. I highly doubt he is going to give away his only daughter to a perfect stranger," the elephant remarked.

Uncoiling himself from his perch on one of the chairs, Sedgewik slid across the floor and up to the bed.

"I think that we should ask the council for help one last time. We have nothing to lose if they refuse us again," he said. Kona nodded in agreement. There was a moment of silence while the five companions thought over their present situation, each trying to come up with a better plan.

Kona fiddled with the ends of her sleeves. "I just wish we could come up with something to help Queen Naryana. She needs to marry... and soon."

"Do not try playing a matchmaker, Kona. Chances are you will get Queen Naryana into worse trouble than she is in now. I mean, look what you did to me! I was perfectly content living a quiet life in Utomia, but you had to go off on this mindless quest and drag me along with you," said Cika teasingly.

Aren smiled and took Kona's hand. "Thank you for setting out on that mindless quest, Kona. I am eternally grateful that you did."

"Uh oh... the lovebirds have landed."

Everyone laughed at Cika's good natured teasing. Kona got off the bed and gathered up the scrolls, replacing them on the large table in the center of the room.

"I will go to the council now. Be ready to leave. I do not know what their reaction to my second request will be," said the princess quietly. She caught a worried look from Aren, and smiled at him reassuringly.

She hurriedly fixed her hair and put on the forest green dress that the queen had sent down as a gift. The emerald color brought out the gold of her hair. Matching earrings were the final touch. Kona turned to see her friends watching her. She smiled.

"Well? Do I look like a princess?" she asked teasingly.

"Like a princess indeed," replied Cika. "You look lovely, Kona. I do not think the council will be able to refuse your request."

Kona's smile faded slightly. "I fervently hope you are right, Cika. Still, I cannot expect anything. Lord Kazih did not seem to like the idea of us being here this long as it is," she pointed out.

"Let me go with you," said Aren. Before Kona could protest, he had scooted to the edge of the bed and was attempting to stand.

Cika moved to his side just as he was about to fall. He grasped one of her tusks for support, a pained grimace on his face. Kona hurried over to him, fussing like a mother hen.

"Aren! What a foolish thing to do. Your wound is just beginning to heal, and you are going to undo all the work I have done. Lay back down on that bed. You are not well enough to go anywhere, much less to see the council!" she scolded him, her eyebrows furrowed.

A small grin replaced Aren's grimace of pain. "Who knew you were such a little warrior," he teased breathlessly. "But I am going with you. I will not sit here while you face those men alone. Perhaps my presence will help persuade them."

"Aren, you are wounded. Give me one good reason why I should not have Cika put you right back on that bed," said Kona sternly, one eyebrow arched.

"I came all this way; I am not going to lay here while you face the council alone. I want to go with you. I might as well do something useful," replied Aren with an impish smile. Kona gave him a half hearted glare.

"You know I cannot say no when you smile like that," she said accusingly. Aren smiled again.

"No I did not know… but I will keep it in mind for the future." He kept his hand on Cika's side heavily, still not able to stand without her support. The elephant gave Kona a worried glance.

"I think I had better come along as well. I do not want him fainting in front of the council," she said. Aren glared at her and tried to straighten his shoulders bravely, but he winced and pressed his free hand to his side again. Kona shook her head and went to Aren's side. She reached up and kissed his cheek gently.

"You do not always have to be a hero, Aren. I am going to love you no matter what. So please, do not strain yourself. You will make me happy if you heal sooner," she told him.

Kona led the way out of the guest quarters, closely followed by Cika and Aren. The princess' limp was evident, but it was obvious to Aren that she was doing her best to hide it. The three of them took their time going down the stairs, Aren taking them one step at a time, still supported by Cika.

When they finally reached the council chamber, the guards opened the doors for them. Lord Kazih sat at the far end of the chamber, his dark eyes surveying the Leyowanians with irritation.

"What can the council assist you with this time, Princess?" he asked mockingly. Kona squared her shoulders.

"You have neither assisted us nor made any effort on our behalf, Lord Kazih. I am here once again to plead for the help of your country. My father can offer you the alliance of our nation if you give us aid through these dark times. I beg you to reconsider your decision."

Lord Kazih began to laugh. "You beg me? How unbefitting a princess, Your Highness. Besides...I do not see you on your knees."

There was a moment of silence. Aren silently simmered in fury at the way the council was treating Kona. But the princess of Leyowan took a step forward toward the men, her head raised high.

"No princess belongs on her knees, Lord Kazih," she said, her voice low and steady. "I do not beg you for mercy. I beg you to consider this for the sake of my people. But my words fall upon deaf ears, upon the ears of men who are so hardened to the plight of others that they think no more of this famine and its merciless effects on our people than the dirt upon which you trod."

There was no anger in Kona's voice, only sadness. Aren and Cika stood behind her silently, watching the princess as she addressed the council of Terikanha, looking every bit the majestic daughter of Kikpona.

It seemed that even the council was struck mute by her strong words. Lord Kazih cleared his throat uneasily.

"Be that as it may...Terikanha owes Leyowan no allegiance or aid. We do not desire their alliance. Therefore the council retains its decision. We will not send aid to Leyowan."

Kona closed her eyes, but did not show the defeat she felt in her heart. She gazed directly at Lord Kazih, her eyes locked with his until he finally looked away.

"I must say, Lord Kazih, for a man to hear such moving words from so beautiful a young woman and be untouched, it raises much doubt as to his character," said a deep voice behind the three companions. Kona whirled in surprise. She knew that voice!

There in the doorway stood Jathren. He was dressed in leather armor and a long cloak, and dirt covered his tall boots, attesting to the long journey he had made.

Joy filled Kona's heart, and she gave her uncle a bright smile. She wanted nothing more than to run to him and throw her arms around him in an embrace. She did not realize how much she had missed him. But she was still in the council chamber, in the presence of the lords of Terikanha. She would not break the rules of court etiquette.

Surprise and then anxiety flashed across Lord Kazih's face. "Ah... my lord Jathren! This is a most unexpected...pleasure. We were not expecting the ambassador of Leyowan to appear upon our doorstep!"

"I have come for my niece, Lord Kazih," replied Jathren smoothly. "Her father the king is most worried for her health and safety. We were not aware that she had journeyed to your country for some time. If you do not mind, I believe my niece and I have much to talk about. We will return to you at a more convenient time."

Amazed, Lord Kazih only nodded in agreement. Kona was astonished at the smooth, steady way her uncle had dismissed the council, and in their own chamber no less!

Cika and Aren led the way out the door, and Jathren offered his arm to Kona. The princess smiled and took it graciously. The Leyowanians left the chamber, leaving behind them a very miffed council.

. . . . .

Jathren said not a word to his niece until they reached the guest quarters. He followed Cika and Aren quietly into the large room, and did not seem to notice the curious looks he immediately received from Roniki and Sedgewik. He sat down in one of the luxuriously cushioned chairs and glanced expectantly at Kona. The princess reached down and hugged him tightly before sitting down in another chair.

Cika helped Aren back to the bed. The boy was exhausted from the strain it had taken to stand for so long, and the pain of his wound.

As Kona glanced back to her uncle, she saw him watching Aren carefully, and felt a pang of uneasiness. Jathren looked at her again.

"You are well?" he finally asked her, worry filling his eyes. Kona nodded reassuringly.

"Very well. Thanks to my friends. Uncle Jathren, this is Sedgewik, and Roniki," she said, pointing to the two animals. "And … this is Aren." The princess rose from her chair and went to the bed, reaching for Aren's hand. The boy smiled at her and interlaced his fingers with hers.

Jathren's eyebrows lifted. "Aren… who are you, lad? Where are you from?" he asked warily. Kona could tell that he was not pleased with the obvious affection that his niece was showing this strange boy.

"My parents had an estate near the town of Bailin. That is where I grew up. My parents were killed by raiders when I was nine. After that, I wandered from place to place," Aren answered softly. He returned Jathren's steady gaze unflinchingly.

Kona stepped in. "If it were not for Aren… I would not be alive right now, Uncle Jathren. We owe him our thanks."

At that, Jathren's face softened. "Perhaps you had better tell me everything. Start with the night you left."

20.

It was evening before Kona finished her retelling of their travels, not leaving anything out, even her talks with Aren. The others filled in bits and pieces. Jathren said nothing, but listened with grave solemnity to his niece's tale.

"…and when we went to the council the second time, you came in," finished Kona breathlessly. She pushed a wayward strand of hair out of her eyes.

Jathren was silent for a long moment. He leaned back against the cushions and ran his hands over his face before looking at Kona. "That is one of the most incredible stories I have ever heard," he said. "Your mother would be proud of you, Kona."

He glanced up at Aren. "And you, young man. I owe you the gratitude of a nation for keeping our princess safe. However, there is a problem that we must face. You are not of noble blood, and King Morgo will not easily agree to the love you share with Kona. He has already chosen a betrothed for her."

Aren frowned. "I know, but Kona did say that her leaving would mean that the betrothal would have to be broken. That both she and her betrothed would be free of the bond."

"Unfortunately, Nobio's father chose to keep the betrothal intact until Kona was found. He is very adamant about this union, as is King Morgo himself," replied Jathren.

"No! He could not have…" Kona's voice softened. "Do they not know that Nobio loves another? How could they force him into a marriage with me?"

Jathren shook his head. "Nobio would never admit such a thing to his father; he is far too obedient of his father's wishes for that. He has agreed to the marriage."

Sitting up, Aren's eyes flashed angrily. "I will not allow this! I will do anything in my power to see that Nobio does not marry Kona. I love her, and I will not stand by as some other man marries her!"

Kona put a hand on his arm gently. "Aren, you know that my heart is yours. Forever. We cannot do anything until we return to Utomia and speak with my father. I promise you, I will do everything I can to reverse this betrothal. But right now, we have a bigger problem. We have to find a way to free the queen."

"You said that the law states that she can only be freed if she marries a prince or king?" asked Jathren thoughtfully. Kona nodded.

"Yes, we looked over all the scrolls she gave us, but we cannot find any loopholes that would allow her to bypass that law. She said that she has not found anyone thus far who is able or wishes to marry her. She said she even considered Father, but did not dare ask him to replace Mother," the princess replied.

"I would like to speak to the queen," said Jathren. "I wonder if there is not a way to resolve all this."

Kona sighed. "We have thought of every possible idea, and none of them work. Without the queen, we cannot take any food or supplies back for the people of Leyowan. She has to be careful about speaking with us. If the council knew what we were trying to do..."

Rising from the chair, Jathren walked over to his niece and wrapped his arms around her, tipping her chin up with one finger.

"The queen knows me. I have been here several times before as Ambassador. The council would not dare interfere with my business. They fear me too much. I am the brother of Kikpona, after all," he finished with a smile. "Now do not worry. The queen and I will find a solution, I promise."

Jathren turned and left the room, closing the door quietly behind him. Kona sank back to the bed and turned to look at Aren.

"Well, at least we know that we have one ally to our love," she said softly, noting the downcast expression on Aren's face. He looked across at her and patted her hand.

"One?" Cika retorted indignantly. "I believe four would be the correct number."

Roniki jumped up to the bed and scurried over to Aren's lap. "Yes yes! Roniki big help, you see!" she exclaimed.

Everyone laughed at the little rodent's enthusiasm. Kona picked up the rat and hugged her. "I know you will be, my friend."

. . . . .

Kona gazed out the window of the chamber silently, watching the stars shine brightly in the sky. Jathren had returned several hours after he had left them, but had told the companions nothing of his audience with the queen, other than saying that they had a plan, and would talk to the council the next morning.

The princess knew that the next morning would be the last chance they had to free the queen and get the help they had come for.

"Kona, you must sleep," whispered Jathren from his pallet on the floor. Kona glanced down and saw her uncle watching her worriedly. She smiled and returned to her own mattress, lying on the floor next to the bed, where Aren was sleeping.

As she closed her eyes, Kona wondered what tomorrow would bring. Either way, it would change the lives of her people. But would it be for the better, or for the worse? That remained to be seen.

. . . . .

Morning dawned, bringing with it the bright light that shown in the windows of the guest chamber, illuminating the sleeping Leyowanians within. Aren was the first to wake. He opened his eyes slowly, letting them adjust to the brightness of the room. He glanced to the side, and saw Kona sleeping on her back, her hands folded serenely over her stomach. Her golden hair spilled out over the pillow. The morning sunlight cast a radiant glow over the princess as she slept.

"Beautiful..." murmured Aren to himself, unable to take his eyes from the sight before him.

Jathren awoke, and saw the boy sitting up in the bed, looking down at Kona. The look in Aren's eyes was so tender, so loving. Jathren smiled slightly as he rose from his pallet, carefully avoiding stepping on the long python tail that had moved next to his bed during the night.

"I will wake the others," said Jathren. Aren carefully got off the bed, wincing as his side burned from the movement. He half knelt, half fell to his knees beside Kona's mattress, and reached out for her shoulder.

"Arise, Princess," he whispered into her ear, shaking her shoulder gently. Kona's eyes opened, and she looked up to see Aren bending over her.

"It is morning already?" she asked sleepily.

Aren nodded and chuckled. "Yes. And today we are going to do what we came here to do. Your uncle says that the queen has a plan."

"A plan indeed," said Jathren. "We will reveal it when we go before the council today. Mark my words; this day will see the end of their greed and malice. Terikanha will be free from them once and for all."

A smile came to Kona's face. "Really? That is wonderful news! I cannot believe it..."

Jathren set up the dressing screen for Kona. "But we are going to be late if you do not hurry and dress. Cika and Roniki, would you assist the princess, please?" he asked.

The elephant and the rat hurried after Kona behind the screen, and began fussing over her hair and dress. Jathren sat down on the bed next to Aren, and looked at the boy closely. Aren returned his gaze.

Finally, Jathren spoke. "Aren, I am grateful to you for all that you have done for my niece and our country. But I must know…do you truly love her? Or is this a scheme on your part? Marriage to the princess of Leyowan is not a small matter."

The boy's green eyes turned toward the window. "I know. It means that I will become the Prince of Leyowan. But the title does not please me… I never wanted a life of nobility. I wanted to be free to come and go when and where I pleased."

Aren turned back to face Jathren, and he managed a small smile. "But when I met Kona… all that changed. I would give up my freedom to be with her. I would travel the world just to win her hand. She alone holds my heart, and she always will."

There was a pause, and then Jathren nodded solemnly. "If what you have said is the truth, then I will do what I can to help you when we return to Leyowan."

"Thank you."

Kona reappeared from behind the screen, wearing her emerald colored dress. Her hair was piled on top of her head in a mass of neat curls. A strand of diamonds hung at her throat, another gift from the queen.

"Are we ready, then?" she asked with a smile. Jathren stood and helped Aren do the same. Cika returned to her place beside the boy to support him as he walked. Roniki jumped up to Kona's shoulder, and Sedgewik slid along beside Cika.

Jathren led the way out the door and down the hallway. The queen waited for them at the stairwell, dressed in a luxurious blue gown, her ebony hair left free to tumble down her back in a rippling black sea of curls.

"All is well, Your Majesty?" asked Jathren, bowing low. The queen smiled and nodded.

"Today is a new day, Lord Jathren. A new day for all of us," she said, looking back at the princess and her friends, who also bowed. The queen took Jathren's proffered arm, and they descended the stairs.

The doors to the council chamber were opened once again, but this time, Queen Naryana herself stepped through them confidently, escorted by the Ambassador of Leyowan, brother of Queen Kikpona.

Lord Kazih stared openly at the queen, startled by her presence. "Your Majesty, I was not aware that you were *invited* to this meeting," he said condescendingly.

The queen smiled regally. "I am the queen of Terikanha, Lord Kazih. I believe that if I wish to attend a meeting of this council, there is no law in place which forbids me to do so."

Jathren stepped forward. "You owe the queen your respect, Lord Kazih. After all, it is her word, not yours, that is law in this country."

"My lord, you are sadly mistaken," returned Lord Kazih. "We have in place a law of restriction over her Majesty to ensure that the lands of Terikanha are ruled as they should be...by the council."

"A law which is now negated," proclaimed the queen. Naryana stepped up to Lord Kazih, standing a mere foot or two away from her oppressor. "I am going to marry, and therefore, your rule is over."

Surprise filled Lord Kazih's eyes, and murmurs of astonishment rippled throughout the council.

"Your Majesty, you cannot marry without the approval of this council," returned Lord Kazih confidently. At that, Jathren stepped forward to stand beside the queen.

"That is true, Lord Kazih, unless the suitor is present at this council meeting, which he is. I am Prince Jathren of Leyowan, son of Queen Elaria, brother of His Majesty King Morgo, and his late wife, Queen Kikpona, and I am here before you to marry Queen Naryana of Terikanha."

A shocked silence filled the room. Kona clenched her hands into fists at her sides, unable to believe what she was hearing. Her uncle Jathren was going to marry the Queen?

Lord Kazih scrambled to regain some form of composure. "I...well surely there is... you cannot simply..."

"I can, and I have. Queen Naryana and I were married last night by your very own palace priest, Lord Kazih. You owe me your allegiance and your respect. And as my first act as King of Terikanha, I negate this council and all its holdings over my wife, the Queen. You are dismissed from Talda, and banished from these lands."

Speechless, Lord Kazih glared at the queen, and then brushed past her out of the room. One by one, the other council members filed out of the chamber, leaving the new king and his queen alone with the five companions.

Jathren turned to face Kona, who was trembling, tears running down her face. He took three long strides toward her and gathered her to him.

"Why do you cry, dearest? This was the only way to free Naryana, and I know that I love her. We will be happy," he said soothingly, rubbing her back. Kona sighed and leaned back, wiping the tears from her cheeks.

"But you were supposed to be King of Leyowan," she said. Jathren laughed, surprising the princess. He looked at her with a broad smile.

"My dear niece, I would never have been King of Leyowan. That is your throne, and your future husband's throne. I would never have ruled our lands. My heart will always be in Leyowan, but now my duties lie here, with Queen Naryana. You can come and visit us whenever you like."

Kona frowned. "But you promised that you would help us," she said, motioning to Aren. "You said you would plead our case to my father. We cannot do this alone."

Reaching into his pocket, Jathren withdrew a scroll. "I have written a letter to your father, explaining where I stand in this matter. You will give it to him, and I believe it may make a difference in his decision."

"You cannot stay here," said the queen. "Your father already has missed you long enough, and you have accomplished what you came here to do. We will send caravans with you to return to Leyowan, with food and supplies for your people. Terikanha has plenty to spare, and we will give you what we have."

Kona's eyes misted again. "Thank you... may I call you Aunt Naryana?" she asked shyly. The queen smiled brightly and opened her arms. Kona embraced her new aunt without hesitation.

"Of course you may, Kona. I have always dreamed of having a niece. And now I have one who is the most lovely, intelligent girl in the world! And I owe *you* thanks, because without your help, I would never have been able to negate the law. If you had not come to Terikanha... Jathren would not have come either," she said, smiling tenderly up at her new husband.

Jathren pressed a chaste kiss to the queen's cheek, and then turned his attention to the companions. "Now then... the caravans should be about ready to leave. We had them start packing food and supplies last night. If you leave today, you should make it back in about three weeks."

Surprise flashed through Kona's eyes. "Three weeks? It took us much longer than that to get here!"

Once again, Jathren chuckled. "The route you took was much longer than the routes the caravan will take. There is a secret trail between here and Leyowan that is centuries old, but it is the straightest path between the two. Come, let us get you packed."

.....

Kona watched the city of Talda fade into the distance from her cushioned seat in one of the caravan wagons. Aren sat next to her, holding Roniki in his lap. Sedgewik had chosen not to ride in the wagon because Cika had to walk, so he was keeping her company.

There were tiny little snores from Roniki as the rodent slept comfortably in Aren's lap. Kona glanced at the smallest member of their group with a smile. She reached over and stroked Roniki's head gently.

"How does it feel, to be finally returning home?" asked Aren quietly. Kona looked up at him.

"I do not know. I feel relieved, knowing that we are bringing food that our people desperately need, but I am also afraid. I do not know what my father is going to do when I return. If he really is angry with me, we may not have a chance to speak with him about us until it is too late."

The princess searched Aren's eyes with her own. "Are you sure you want to give up the life you know for me? A prince of Leyowan is bound to the throne. You would be King one day."

Aren leaned back against the cushions. "I would give up any life for you, you know that. But to be king..." he paused. "I know that I am not prepared for such a task."

Reaching out, Kona took his hand. "But that is years from now. My father will be king until he thinks his heir is worthy to take the throne. And by then, you will have learned much about the ways of ruling a nation. And you will not be alone...I will always be with you. Every King needs a Queen."

Aren smiled and leaned over. Kona kissed him gently, but drew back when she felt him wince. "You should be more careful, Aren."

He chuckled and kissed the tip of her nose. "You are right. I should be more careful. Kissing you is getting to be a very dangerous experience," he teased her. Kona smiled and shook her head.

"Is your wound feeling any better?" she asked.

Aren shrugged. "Better than it felt when I first received it," he said with an impish grin. Kona sighed and threw her hands up in the air.

"Can you never be serious?" her blue eyes gave him a half-hearted glare. Aren smiled and squeezed her hand.

"That depends..." he replied, leaning in for another kiss. "I can be serious for certain things... like this. Or this," he said, kissing her again. Kona laughed and pushed him away gently.

"Alright enough of your games," she said. "You will have plenty of time to heal on the way home. At least this time it is a bit more comfortable, and we will not have to worry about whether or not we have enough food."

Aren nodded. He watched as Kona closed her eyes wearily, her hands folded carefully in her lap. After a few minutes, her head fell to rest on his shoulder. A tiny smile lifted the corner of Aren's mouth, and he reached up to smooth a lock of golden hair back behind her ear.

"Sleep well, my love."

. . . . .

The three weeks of travel passed quickly, and it was not long before the caravan was across the border of Leyowan, headed for Utomia. Before they had left Sumeria, Kona had requested that the wagons stop in the town of Nevor. She could still see the look on Noora's face as they'd brought in enough food to last her and Pickins through the famine. The old dog was so grateful that he had even licked Kona's hand.

Several wagons had branched off from the main caravan, taking supplies to the other parts of Leyowan under the direct order of the princess.

Utomia drew nearer and nearer, until at last, the caravan rumbled right through the wide open gates of Leyowan's capitol city.

. . . . .

Kona gripped the side of the wagon tightly, tears rolling down her face at the sight of her mother's city. The beautiful limestone walls rose up into the sky, protecting the domed roofs of the buildings behind them. Thousands of people and animals were lining the road, cheering with a noise so deafening that it made Kona's ears ring. She stood up in the wagon and waved, smiling past the lump that had risen to her throat.

Aren looked up at her, radiant and beaming out at the people she served and loved, and felt very out of place. He looked out at the faces of those that cheered for their princess, and realized that he should be with them, not sitting there in a cushioned wagon with the heir to Leyowan's throne.

He sat back against the side of the wagon, and ignored the curious look that Roniki gave him. The wagon rumbled to a stop in front of the palace courtyard. Kona looked down the path, and saw some very familiar faces awaiting her. Vanddai came running towards the wagon, calling out Kona's name. The princess climbed carefully over the side and limped the last few steps to her aunt. Vanddai wrapped her arms around the princess and held her tightly.

"You are the most foolish, reckless, beautiful, incredible girl I have ever known," Vanddai said, her voice breaking slightly at the end.

Kona laughed, and drew back from her aunt to see Quetoro standing next to them, his dark eyes shining happily. "Welcome home, daughter of the Queen," said the old horse.

"Thank you, Quetoro. It's so good to be home, I cannot believe it has been so long since I left," she replied. "Where is my…" her voice trailed off as Vanddai and Quetoro stepped aside. Ten feet away from the princess, stood King Morgo. The king faced his daughter silently, his eyes shadowed. Not sure what to say, Kona dropped in an awkward curtsey.

"My loyalties, as always, Father," she said respectfully. She raised herself shakily, trying to balance some of her weight on her bad leg. She lifted her eyes to those of her father, and saw them smoldering with a deep fire. But to her surprise, it wasn't the fire she expected.

Morgo's stony mask crumbled and he took two long strides toward his daughter. He threw his arms around her, lifting her up in the air. Kona shrieked in surprise and joy as her father swung her around and around.

He set her down gently, still holding her tightly to himself. "I am so proud of you, Kona. And I know that if your mother were here, she would be bursting with pride at what you have done for your country."

Kona could not remember a time when she had felt any happier. "Thank you, Father. Thank you so much. I love you."

Morgo drew a hand across his eyes. "I love you too, Kona. I love you too."

The princess stepped back, and gestured toward her companions, who were watching curiously. "Father, these are my friends, the ones who got me to Terikanha and back safely, besides Cika, of course. Sedgewik, Roniki and Aren."

Walking up to where Aren was standing next to the wagon, the king reached out a hand. After a moment of hesitation, Aren nervously gripped it with his own hand. The king looked at the boy and then at Sedgewik and Roniki.

"You have my eternal thanks for protecting my daughter from harm. All three of you may have whatever you ask for. Gold, land, anything that you desire will be yours," he said generously.

Roniki raised a paw. "King, can Roniki's ratta tribe have food?" she asked timidly. The king laughed aloud.

"Of course, little one. Your tribe will have more food than they can possibly eat!" he replied. Roniki bounced up and down excitedly. Sedgewik raised himself off the ground slightly and cleared his throat.

"Begging your pardon, my lord... but could I possibly have food sent to my tribe as well?" the python asked quietly. The king smiled and nodded.

"Noble requests indeed, but surely there is something else that each of you desires? Come now, I will not rest until I have given you gifts."

Both Sedgewik and Roniki looked flustered, and they fell silent. Kona placed a hand on her father's arm, and whispered something into his ear. He patted her hand and faced the two animals before him again.

"My daughter wishes that you each be given a title of nobility, Lord Sedgewik and Lady Roniki. With this, you will be granted all the rights and responsibilities of nobles," he said. Looks of amazement and gratitude flashed over Sedgewik and Roniki's faces.

The king turned to Aren, and was met by the gaze of two green eyes. "And you, boy? What is it that we can give to you?" the king asked. Aren blinked and licked his lips nervously.

"May I have anything I wish for, great king?"

Morgo raised his eyebrows in surprise. "Of course, you may have anything you request. Wealth, land, a position in my army…"

Swallowing hard, Aren took a deep breath. "There is only one thing that I would ask of you, my lord. I wish with all my heart to marry your daughter."

21.

Morgo paced the great hall, his hands clenching and unclenching. After Aren's request outside the palace, the king had not said a word to either him or Kona, but had the whole group moved inside. He had taken Vanddai, Quetoro, Aren and Kona into the great hall, and requested that everyone else leave them in privacy to discuss things.

The king looked at Kona. "You cannot marry him, Kona. I will not allow it. He is a peasant, not the sort of boy who could be a prince of Leyowan. I am sure he is a fine fellow, but sometimes the heart leads us astray."

"Father please, you do not understand. My heart knows its place, and it is right here, with the man I love. He is the man who saved my life and sacrificed so much for a cause that was not his own. I have never known anyone that I loved and cared about this way," she said softly, interlacing her fingers with Aren's.

Morgo glanced at their joined hands. "As much as that may be true, I could never justify this, Kona. You are betrothed to Nobio, a boy who has been waiting for your return since the hour you left, and you have not even greeted him yet."

Looking down at the floor, Kona replied, "No Father, I have not."

"Go to him. He will want to know that you are home safe. I want to talk to Aren for a while," said the king. Kona looked at Aren questioningly, but he managed a tight smile and nodded.

"Go on, I will be fine," he said. Kona stood up and limped out one of the doors toward the guest quarters of the palace.

Morgo brought a chair over and sat it down across from Aren. The boy clenched his hands into fists in his lap, inwardly he was terrified, but he dared not show it. The king saw the bandage that was wrapped around Aren's stomach underneath the thin shirt the boy wore.

"That must be quite a wound, son. How did you come to receive it?" Morgo asked quietly.

Surprised, Aren's eyes lifted to the king's. "It wasn't anything... just a... I... really it wasn't anything. I did something I had to."

"Surely there's more of a story in it than that," replied the king patiently. He waited for a long moment. Silence filled the room, and finally Aren spoke again.

"I was knifed," he said softly. "I had to do it so the others could escape. We were imprisoned in a guardhouse, captured by the border patrol in Terikanha. I have never seen such warriors, robed in black and cruel. Sedgewik let us out of the cells, but Roniki was still in the guardhouse with the warriors. I got her out, but when I tried to retrieve my weapons... they woke up. One of the warriors pinned me to a wall and stabbed me."

"Were you afraid?"

Aren was taken aback by the king's question, but he gazed back at Morgo, meeting the older man's eyes. "Yes sir... I was."

A smile touched Morgo's lips. "I would have been afraid too, had I been there. Why were you afraid, Aren?" he asked. There was a long pause, and Aren looked down at his hands.

"I was afraid they would find her again," he murmured. "I love her. I love her more than anything in this world. I cannot imagine living my life away from her."

A wistful look came to the king's eyes and he sat back in his chair. "I can see that. And I know... exactly what kind of love it is that you have told me about. Long ago, I loved someone the same way you love my daughter."

Aren looked up. "The queen, my lord?" he asked. Morgo nodded.

"Not just a queen, Aren. Kikpona was the most incredible woman I have ever known. She was *the* queen, and everyone who ever met her knew it. I was the most blessed man on this earth when she agreed to marry me," Morgo said. "And when she died, a part of me died with her."

"My greatest sympathies, my Lord. I cannot imagine what I would feel if Kona were to die," replied Aren quietly.

Heaving a great sigh, Morgo leaned forward once again. "I cannot allow this marriage, no matter how much either you or my daughter might wish it. You are not noble, and to allow you to marry my daughter would divide the people."

Aren closed his eyes tightly. "Forgive me my lord. But the truth is… I am noble by blood. My parents were Lord Arnero and Lady Mathena of Bailin."

Shock registered on Morgo's face. "They were ruthlessly murdered by bandits… nine years ago… I was told that their son was killed also."

Shaking his head, Aren responded, "I left Bailin as soon as I found out my parents were dead. I did not want anything to do with a life that would remind me of them. So I became a peasant. Until now."

Morgo ran his hands over his face. "I cannot believe this. First my daughter disappears, then my brother-in-law marries the queen of the country my daughter disappeared to, and now the son of one of my most loyal advisors turns up alive after nine years."

"I am sorry, my lord." Aren swallowed hard. "Forgive me, I did not mean to cause any trouble for you."

"Well, that clears the problem of your birthright. But there is still a very real obstacle that remains in your path. I have promised that Nobio will marry Kona, and the only way that I can release that bond is if Nobio's father negates the betrothal."

Aren felt his heart drop. "I see."

The door to the great hall opened, and Kona came in, escorted by Nobio, and followed closely by Lord Albios.

Aren immediately stood up from his chair, ignoring the slight twinge in his side, and faced Nobio. The two young men looked at each other for a long moment. Nobio reached out a hand.

"It is a pleasure to meet you, Aren," he said. Aren hesitated, and then shook the other boy's hand.

"And you, Nobio. I have heard many good things about you from Kona. She says you have been a very good friend to her, and for that, I thank you," said Aren honestly. Nobio smiled.

"She is easy to be friends with. She is a very giving person. And I hope that we can resolve this so that she can marry the man who loves her the most," replied Nobio. He blinked several times and patted Kona's hand. The princess gave him a quick hug.

"Thank you," she whispered in his ear. She turned and went to stand at Aren's side.

Lord Albios looked sternly at his son. "Nobio, you realize what this marriage means for our family? We have spent your whole life planning for this day, and yet now you squander your chances of marrying the princess?"

In that moment, something seemed to change in Nobio. He returned his father's stern gaze. "I will not let our family down, Father. And I will not squander my chances for my future. I also will make the best choice for this country with my father's blessing."

Nobio looked at Kona, who gazed back at him in confusion, fear in her wide blue eyes. Nobio smiled reassuringly. "I will be a friend to the Princess as long as she may need me. But I will not steal away from her the future that she deserves, the future she has with Aren. My heart is already given to a beautiful girl named Lilleth."

Lord Albios spoke. "I am disappointed... that I did not realize how mature my son has become. I am proud of you Nobio."

Nobio turned to face the king. "My lord, with all respect, I negate any and all bonds between myself and the princess."

The king placed a hand on Nobio's shoulder. "Are you sure that you are willing to do this, Nobio? You still have the chance to marry the princess if that is what you desire."

Shaking his head, Nobio glanced at Kona and Aren. "No. I will not marry the princess."

Unable to contain his joy, Aren turned and hugged Kona to him. She laughed brightly and embraced him back. But then she walked toward Nobio, and reached out her hands. The boy placed his own hands in hers.

Kona smiled through her tears. "What you have done for me today... I will never forget. You will be my friend for all time, and when I am queen, you will have a place in the Royal Council as my close advisor."

Gratitude filled Nobio's eyes, and he bowed slightly. "You are very generous, Kona. For that I thank you."

Kona reached behind her neck and released the chords of the necklace that Nobio had entrusted to her at the beginning of her journey. "I believe this belongs to you and Lilleth," she said, placing the piece in his hand. She gently folded his fingers over the necklace. "When you and Lilleth are married, you will have a royal wedding."

The princess smiled and released his hands as Lord Albios led his son away. Morgo called after them.

"Remember, you are both invited to the festival tonight!" he said. Lord Albios called back that they would be there, and then the two men left the room. Morgo looked at Kona, and saw her puzzled expression.

"Festival?" she asked curiously.

"Yes. We have been planning a festival in honor of your return. The whole city will be there," he replied with a smile. "It will also be the perfect time to announce your betrothal to Lord Aren."

Kona started at that. "Lord Aren?"

Morgo smiled. "It seems as though your betrothed is much more than he seems. He is the lost son of Lord Arnero and Lady Mathena of Bailin. So he is not a peasant after all."

Looking at Aren, the princess saw the sheepish grin on his face, and knew that her father spoke truth. "Why did you never tell me?" she asked.

Aren shrugged. "I just never found it relevant. I was not ready to be known as Lord Aren yet. My parents' death was still very real to me." He looked away from the princess. "And still is."

Glancing at her father, Kona spoke quietly. "Father… will you give us a moment?" she asked.

The king kissed her forehead and nodded. "Of course. I will come back in a few moments… you do not want to miss the festival."

Morgo left the great hall, leaving the two lovers in silence. Kona sat down on the hearth of the fireplace, letting the heat from the flames warm her suddenly chilled body. Aren came to sit beside her.

"What troubles you, Kona?" he asked gently. "I am sorry that I did not tell you who I was sooner, but I did not want it to change anything about the way you felt about me. And my parents...I can still feel the pain I felt that day when I found them."

Kona shook her head. "No, it is not that. All this," she said, gesturing through the air with her hand, "everything that has happened... it is all so much. I love you more than anything, and now you are my betrothed, just as we hoped for. Someday I will be Queen of this country, and sit on my mother's throne. It is all happening just the way I wanted it to."

"Then why are you troubled?" Aren asked again, watching the princess closely. Kona sniffed softly and her eyes misted.

"Aren... how can I ever face the throne that my mother built? How can I rule an empire in her stead? How can I ever hope to be the woman that she was? I am so much less than she was. I am a cripple; I cannot even wield a sword."

A calloused hand gently cupped her face. Aren looked into her eyes. "Kona, my beautiful love. You are stronger than you realize. You are not a cripple in my eyes. You are a whole, perfect, gentle-hearted woman who has so much to give her country. You will never be your mother, nor should you be.

You were given your own life to live, and I know that your mother would be proud of you."

One solitary tear trickled down Kona's cheek. "I cannot walk through life as a cripple, Aren," she said softly, her eyes searching his.

A small smile touched Aren's lips. "You will not have to. I will always be here to carry you."

Love shone in Kona's eyes as she leaned in to kiss Aren. Their lips touched gently, sweetly. Aren broke the kiss to lean his forehead against Kona's.

His fingers brushed against the gold medallion that still hung around the princess' neck. A soft smile touched his lips.

"I gave you this, hoping you would choose to wear it always."

Kona's eyes met his. "Then I always will."

"Come... the festival is starting, and we would not want the guest of honor to be absent, would we?" he asked quietly. Kona leaned against him again, not wanting to leave the safety of his arms.

"I would miss a thousand festivals just to stay here with you," she whispered.

Aren smiled wistfully. "I know you would, Kona. But for a princess to miss her own festival is something no one would appreciate."

The princess allowed Aren to lead her towards the door. She concentrated on concealing her limp. Aren led her toward the palace's rear courtyard, and Kona began to hear the loud sounds of music and voices.

Morgo met them at the gates of the courtyard, and smiled at his daughter. "Are you ready?"

"I am," she replied. Morgo held out his arm for his daughter, and she took it silently. Aren walked behind them as the king escorted Kona out to the festival. As soon as they exited the gates of the palace courtyard, the revelry was nearly deafening. Kona's eyes swept to and fro, trying to take it all in.

Garlands of leaves were hung everywhere on tall pillars that surrounded a large circular clearing. All manner of animals and people were dancing merrily. Beautiful old Leyowan melodies flowed from the flute and drum players that stood to one side.

Leaning in to Kona's ear, the king whispered, "We all would be most indebted if the princess would sing us a tune."

Nervous butterflies flew around in Kona's stomach as she considered her father's request. She did so dearly love to sing, but in front of all these guests? She wasn't sure she was brave enough.

"Please do, Kona. I do not believe I have ever heard you sing," murmured Aren into her ear softly. The princess felt a tingle run down her spine at his voice, and shyly smiled.

"Very well…" she agreed. "I shall need only one flute player to accompany me."

Morgo walked over to the musicians and spoke to them. A hush fell over the crowd as the king turned to speak to the whole gathering.

"Princess Kona has agreed to grace us with a song!" he proclaimed. The crowd cheered as Aren helped the princess up to the platform where a single flute player was waiting for her. The man bowed as she faced him and smiled brightly.

"I'm ready whenever you are, m'lady," he said kindly. "You start singin' and I'll join in with my flute."

Kona looked out over the eager, waiting faces of the crowd, and suddenly felt her butterflies disappear. She imagined that her mother was among the guests, listening; and that seemed to quiet her nerves. She saw the faces of her dearest friends in the crowd: Sedgewik, Roniki, Cika…Aren… Opening her lips, she began to sing.

See ye stars above in midnight sky
O'er yonder meadow shining
Morning comes, drawing nigh
Night no more my heart confining

Dawn brings with it golden hues
Lift, ye hearts in joy today
Night fades into lighter blues
Darkness defeated, come what may

Strength and joy return
Night is o'er, let peace now reign
For my lover now I yearn
He'll come back to me once again

Kona fell silent as the last notes of the flute faded into the night breeze. The crowd seemed to be under the spell of those sweetly sung words, for no sound was heard for several moments. The princess bowed her head, and waited.

Cheers broke out from the crowd, and Kona smiled and waved. "I thank you all for welcoming me home. I believe that my father wishes for me to make an announcement regarding my betrothal," the princess said. The crowd fell quiet again.

Kona's eyes found Aren, and she smiled. "During my travels, I was blessed to meet a young man who has stolen my heart. Who is now my betrothed, the future Prince of Leyowan, Lord Aren of Bailin."

Aren waved to the cheering crowd, feeling hands patting him on the back as he joined Kona on the platform. He jumped up to the wooden structure and put his arms around Kona. The crowd roared their approval as Aren lifted Kona up in his arms and kissed her.

Blushing, Kona drew in a deep breath as Aren set her back down to her feet. She took his hand and let him help her off the platform.

The musicians struck up a lively tune, and the dancing began all over again. Kona accepted endless congratulations from people and animals that came up to the happy royal couple to wish them well.

One of the well-wishers was Nobio. He came up to Kona wearing a broad smile, a brown haired girl holding his arm.

"Kona, I would like you to meet my betrothed, Lilleth," he said happily. The girl curtseyed daintily. Kona reached out and embraced her.

"I am so very happy to meet you, Lilleth. And I am so glad that you can be with Nobio. He will make you a very fine husband. My best wishes for your lifelong happiness together," she said to Lilleth, meaning the words with all her heart.

As Lilleth and Nobio moved away to dance, Aren looked down at the princess, his eyes twinkling merrily.

"As your betrothed and future prince of Leyowan, may I have this dance, m'lady?" he asked her solemnly. Kona placed her hand in his, and raised an eyebrow while she answered him.

"As *your* betrothed and Princess of Leyowan, I accept your offer," she said. The familiar impish grin that she loved so much spread itself across Aren's face as he led her toward the whirling couples.

Aren held her to him tenderly and wrapped his arms around her waist. Kona lifted her hands to his shoulders, and let him lead her in their own personal way of dancing. Kona felt as though her heart weighed less than a feather, and her limp disappeared from her mind.

I know that Mother would be so happy to see this... thought Kona to herself, a smile coming to her at the thought.

From that moment on, it seemed as though it was just her and Aren, alone in their own world of love and joy. The sounds of the festival and guests faded into the background as the two young lovers danced.

The End

EPILOGUE

Kona and Aren married a year later on the princess' eighteenth birthday. Thousands of Leyowanians attended the wedding, which was the grandest in the history of the land. Many guests came from Terikanha also, including King Jathren and Queen Naryana, who were expecting their first child. A certain old woman and dog also attended the festivities. King Morgo gave his daughter the wedding gift of her mother's iron spear, re-forged and made whole once again.

Sedgewik returned to his snake tribe, and was made clan chief because of his courage and bravery on the journey he had made with Kona. Under his leadership, the python tribe became prosperous and well-regarded throughout the lands of Leyowan, and peace was made between the snakes and the other inhabitants of the country. Sedgewik finally was respected and loved by his own, and he always remained a faithful friend of the Royal House of Leyowan.

Roniki never returned to her original home, but rather sent for her whole family to join her in living comfortably at the palace in Utomia. It was not uncommon for the passersby to have to watch their step in the halls of Kona's lavish home, lest they find themselves apologizing to an angry rat with a bruised tail. Roniki herself could usually be found perched on the shoulder of either the princess or the prince, especially at mealtimes. She enjoyed an abundance of sugar biscuits.

As for Cika, the elephant remained in Kona's service at the palace. She married her own betrothed, and fretted over the demands of a rambunctious elephant infant. She had been promised a place as one of Kona and Aren's chief advisors when they took the throne, but for now she was content to pass her time with her new family and her dearest friend.

What of Nobio and Lilleth, you might ask? They lived quite comfortably at Lord Albios' estate. Nobio earned his right to be an Advisor to the new prince and princess of Leyowan, as well as a grand wedding for he and his bride planned by Kona herself.

Author's Note for the Iron Spear

Greetings again to my faithful fans! It has been a blast working on the sequel to IronHeart, and I hope all of you enjoy reading it as much as I enjoyed writing it. This was a fun cast of characters to build and develop, and I'm hopeful that you all will find favorites in this group as quickly as in IronHeart.

I tried to make the culture and music of Leyowan a bit more present in this book. The songs in particular were fun for me to write because I based a lot of the culture ideas from my own views and beliefs. I find so much beauty in the wonders of God's nature: sunsets, forests, the ocean, etc., and decided that I would incorporate that into the culture of the Leyowanians. They write songs about what they find beautiful, which is obvious through the poetry and songs that I've included in The Iron Spear.

Another thing I'd like to mention is that it was very interesting working with Kona. She was so much like Kikpona yet so different in many ways. This book symbolizes peace and rebuilding of the empire that was at war in IronHeart.

My personal favorite character in this book would definitely have to be Roniki. Her speech patterns and personality were so much fun! There were several times while writing this book that I had to laugh when writing pieces for her. I love her enthusiasm and her loyalty to Kona. It was a beautiful thing to build and create.

Aren... where do I start? Ever since I started this book, I had an image in my head of this handsome yet impish peasant boy with a pair of daggers... that's kind of where his character started from. Originally he didn't fall in love with Kona. Nobio was Kona's love in the first draft plan, but as I started working with them, I realized that those two boys should reverse roles.

Nobio is my second favorite character. He's the typical schoolboy that everyone falls in love with. But I wanted him to really mature by the end of the book and make his journey to manhood, which I think he did.

I really hope that this book meets all the expectations that were put before it. I will admit that it was a daunting task to try and create a sequel for such a well received novel like IronHeart.

Well, that's all from me for now... hopefully you enjoyed The Iron Spear... until next time, remember, never take the little things in life for granted.

Love from Victoria